*The Willful Wallflower*

# THE WILLFUL WALLFLOWER

A Zodiac Regency Romance, Book 2
A Wallflower's Revenge Novel, Book 4

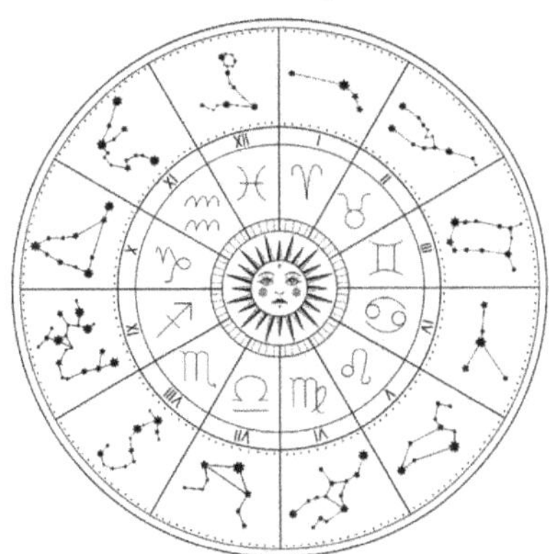

## Meredith Bond

Published by Anessa Books,
http://anessabooks.com

**Taurus**: (April 19-May 20) The Taurus is best known for being stubborn. Once they get an idea into their head, it is nearly impossible to get it out again. And don't even try to argue with them because they know they're right. A positive aspect of this stubbornness is that once they start something they will finish it, no matter what. They are tenacious and hardworking. This earth sign embodies stability. When everything else seems to be falling apart, Tauruses are a rock of dependability in an oasis of calm. They believe strongly that practical knowledge and experience will carry the day.

**Cancer**: (June 21-July 22) People who fall under the water sign of Cancer are passionate people. They are highly emotional and sensitive and prioritize matters related to family and home. They are very loyal and empathetic to the pain and suffering of others. They are often unaware of their own positive qualities and may endanger their own comfort in the service of someone else's cause. They know where they are going, but they sometimes find themselves heading in the wrong direction until they learn their lessons and begin to rely solely on themselves.

# Chapter One

1810

Lady Emilie Pelham had been having a perfectly wonderful evening with the rest of the wallflowers at Lady Hardcastle's ball. The strains of the music being played wafted over her and her friends as they stood on the far side of the ballroom. As usual, Miss Merrill had been sighing over Lord Dunright. Miss Smyth had been making snide comments about all the girls dancing, criticizing their gowns, their hair, and even the way they giggled; and Miss Winter had been complaining about her mother and how the woman never made any sort of effort to introduce her to eligible gentlemen because she was too busy throwing herself at them instead—not that she would do anything improper, of course. Baroness Winbourne just liked to flirt, as Miss Winter assured them all again and again.

Emilie was simply content to listen to the other girls and keep an eye out for whoever her mother might force on her next. Every time they went to a party, there was one poor fellow who her mother would hound until he finally gave up and asked Emilie to dance. Every single time she would have her toes stepped on and have to suffer through twenty minutes of inane conversation just so her mother would leave her alone for the rest of the party.

They had an unspoken understanding, Emilie and her mother. Emilie would dance once with a gentleman of the lady's choosing, and then she would be left alone for the rest of the evening to do as she pleased—which was to watch and feel sorry for all the other girls dancing and having their toes stepped upon. Since her mother was still convinced that Emilie was going to find a husband—despite her arguments to the contrary—and insisted she at least *try*, this seemed to be the best arrangement Emilie could hope for.

This evening she had already had her dance. It had been with Lord Boring, er, Borling, it was Borling. Goodness, she's nearly called him Lord Boring to his face! She'd caught herself just in time, she remembered with a little laugh.

"What's so funny?" Miss Smyth asked. "Is it Miss Talbot? Is it that dress she's wearing with the... what is it? Twelve flounces? I don't know—I've lost count." Miss Smyth gave a little smirk.

"What? Oh, no. I was just remembering how I nearly called Lord Borling *Lord Boring*," Emilie told her.

Miss Merrill spun toward her. "You didn't!"

"I didn't, but it was a near miss," Emilie said with a little giggle.

Miss Smyth nearly laughed right out loud but caught herself just in time. Instead, the crinkle of her mud-brown eyes was the only way to tell that she was laughing inside. She wasn't a bad-looking young woman, but she did have rather sharp features and a strong chin. She looked as if she never ate a thing, although Emilie had seen her consume an almost indecent amount of food once.

"Girls, I am so glad to see you are enjoying yourselves this evening," Lady Tremelling, Emilie's mother said, coming up to them with a young gentleman in tow. The lady herself was looking as lovely and determined as ever. Her deep-blue gown made the steel gray of her eyes stand out sharply as she took in the girls all standing in a row. Her hair was still the same color as Emilie's—a rich dark brown—but there was a stray glint of silver caught by the light every so often.

*What was this?* Emilie thought. She'd already done her duty for the night. A second dance was not part of their deal.

Emilie's friends all immediately lost their smiles and stepped away from the man, as if he had the plague.

"We are, thank you, Mother," Emilie said, deliberately ignoring the gentleman.

"Excellent. Lord Easton, may I present my daughter, Lady Emilie Pelham?" her mother said, turning to the man. He was handsome enough with broad shoulders and good height, but it was clear that he didn't miss a meal and enjoyed them immensely.

He smiled at Emilie and bowed. "It is an honor, Lady Emilie."

Emilie pulled up a polite smile as she curtsied. "How do you do?"

"Quite well, thank you," he answered, as if she actually cared. "Lady Emilie, might I lead you out for the next dance?"

Emilie narrowed her eyes momentarily at her mother. This was most definitely not part of their understanding, and she wasn't going to put up with it. She gave the man a sad smile. "I am so very sorry, my lord, but I'm afraid I turned my ankle when I danced with Lord Borling and it is paining me ever so much. You will please excuse me?"

"Oh dear, I am so very sorry to hear that," the gentleman said, feigning concern, but in truth, Emilie wasn't entirely certain there was a hint of relief in his eyes.

"Perhaps a slow promenade about the room instead. That shouldn't hurt your *ankle*," her mother suggested, putting undue stress on the last word. It was clear she didn't believe Emilie's excuse for the slightest moment.

"Oh, I don't—" Emilie started.

"Yes, of course! What a brilliant idea, Lady Tremelling," the gentleman said, giving her mother a nod. "We will, of course, go slowly so as not to aggravate your injury."

"You are too kind, my lord," Emilie said. She had no choice but to take the man's arm and allow him to lead her away. She didn't even look at her mother to see the self-satisfied smile she was certain was hovering on the lady's lips.

Later that evening as they drove home in their carriage, Emilie didn't hold back. "Mother, how could you bring a second gentleman over for me to meet? I'd thought we had an understanding."

"Understanding? What understanding?" her mother snapped. She was clearly just as unhappy with Emilie.

"That you would only force one gentleman on me per evening," Emilie spelled out for her.

Her mother's jaw dropped, and her eyes widened. "Well, I never agreed to such a thing!"

"But it's what you've always done," Emilie argued.

Her mother paused, thinking about it. She gave a sniff. "Well, if it is, it is only because you are so ungrateful and unwilling to even give any of the very kind gentlemen I introduce to you a chance."

"I give them a chance. I never complain when they step on my toes as we dance. I always make polite conversation. I hold up my end of the bargain."

"You dance with them and then don't speak with them the rest of the evening."

"I stand with my friends," Emilie pointed out.

"You stand with all the other wallflowers when you could be out enjoying yourself and meeting eligible men. You will never find a gentleman to marry if you only dance with one man at every party we go to."

"I told you. I have no interest in—"

"Yes, yes," her mother waved away her words with a nonchalant hand. "And I have told you that you *will* marry, whether you want to do so or not. Dancing with one man per evening will never get you to the altar. What a ridiculous notion! Now, am I going to have to ask your brother to find a husband for you, or will you cooperate?" Her voice had suddenly become much sharper as she turned to stare right at Emilie despite the darkness of the coach.

"I will not—" Emilie started again.

"That's enough! Enough of this absurdity, Emilie. I am through with coddling you. You will find a gentleman to marry or... or..."

"Or what?" Emilie asked, challenging her.

"Or I will find one for you. No, wait." Her mother stopped speaking and turned to look out the window for a moment. "I just remembered something. I overheard Lady..." Her voice trailed off as she struggled to remember whatever it was. She then said softly to herself. "Yes. I will have to send 'round a note... or better yet, pay her a call." Lady Tremelling turned back toward Emilie with much more determination. "Don't you worry about a thing. I shall handle everything."

"Worry? Indeed, I am very worried—now."

Gabriel, Marquess of Willington, followed the sound of his grandmother's voice. It wasn't a difficult task as it could be heard throughout the ground floor of the enormous, ancient Kilby Castle. He found her in the middle of the great hall, dwarfed by the enormous fireplace that took up a great deal of one stone wall.

"What do you mean you can't beat this tapestry?" His grandmother stomped her cane on the floor to emphasize her words. "Why in all that is right can you *not* do as you are told?"

"Maybe because that tapestry has been hanging on that wall for the past four hundred years, Gran," Gabriel asked, approaching the Dowager Marchioness. Her pale-blue eyes glittered with anger. "If she beats it, who's to know what might come out? Or it might simply fall apart all together, or fall off the wall where it has hung for so very long," he suggested, giving the maid, who was standing nearby looking terrified, a reassuring smile.

"Don't be ridiculous, Willington. The maids have beaten this tapestry for the past fifty years with no mishaps whatsoever. It is only this one girl who is too scared to even get near it. Look at her cowering, standing a full five feet away from it," his grandmother snapped.

"And I don't blame her. Sally, why don't you go fetch Thomas and tell him I said he should be the one to beat the tapestry, and to do so gently—just in case."

"Gently? How will it get clean if it is beaten gently?" Lady Willington asked. She turned her scowl to Gabriel.

"Well, we don't actually want it destroyed, now, do we? Goodness only knows what drafts it is keeping hidden behind it."

"What vermin, you mean," his grandmother said.

"Well, there could be that too. Although, I haven't seen a mouse since you took over the running of the castle."

"I should say not!" his grandmother said, affronted. Then she added more quietly, "Your mother was never one for housekeeping, I'm afraid."

"No, she wasn't," Gabriel agreed. His mother hadn't been interested in very much beyond her paints and her most recent lover—and all too frequently, the one found himself duplicated in the other. Gabriel had disposed of more paintings of naked men after his mother died than he'd care to remember. He refocused his attention on his grandmother. "And I think it is high time you took a break from these labors as well."

"What? Whatever can you mean?" his grandmother asked, walking over to the sofa, her beautifully carved cane tapping loudly on the black-and-white marble floor before it was muffled by the red and cream carpet, delineating the seating area before the fireplace.

"I think we should go to London," he said, following her and, once she had seated herself on the red damask sofa, took the matching chair across from it. "The Season has already started, but I'm certain once word has gotten about that you are returned, we will be inundated with invitations."

"But it's barely been..."

"It's been a year and a half since my parents died. I'm certain it doesn't feel that long to you since you were ill and then recovering for an extended period of time, but it has most definitely been long enough," he said, his voice becoming gentler.

His grandmother gave a heavy sigh. "I suppose it has been," she agreed.

"So, it is high time you returned to London and left the poor servants here to manage as they have always done so."

"Not very well," she snapped half-heartedly.

He gave her a smile, leaning forward toward her. She reluctantly lifted a corner of her lips as well.

"Do you think anyone will remember me?" she asked, sounding slightly nervous.

"Gran, you've been gone from society for less than two years. I'm certain everyone will remember Watchful Willington."

She gave a little snort of laughter. "Better than what they used to call your moth—" She stopped abruptly, but Gabriel knew what she'd been about to say.

The scandal sheets had dubbed his grandmother "Watchful Willington" for the way she watched out for the young ladies of the *ton*, ensuring that everyone who wanted to dance had a partner to do so. His mother, on the other hand, had been called "Too Willing Willington" in reference to all the men she took to her bed. He still didn't know how his father had resisted the urge to bring her here and lock her in the highest tower. No, he'd just ignored it. Ignored her. Ignored Gabriel. Ignored everyone. He had shut himself up here rather than deal with the sniggering behind his back and the parade of men going in and out of his townhouse.

Gabriel still didn't understand how his father had managed to stay so calm, to keep himself above it all. But it was that uncaring, that lack of feeling which Gabriel respected most in his father... and what he strived to attain himself. He'd already felt— too many times—the consequences of not locking away his feelings, of letting his passions rule. It had never led to anything good.

As if reading his mind, his grandmother cocked her head at him. "Well, if I am going to return to society, it will be with one goal in mind, Gabriel."

He blinked at her. It was never a good thing when she called him by his given name.

"You are going to marry, my boy," she informed him with a wag of her finger.

His immediate reaction was to say no, but he stopped with the word on his lips as he thought about it.

His grandmother continued for him. "You need an heir now that you're the marquess. You need companionship. And, to be quite frank, you could use some happiness in your life."

"First of all, you bring me all the happiness I could need," he started.

She chuckled but shook her head. "You don't need *grannie* happiness. You need a wife who will make you happy. It's a very different thing."

"Which brings me to my second point—a wife won't necessarily bring me happiness, Gran."

"Of course she would! If you choose the right one."

"And how do I do that?" he asked with a disbelieving smile.

"You meet women. You speak with them. You fall in love," she said, leaning forward slightly.

Gabriel just shook his head. "I am not going to fall in love."

"Why not?"

"I..." he paused. How could he explain to his grandmother that he'd done so once already, and it had turned out disastrously? He might have only been nineteen at the time, and he might have only known the girl for a short time, but it had been enough. More than enough, really. He'd been ruled by his emotions in his youth. He'd allowed his passions to rule his head and his heart. And he learned the hard lesson of where that got him—with a face full of fist from her angry brother and the loss of not only the girl, but a good number of friends at school as well. No, no, he was never going to do that again.

No, if he ever married—and he was not against the institution at all—it was going to be a traditional society match without an ounce of feeling involved.

"I think it's an excellent idea," he said, finally.

His grandmother's mouth nearly fell open.

He gave a short laugh. "You were expecting me to argue," he stated.

"I was," she agreed.

"But you're right, I *do* need to marry, so go right ahead, Gran, choose a bride for me."

His grandmother frowned. "I am not going to choose your bride—that's for you to do."

Gabriel shook his head. "I don't really care who she is, so long as she's passably pretty."

"But what about love?"

He waved the idea away. "I have no interest in it."

"What? How can you say that, Willington? Love is... is the most wonderful—"

"I am not interested in love. It's not for me," he repeated himself.

She lowered her eyebrows and peered at him. "So, what they say is true. You are a cold, unfeeling man—just like your father."

The words hurt even though it was not only the truth, but something he'd worked very hard at. And he'd had enough of this conversation. "I have work that I need to return to. We'll leave by week's end." And with that, he got up and walked away.

# Chapter Two

When Emilie and her mother walked into Lady Haddenfield's drawing room, she was incredibly relieved to find her elder sister, Eliza, already there. Eliza, or more properly, Elizabeth, Countess of Alford, was sitting on a sofa speaking with another lady Emilie didn't know. She too had inherited their mother's brown hair, but she'd also gotten her gray eyes. In fact, aside from her height, which the lucky thing had inherited from their father, she could have been a younger version of their mother.

As Emilie and Lady Tremelling were greeted by their hostess, she nearly burst out laughing at the look of relief that flashed on and off her sister's face. Could it possibly be that Eliza was not enjoying the company of the lady she was speaking with, Emilie thought with a silent giggle.

"Ah, there is your sister speaking with Lady Humphrey," Lady Tremelling said to Emilie.

"If you don't mind, I think I'll join them," Emilie said, giving the two ladies in front of her a polite smile.

"An excellent idea," her mother agreed.

Eliza stood as Emilie approached her. "Emilie, how lovely to see you!" her sister said with a little too much enthusiasm.

"And you, dearest sister," Emilie said, giving her a big smile. She turned to Lady Humphrey, a middle-aged woman who Emilie now remembered as being seen in the company of the gossips of society, to greet her as well.

The lady also stood. "I don't believe we've been introduced."

Eliza immediately remedied the situation, and Emilie curtsied to the lady.

"I was just telling Lady Alford how surprised I was to see Lord Easton at Lady Hardcastle's last night. Oh, but I do believe you met him as well, didn't you?" the woman asked, turning to Emilie.

"He was kind enough to promenade with me," Emilie said, trying her best to keep the polite smile on her face.

"Is there something about the gentleman we should know, Lady Humphrey?" Eliza asked, cocking her head a little.

"Oh no! Not at all, I'm sure," the lady demurred.

"Which means there is. Come now, I would hate for my sister to be seen in the company of an inappropriate gentleman," Eliza said, prodding the woman a little. It was all it took, sadly.

"Well, I'm certain I shouldn't say as much, but I did hear how he has recently been seen in Lady Winbourne's company—a great deal," the woman admitted.

Eliza blew out a little puff of air. "There are a great many gentlemen seen in Lady Winbourne's company. It means nothing."

"Are you certain? I mean, she is a married woman, but..." Lady Humphrey said, lowering her voice to a whisper.

"I do beg your pardon, my lady. I'm afraid we must take our leave," a gentleman said, joining them.

Lady Humphrey was spared the necessity of explaining herself further, for which Emilie found herself rather grateful.

"Oh, of course. You will please excuse me?" She gave them a nod and then went off with the man.

"And who was that?" Emilie asked, watching them go.

"I have no idea. Her son? Her husband? A brother? It's impossible to tell. I heard someone say she's in her mid-thirties, but he could be anywhere from twenty to thirty-five, don't you think?"

"I do. Well, that's fine with me. She didn't seem to have a great deal of sense if she was worried about a gentleman who'd been seen with Lady

Winbourne," Emilie pointed out, keeping her voice low.

Eliza chuckled. "No, honestly, half the men in the *ton* have been seen with the lady. I'm certain it means nothing."

Emilie nodded and then turned to look around the room. As she did so, she noticed her mother standing and speaking with Lady Haddenfield in a far corner. Lady Haddenfield was looking straight at her. The lady, however, quickly turned back toward Lady Tremelling, as if she didn't want to be noticed looking in Emilie's direction. A moment later, her mother, too, looked over at her.

"All right, what do you think that's about?" Emilie asked Eliza.

"What?" Eliza looked about the room, not seeing what Emilie was referring to.

"Mother and Lady Haddenfield are talking about me. They both just looked over here and then away, as if they didn't want me to notice I saw them looking."

"Really? I have no idea," Eliza said, locating their mother.

Just then, the two ladies split apart with a nod and went in opposite directions.

"Go and find out, will you?" Emilie asked, giving her sister a nudge in Lady Tremelling's direction.

Eliza gave a nod and headed over to greet their mother. She really was the best of sisters, Emilie thought to herself.

Emilie allowed herself to get drawn into another conversation concerning those who had been seen eating Günter's ices—all terribly important information if one judged by the excitement in the voices of the two young ladies taking part in the conversation. As she listened with half an ear to the conversation in front of her, she kept stealing glances at her mother and sister. Lady Tremelling seemed to be quite pleased about something, but Eliza was looking ever more frustrated. Finally, Lady Tremelling began to move away, leaving Eliza where she was.

"And what is your opinion, Lady Emilie?" Emilie heard one of the girls say. "Oh, I think the chocolate flavor is by far the best," she said, with absolutely no idea what they had been asking her opinion on. The two girls gave her a confused look, but she just smiled and excused herself to accost her sister.

"So?" she asked as soon as she'd reached Eliza's side.

"She won't say! But she certainly looked like a cat who'd gotten into the cream," Eliza said, still looking after their mother.

"I saw that, but you couldn't get any information out of her?"

Eliza finally looked at Emilie, shaking her head. "Not a bit. I'm sorry, but whatever it is, she is being very tight-lipped about it."

"How very frustrating!" Emilie exclaimed.

"I imagine you'll find out soon enough."

Gabriel wasn't certain how his grandmother had talked him into paying morning calls, but here he was, handing her down from his coach just outside of Lady Haddenfield's home.

He turned to watch another coach start off from just behind them—someone else leaving the same gathering, no doubt. He caught a glimpse of the crest on the door as the vehicle drove by—Tremelling. Well, perhaps it was a good thing Gran had taken so long to get ready. Gabriel certainly wouldn't have wanted to meet the earl. They hadn't spoken since that day so very long ago when Gabriel had been a guest at the Tremelling home over the Easter holidays—the day his life had changed; the day he'd learned the truth.

"Are you just going to stand there daydreaming, or shall we go in?" his grandmother asked from just beside him.

"I do beg your pardon," Gabriel said, coming back to the present. "By all means, let's go in and get this torture over with."

His grandmother snickered as she led the way inside.

Gabriel stopped just inside the door to the drawing room as his grandmother waited to be greeted by Lady Haddenfield, a plump lady with ruddy cheeks. She looked to be saying goodbye to another lady, a very pretty woman with dark-brown hair and a slender, statuesque physique. There was something about her that teased at Gabriel's memory, but he couldn't place it. He must have met her before, he decided.

"Thank you so much for joining us today, Lady Alford," Lady Haddenfield was saying.

"Oh, it was entirely my pleasure," the lady replied with a slight curtsy. "And I am so glad you and my mother got a chance to speak. It seemed as if she had something very important to discuss with you." The lady was clearly fishing for some information as she looked at their hostess hopefully.

Lady Haddenfield just gave a little chuckle. "Indeed, Lady Alford, and I was very happy to provide her with what she needed."

A slightly disappointed smile graced Lady Alford's face, but she gave a nod in good grace. It was then that she happened to turn toward the door and see Gabriel and his grandmother standing there. A look of shock crossed her face for just a moment, but she quickly schooled it into a polite smile. "Oh, Lady Willington, I am terribly sorry I didn't see you. If you will excuse me, I'm just on my way out." She gave Gran a curtsy and Gabriel a very brief nod before making a quick escape. Even Lady Willington turned to watch her go, as it was so abrupt.

Gabriel wondered if he'd ever done anything to make the woman dislike him—perhaps he'd danced with her? Or hadn't when she expected him to do so? He had no idea. He gave a little mental shrug and returned his attention to what was happening directly in front of him.

"Lady Willington, what a wonderful surprise!" Lady Haddenfield said, reclaiming Gabriel and his grandmother's attention. "I didn't realize you were in Town."

"Wasn't until yesterday," Gran told her.

"Well then, I am exceedingly honored to be your first social call. How are you doing?" she asked solicitously.

Gran gave a little sigh but smiled. "I must admit it hasn't been easy, but with Willington's assistance, I have been managing."

"Oh, but it must have been such a difficult time for you both," the lady said, now including Gabriel in the conversation.

"Indeed. Losing both of his parents was not easy on the boy," Gran said, giving Gabriel's arm a pat. He attempted to look saddened by the loss, but honestly, he'd gotten over the worst of the shock months ago. At times, it still hit him that he no longer had any parents, but then he would allow himself to get distracted from such morose thoughts and continue on, taking care of his responsibilities. It was easier since he hadn't been particularly close to either one of them.

"Of course not!" Lady Haddenfield gave him a consoling smile before turning back to Gran. "But please, allow me to introduce you to some of the newer members of society who are here. And, of course, you remember Lady—"

Gabriel stopped listening the rest of the lady's chatter and allowed his grandmother to be led away to meet people he had no desire to interact with.

He found Lord Merriton over by the fireplace, watching the proceedings.

"Willington." The man nodded.

"How do you do, Merriton? Enjoying your afternoon?" Gabriel asked with a smirk.

"It's been tolerable so far. Escorting your grandmother about?" the man asked with a matching expression.

Gabriel nodded. "I've allowed her to convince me to look about for a wife," he told the other man. You never knew who might know of someone appropriate, and Merriton wasn't a bad sort. They'd been at school together.

The man grunted his acknowledgement of the information.

"Are you here for the same reason?" Gabriel asked.

The fellow stood straighter. "God forbid! No, I'm escorting my sister about. Just made her debut," he said, nodding toward a pretty thing sitting on the sofa nearby.

"Oh," Gabriel said, taking the girl in. She was very fair, like her brother, but too pale and colorless for Gabriel.

"No offense, but she isn't the sort for you," Merriton said.

Gabriel turned toward him with a questioning expression.

"Looking for a love match," Merriton explained. "Or at the very least, someone warm and friendly who she can grow to love."

"*Not* like me," Gabriel agreed, shoving down the odd feeling of hurt sinking to the bottom of his stomach.

The man gave a little chuckle. "Definitely not like you." He caught sight of Gabriel's face and quickly lost his smile. "Er, you do understand, don't you, old chap?"

"Absolutely! I am definitely not looking for a girl who would swoon over me. Glad you warned me off," he said as affably as he could.

Merriton relaxed a touch. "I figured as much. You're not the romantic type, spouting poetry and all that rot."

Gabriel gave a little laugh. "Good God, no!" He gave the other man a nod and moved over to a table laden with refreshments. He could really have used something stronger, but he supposed tea would have to do.

# CHAPTER THREE

Gabriel had never enjoyed going to society parties and especially not balls. In fact, he'd made a point of avoiding all such entertainments for the longest time that it felt rather odd attending two balls just days apart. But for his grandmother, he found he would do whatever it took to make her happy, and clearly, attending society events—even balls—did so. And so, he found himself at Lady Orford's ball just a few evenings later.

"Oh, I see a dear friend of mine," Lady Willington said soon after they arrived. "Do excuse me, my love."

He could do nothing but stand by the door and watch as the lady made her way carefully among the partygoers.

"Looks like you've been abandoned by your lovely companion," a man said with a laugh as he joined Gabriel.

He turned and found Lord Brice, one of the boys he'd known at school. They had never been friends, as Brice was a few years older, but they'd known of each other. Brice was a good-looking fellow if rather thin. Gabriel had heard that the ladies liked his blond hair and piercing green eyes, but for himself, Gabriel always found the odd glint in the man's eyes a bit off-putting—as if he knew something you didn't, and he wasn't about to tell.

Gabriel gave a little laugh. "Yes. I'm afraid she does that pretty frequently. Sometimes it's hard to keep track of her for all her flitting about."

"Really? You wouldn't expect that of someone her age."

"I'm afraid I'm teasing you, Brice. She does tend to stay in one place for much of the evening. It is I who she sends away usually." The thought brought to mind Brice's reputation as quite the rake. "Say, you are a favorite among the fairer sex, aren't you?"

The man gave a little chuckle. "I believe I might have the distinction. I can't say anyone's ever declined an invitation."

Gabriel nodded. "Perhaps you might, er, introduce me?"

"Be happy to! Who would you like to meet?"

"Anyone pleasant to look at and on the lookout for a husband," he said, not without a little foreboding.

His friend's eyes went wide. "Do not tell me that you—"

"Good evening, Lord Brice," a warm voice purred from Brice's other side.

Both men turned to greet the lady. She was a handsome woman with dark-brown hair and light-blue eyes, probably in her mid-thirties and dressed in a deep-red silk gown that was cut so low Gabriel wondered if a mishap wasn't about to occur.

"Ah, Lady Winbourne, what a delight to see you this evening," Lord Brice said, taking the lady's proffered hand and placing a kiss on the back of it.

"I'm certain it is. And who, pray tell, is your handsome friend?" she asked, not taking her eyes off Gabriel.

Brice didn't seem to mind being so quickly dismissed. "My lady, may I present Gabriel, Marquess of Willington?"

"Willington? I believe I've heard of you," the lady said, looking Gabriel over critically.

Gabriel bowed. "It is a pleasure, my lady."

"Now, what have I heard?" she asked, while managing to move herself between the two men. She reached out and smoothed a hand down his coat lapel. "Why does your name ring a bell?"

Gabriel had a hard time not recoiling from this woman between her overwhelming perfume and her breath, which smelled of liquor. "I honestly cannot say, but I would kindly request you remove your hand from my person," he said.

She frowned. "Oh, yes, that was it." Her hand dropped to her side. "I heard you were a cold fish.

What a shame, I have a lovely, marriageable daughter. Well, I shall just have to find someone else for her." She heaved a great sigh, then turned to Brice. "Lord Brice, if only you were interested."

"I am so sorry, my lady, but marriage is just not for me. However, I would be more than happy to—" he leaned down and whispered something in her ear. She threw her head back with a great laugh, drawing the eyes of everyone nearby.

"Oh, my lord, you are too much!" she exclaimed. She gave him a sly smile. "We shall certainly meet again very soon. Will you go to Lord Mentrose's tomorrow night?"

"Of course! I wouldn't miss it," Brice said.

"Good, I will see you there." And with that, she sauntered away.

Gabriel watched her go and then turned back to Brice, whose shoulders were shaking with silent laughter.

"I don't know Mentrose," Gabriel commented.

"Oh, he throws the best orgies. If you're interested—"

"No! Thank you. Er, not my thing," Gabriel interrupted him. He was beginning to think he'd made a mistake asking this man for introductions. Clearly, he didn't associate with the sort of women Gabriel was interested in.

"Well, you just managed to offend one of the most well-known ladies of the *ton*."

"What is she known for, sleeping around?" Gabriel asked with a frown.

"Precisely. I think she has graced the bed of nearly half the men in this room."

Gabriel couldn't help but make a disgusted sound. "Well then, excuse me if I am not terribly upset at the lady's lack of interest."

"Goodness, you are a cold fish!" Brice said with another laugh. "Come on then, let me introduce you to others of your ilk, only in female form." He led the way while Gabriel was beginning to be grateful for his reputation. A cold, distant young lady was precisely the sort he wanted to marry.

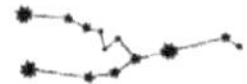

Emilie found her friends at Lady Orford's ball doing what they always did, discussing the happenings all around them.

"I simply cannot believe that gown," Miss Smyth said, watching the dancers. "It not only has four flounces but lace as well!"

"Is that Miss Talbot?" Emilie asked, turning to look.

"Who else?" Miss Winter asked with a little giggle. Her black hair was pulled up in a complicated coiffure that Emilie thought a little much. Unlike her mother, however, Miss Winter hid her bold curves with a neckline to her dress that nearly came up to her throat.

"Where is Miss Merrill?" Emilie asked, noticing one of their usual group was missing.

"Dancing! Can you imagine?" Miss Winter said, nodding toward the floor.

"Not with Lord Dunright?" Emilie asked in shock.

"No! With Lord Easton," Miss Smyth answered.

"Oh, he's the one I promenaded with the other night. He's not so bad," Emilie said, remembering the gentleman. "He hadn't been able to trod on my toes as we were merely walking and not dancing, and his conversation was less than erudite."

Miss Winter giggled again.

"I don't know about his footwork, but would you look at that waistcoat! Have you ever seen a gentleman in such a shade of pink before?" Miss Smyth asked.

With this description, Emilie easily found the gentleman. "Oh my! It certainly is, er, vibrant," she agreed.

"Why couldn't he be more understated and elegant like the man near him. Now that is exactly the sort of thing a man should wear," Miss Smyth said.

"I cannot agree more, Miss Smyth," a lady's voice said from behind Emilie. She spun around to find Lady Winbourne standing next to her daughter. Not one of them had seen her approach, they'd been so focused on the people dancing.

"Oh, Mother!" Miss Winter said, her cheeks turning pink.

"Good evening, ladies," Lady Winbourne said, giving them all a smile. "Now, while I do approve of your excellent taste in gentlemen's clothing, Miss Smyth, I would warn you against the gentleman wearing that very elegant waistcoat.

Emilie turned back around. She hadn't even had a chance to follow who Miss Smyth had been talking about. "I didn't see the gentleman in question, which one was it?" she asked her friend.

"The man two gentlemen down from Lord Easton," Miss Smyth said, also looking back at the dance floor. "He's wearing a black coat with a deep-gray waistcoat with silver embroidery."

Emilie followed Miss Smyth's directions and... gasped.

"It sounds as if you are already acquainted with the gentleman," Lady Winbourne said. "I admit he is a handsome devil. One might wish he were a bit more, well, devilish. A colder man I have never met," the lady said with a sniff.

Emilie met Miss Winter's gaze. Her friend rolled her eyes.

"Why do you say that, my lady?" Emilie couldn't help but ask. The young man she remembered wasn't cold at all—in fact, just the opposite. She could still remember the heat of his lips on her own. She could still smell the fresh, clean scent of soap on him, as if he'd just washed his face, and remember the feel of running her fingers through the soft curls of his dark hair. His deep-brown eyes had looked into her own with so much passion she'd felt scorched by it. Oh, no, there was absolutely *nothing* cold about Lord Gabriel.

Lady Winbourne frowned at her daughter. "And no, Helen, it is not because he rebuffed me. Ask any woman here who has had the displeasure of meeting Lord Willington, and they will tell you. He is cold, unfeeling, and, not infrequently, downright rude."

"Really?" Emilie asked. This wasn't at all the boy she remembered. Of course, the fact that he'd kissed her could be coloring her memory.

"Oh, so you do not know him?" Lady Winbourne asked.

"I do… er, well, I met him many years ago. He and my brother went to school together," Emilie told her.

"Well, perhaps he has changed since he was a boy, but I've heard he is now on the lookout for a wife, and I would not recommend going after that particular quarry no matter how delightful he is to look at." She turned toward her daughter. "Now, Helen, I came over here to introduce you to a perfectly acceptable young man. Come along, my dear."

Miss Winter looked at Emilie and Miss Smyth with widened, disbelieving eyes before chasing after her mother.

"Goodness, I've never heard Lady Winbourne speak so about a gentleman," Miss Smyth said. "Lord Willington must be quite an unpleasant gentleman."

"Well, I would not dismiss the lady's warning despite her reputation," Emilie said. She, herself, would do her utmost to avoid him, that was for certain—who would want to be with a man who made one feel overly warm? She turned away from the dancers and caught sight of her mother just as Lady Haddenfield was approaching her with another lady. Emilie watched as Lady Haddenfield introduced her companion. The unknown woman was very elegantly dressed in a gray silk gown, which set off her midnight black hair. A pair of small white feathers bobbed above the lady's head as she nodded to Emilie's mother.

"I wonder who that is," she whispered to herself.

"Who who is?" Miss Merrill asked, joining them now the dance had ended. It was easy for her to peer over Emilie's shoulder thanks to her height, and she did so now, trying to follow Emilie's line of sight.

"What? Oh, nobody." She hadn't meant to say it out loud. She turned around and asked, "How was your dance with Lord Easton?"

The girl shrugged. "Fine." She looked back at Lady Tremelling. "Were you looking at the ladies with your mother? That's Lady Haddenfield and Lady..." She paused. "I don't believe I know who the other lady is," Miss Merrill admitted. She turned to Miss Smyth and, before Emilie could stop her, asked, "Do you know the lady with Lady Haddenfield and Lady Tremelling?"

Miss Smyth redirected her attention, narrowing her eyes in the direction of Emilie's mother. "That's Lady Preston, I believe. I don't know her, but she's been pointed out to me once by my brother. I can't recall why."

"Well, I'm sure Lady Haddenfield just wanted to introduce the lady around. Perhaps she's new to London," Emilie offered.

"No, I'm certain she's not. Oh, now this is going to bother me! I don't remember who she is," Miss Smyth said with a shake of her head.

"Don't worry about it. I'm sure she's no one we need to know," Emilie said. "Did you see the gown Miss Fortwell is wearing?" she said, deliberately redirecting everyone's attention to the dance floor once again, much to her relief.

As the girls discussed the gowns, Emilie kept stealing glances over toward her mother. Lady Preston had moved on, much to Emilie's relief. She didn't know why, but she felt it was odd that her mother had never met the lady before. Emilie had always thought her mother knew just about everyone in society—most of the ladies, at least. Well, she supposed you never grew too old to make new friends.

Lady Willington gave Gabriel's arm a pat as he attempted to get her to take a seat in one of the little gilt chairs lining the wall. "You are a very considerate boy, Willington, but I do not need coddling," she told him.

"I just want to ensure that you aren't overtaxing yourself, Gran. Are you certain I can't get you a chair?"

"No! I am perfectly fine on my own feet. And if I get tired, I have my cane to lean on. Now, why don't you go ask some pretty young lady to dance?"

"I danced the last set. I thought I'd sit out this dance with you," he told her, giving her a warm smile.

She reluctantly returned it because Gabriel knew she loved him, whether he annoyed her with his oversolicitous behavior or not. "Very well. In that case, why don't you—"

He would never find out what he could do for the lady because just at that moment Lady Tremelling came over and joined them. He'd been hoping she wouldn't notice him in the crush of people at the ball. Sadly, she had.

"Good evening, Lady Willington, how absolutely wonderful it is to see you grace the ballrooms of society once again," Lady Tremelling said, giving Gran a slight curtsy.

"Ah, Lady Tremelling. Yes, it is a good evening. It is wonderful to be back in Town. I must admit I have missed this!" she said, giving the lady a polite smile. She was only the seventh person to welcome Gran back, each and every one saying exactly the same thing. And Gran replied exactly the same way each time. Gabriel wondered if she was getting tired of that even more than she was of standing on her feet for so long.

"And Lord Willington, how do you do? I hope you will both accept my condolences," Lady Tremelling said, looking at them both.

"Of course. Thank you so much, my lady," Gabriel said with a slight bow.

"I did notice you dancing earlier, my lord, dare I hope along with your new position you have decided to find yourself a bride?"

"Indeed, my lady," Gabriel answered.

"Aren't all your girls married, Lady Tremelling?" Gran asked. "Or is there one more?" Lady Willington furrowed her forehead as she tried to remember.

"I have three daughters, my lady. The eldest is married to Lord Alford and the youngest to Lord Sommets," the lady replied.

"Ah, that's right, that's right. Did the third have a Season at all? You will forgive an old lady for not remembering such details," Gran asked.

"No, actually, she didn't. Lord Sommets is a neighbor. He and Amelia have been close forever. It was only natural that he offer for her the moment she was old enough," Lady Tremelling said with a smile and a slight shrug of her shoulders.

"Well, I suppose that was easy for you." Lady Willington chuckled.

"Indeed." The lady just smiled.

"So, your middle girl is still without. Well, Willington, it sounds as if you should meet the gel," his grandmother said, turning to him.

A shiver of trepidation ran down Gabriel's spine. He knew Lady Tremelling's middle daughter. He knew her much too well, and he was pretty certain things wouldn't go well should her mother reintroduce them.

He had yet to even see the girl again. In truth, he was rather terrified to do so. He had no idea how he would react. He *hoped* he would behave with her exactly the way he would to any other woman—with indifference. He *hoped* his carefully built wall, behind which he now kept his emotions, would stand firm against the loveliness that was Emilie Pelham. But he had no idea and was certain it would *not* be a good idea to put it to the test.

"I absolutely would like to meet your daughter, my lady," he started, "but—"

"There are no buts, young man, go meet her. It's an excellent idea," Lady Willington said.

"I, er..." Gabriel tried again.

"Come right this way, my lord, and I'll introduce you," Lady Tremelling said, indicating he should go with her.

"Actually, we've already met," he said, stalling.

"Of course, you have! I remember it well," the lady said. "I do apologize, I misspoke. Come and allow me to *re*-introduce you."

"But I—"

"When did you meet her, Willington?" his grandmother asked, clearly beginning to see that Gabriel really didn't want to go with Lady Tremelling.

"When I was in school. I spent the Easter holidays one year with Evan, er, Lord Tremelling."

"They had a wonderful time together, if I recall," Lady Tremelling said, giving Gran a smile.

"Oh, well then, you truly must renew your acquaintance with the girl," Gran said, giving him a nod. "It would be very rude if you did not," she added with a warning tone to her voice.

When she spoke that way, Gabriel knew if he didn't do as she said he would hear about it for days. No, he had absolutely no choice but to go meet Lady Emilie—the sweet, beautiful young woman he'd fallen in love with and then kissed senseless before her brother discovered them.

# CHAPTER FOUR

Emilie was watching the dancers when her mother approached from behind her. She really needed to move closer to the wall so people would stop walking up behind her. "Emilie, look who I've found," Lady Tremelling said.

Emilie turned and saw Lord Willington being practically dragged toward her. Oh, no. No, no, no. There was absolutely no question about it, Emilie wanted nothing to do with the man. Not anytime, for any reason—and it wasn't just Lady Winbourne's warnings which made her feel that way.

That wonderful week they'd spent together with her brother and sister. That knee-melting kiss. That dead silence afterward.

"I do beg your pardon, Mother," Emilie said, turning her back and beginning to walk away.

"What do you think you're doing?" her mother's outraged voice followed her, but Emilie kept walking.

Oh, my gracious goodness, she'd just given the cut direct to a marquess! She could not believe she'd done such a thing. Her heart was pounding in her chest, and she felt light-headed, but she was not going to speak to him. She simply would not do it.

She had no idea where she was heading, then realized there was a hallway leading off to the ladies' retiring room. Yes, she would go there and collect herself. What else could she do?

As she made her way, she heard footsteps following her. She paused and turned around to see if her mother was following—she wouldn't, would she?

No. It was Miss Winter, Miss Smyth, and Miss Merrill.

"Lady Emilie!" Miss Merrill said in a loud whisper.

"My goodness, Lady Emilie, you must go back and be introduced to Lord Willington. Ignore what my mother said. You cannot just—" Miss Winter said as she came up behind her.

"I can't believe you just gave him the cut direct," Miss Smyth interrupted, holding back a laugh.

Emilie turned back around and continued walking. "I need to go to the retiring room," she told her friends. "Please, excuse me."

"Oh, absolutely not!" Miss Smyth said with a giggle.

They all followed her inside.

"Who is he?" Miss Merrill asked first as they huddled around her.

"No one," Emilie lied.

"It is Lord Willington," Miss Winter said.

"Lady Winbourne told us he's a cold fish," Miss Smyth told her.

"I do not like him. I do not like men. They are horrid, self-centered creatures, each and every one." The words rushed out of Emilie's mouth in an uncontrollable stream of vindictiveness. "And that man, Lord Willington, is the one who taught me this through his actions and his words—or lack of them. I want nothing to do with him—ever."

"What did he do to you?" Miss Winter asked in a breath.

"I do not wish to speak of it. I am very sorry." Emilie gave a shake of her head before ducking behind a screen where a chamber pot waited for use. She actually had no need of it, but she also didn't—no, she couldn't—explain things to her friends. She just didn't know them that well, and she had no desire to relive those horrid weeks after he'd kissed her.

"I knew this wouldn't be a good idea," he said aloud even as he was cursing himself and Lady Emilie in his mind. No, not Lady Emilie, he would never curse her. It wasn't her fault, it was his. He should never have allowed himself to be led to this like a dog on a lead.

He turned to Lady Tremelling. "If you will excuse me, my lady." He gave her a nod and strode away. He needed some fresh air. No, he needed more than that. He needed to get out of this ballroom and never return. He would have done so too if it hadn't been for his grandmother. He couldn't simply abandon her.

He did the next best thing—he walked out of the ballroom and down a long hallway.

A maid was standing outside of one door, which Gabriel assumed was the ladies' withdrawing room, and a footman stood outside of another—a room where men might take care of their more personal needs.

He stopped in front of the footman. "Where might I find a glass of whiskey and a quiet place to drink it?"

The man nodded toward the door at the end of the hall before reverting his eyes back to stare blankly at the wall across from him.

Gabriel gave a little huff and went off to see what was behind the door.

It turned out to be the library, and it wasn't empty. There were a number of other gentlemen there, also hiding out. One of them looked up from the book he was reading. "Whiskey, port, and sherry are on the table over there," he said, looking over toward the side of the room.

"Thank God," Gabriel said under his breath. A number of the other men chuckled but otherwise stayed quiet. Gabriel helped himself to a glass of whiskey and then took an empty chair.

He glanced around, noticing most of the men were much older, although there was one who looked to be in his thirties.

"Shouldn't you be paying court to the ladies, lad?" one of the older gentlemen asked.

"Even the best of us get tired of doing so," a younger man said, sounding incredibly bored.

"Then why not just leave?" the first man asked.

"Can't. My sister would kill me. Might kill me anyway when she discovers I've slipped away," the second man answered. He finished the liquid in his glass in a slightly desperate-looking move.

"And you?" the older man asked, looking at Gabriel as the other man went to refill his glass.

"I'm here with my grandmother," Gabriel answered.

The man frowned. "You're not Willington, are you?"

"I am," Gabriel said, a little surprised.

A smile grew on the man's face. "I knew your grandmother when she was a feisty, young thing. Watchful Willington, they called her—and not just because she looked out for other girls. She was pretty careful about the gentlemen too."

Gabriel laughed. "She still is feisty, although no longer young."

"So, she's back in society, eh?" the man asked, considering Gabriel.

He nodded. "Holding court even as we speak."

The man made a little noise of interest and then set his drink aside. "I believe I'll just go pay my respects in that case." He got up but stopped next to Gabriel as he passed him. "Don't worry, I won't tell her where you've escaped to." He gave Gabriel a little pat on his shoulder and left the room.

It wasn't until they were on their way home that Lady Willington broached the topic. She began with a heavy sigh and then looked at Gabriel across the dark coach. "Well?"

He didn't need an explanation of she was asking about. That cut had probably been on the lips of everyone at the ball and would most likely be there for a good while after.

"Well, I tried to tell you it wouldn't be a good idea for Lady Tremelling to re-introduce me to her daughter."

"And that is all you've got to say on the matter?" his grandmother snapped.

Gabe stared out the window, wondering what he could tell her. Could he say he'd kissed the girl and then never contacted her again? Could he tell her what her brother had done and said afterward? Could he admit his shame, his reproach at himself for succumbing to his passions?

"Yes." He turned toward his grandmother. "That is all I'm going to say. The rest is in the past, and I'd like to keep it there."

"Well, it's not in the past any longer. Lady Emilie just brought it back to the present with that cut," Lady Willington pointed out. "And people are going to want to know what caused her to do that."

"That is their problem, Grandmother. I am not going to fill the gossips' coffers with tales I would prefer to forget. I have nothing further to say on the matter."

"Do you really think I would stoop so low as to spread tales about you, my own grandson?" Her voice practically shook with outrage. "Do you think so little—"

"I do not. I apologize. I did not mean to imply that you would gossip about me." He was tired. He rubbed a hand over his eyes and then down his face.

"Well then?"

"Then nothing. I am not going to speak of it. I'm sorry." They pulled up at that moment to their home. Gabriel descended from the coach and then turned to assist his grandmother. She had only sadness and perhaps a little confusion in her eyes.

"Very well. Goodnight, Willington." And with that she marched into the house and straight up to her room.

Gabe did the same, only pausing for a moment to ask that a bottle of brandy be sent up.

The following afternoon Emilie was practicing the pianoforte when her mother came into the music room.

Lady Tremelling applauded as Emilie came to a flourishing conclusion to the piece she was playing. Getting up from the piano bench, Emilie gave a little curtsy with a laugh.

"That was lovely my dear, now go fetch your pelisse and bonnet. We have a call we need to make," her mother said as she pulled on her own gloves.

"Oh, of course, Mama. Are we visiting anyone interesting?" Emilie said as she started toward the door.

"I think you will find it so," her mother said, giving nothing away.

Emilie paused to frown at her. "Is that all?"

"Is what all?"

"You're not going to tell me who we're visiting?"

"You will see when we get there, now run along." Her mother made a shooing motion and Emilie continued out the door feeling a little piqued. Lady Tremelling usually told her who they were going to visit. It was odd that she wasn't doing so today.

The house where their coach left them was a little way outside of Mayfair. The other houses on the street were well-kept, but the neighborhood certainly was a step down from the larger homes Emilie was used to.

"You're really not going to tell me who we're visiting," Emilie said, as they got down from the coach.

"You will see momentarily. My goodness, how curious you are. Usually, you hardly even pay attention when I tell you who we'll be visiting," her mother said, as she indicated the footman should knock on the door.

"That's because I usually know who it is. This is quite a mystery." Emilie followed her mother up the steps as the door was opened by the butler. Joseph, the Tremelling footman, handed over his mistress's card. The butler took one glance at it, nodded, and indicated the ladies should enter the house.

"If you would follow me, my lady, Miss," the man said in a strong Irish accent.

Emilie looked to her mother who ignored her and instead followed the butler up the stairs to the drawing room. The room was pleasantly furnished in various shades of green and filled with landscape paintings of rolling fields dotted with sheep or views of the ocean crashing below jagged cliffs. It wasn't the most fashionable drawing room Emilie had ever seen. It was neither obviously new nor threadbare. It felt... comfortable.

"Just one moment, my lady, and I shall fetch my mistress," the butler said with a little bow.

Lady Tremelling gave him a nod and then went to look out the window while Emilie stared after him.

"All right, this is clearly not a normal social call. There's no one here," Emilie pointed out.

"No, it is not. Now do, please, be a little patient," her mother responded, not even turning around to speak to her. She did not seem to be entirely at her ease either.

Emilie wanted to huff her displeasure but knew it would only annoy her mother further, so instead she went to examine one of the paintings.

A few minutes later the door opened and the lady Emilie had seen being introduced to her mother the previous evening entered.

"Good afternoon, Lady Tremelling, how wonderful that you could make it," the lady said, coming over to greet Emilie's mother. Like the butler, she too had an Irish accent, but hers was softer and more tempered.

"How do you do? May I present my daughter, Lady Emilie Pelham?" Lady Tremelling asked, giving the woman a polite smile.

"Of course, of course. I am very happy to make your acquaintance."

"Emilie, this is the Countess of Preston," her mother said, finishing the introduction.

Emilie curtsied. "I am pleased to meet you, my lady."

"Come and sit down, Lady Emilie. I am so looking forward to speaking with you. Your mother has told me a little about you, but I am eager to learn more," the lady said, indicating the sofa.

The door opened before Emilie could get far and the butler entered the room once again.

"Ah, Connor, would you please escort Lady Tremelling to my private sitting room?" She turned to the lady. "I do hope you will excuse us, my lady, but I need to speak with your daughter, and I find young people open up so much more readily when their parents are not in the room. You understand, I'm sure. There is tea set out for you in the other room."

Both Emilie and her mother shared a startled look, but Lady Tremelling conceded quickly enough and followed the butler out of the room. The door was closed behind them.

"There now, we can be quite cozy just the two of us," the lady said, indicating the sofa.

Emilie didn't know what to make of this very strange turn of events. Why had her mother needed to leave the room? What sort of discussion did Lady Preston want to have with her? Emilie wasn't exactly nervous, exceedingly curious was perhaps closer.

"Ma'am?" Emilie asked, taking a seat next to the woman.

"Has your mother told you why you are here?"

"No, she's been extremely coy all the way here. She merely told me we were going to pay a call," Emilie told her.

"Hmmm, yes, some believe that is the better way to do it. I, myself, prefer to be a little more open, but I can understand this method is appealing as well."

Emilie was beyond confused. It must have shown on her face because the woman gave her hands a friendly pat. "Do not fear, I am not here to do anything to you. We're merely going to talk."

"About what, my lady?"

"Do you believe in soulmates, Lady Emilie?" the woman asked instead of answering Emilie's question.

"Soulmates?"

"Yes. They are two people who are destined for one another," Lady Preston explained.

"People who fall in love? Do you mean like that?"

"They usually do," the lady agreed. "But more than that, they were meant to be together—even if they didn't see it at first. I have a particular talent for discovering people who are meant for each other," she explained.

"Meant to marry?"

"Yes, precisely."

"But I am not interested in getting married. I told my mother this."

"Yes, well, she feels otherwise, I'm afraid. And so, she has asked me to find your soulmate in the hope that you will not only want to marry, but perhaps even fall in love with the gentleman and be happy in your marriage." She paused and smiled at Emilie. "Your mother loves you very much and truly wants you to be happy, you know. And she wants you to marry, so..." She spread her hands. "Here I am."

"To find my soulmate?" Emilie asked, not believing a bit of this nonsense.

"Yes."

"And what if I don't have a soulmate?" Emilie asked.

Lady Preston merely smiled. "Everyone does, although sadly most people do not find their true soulmates before they marry. It is my goal to ensure you do, however."

Emilie gave a little laugh. "I appreciate the sentiment, my lady, but truly I have no desire to marry whether I have a soulmate or not."

"May I ask why?" the lady asked with a slight tilt of her head.

The question took Emilie back a little. No one had ever asked her that question before, not even Eliza who was Emilie's closest confidante. "Because men are lying, self-centered creatures with no interest in anything but their own pleasure and doing whatever it is they want. They think of no one but themselves and their own interests."

Lady Preston sat back, clearly startled at the vehemence of Emilie's words. "*All* men?"

"Oh, I suppose there are exceptions, but certainly most men are that way. If I go to a ball and dance with a gentleman, we speak of him and his interests. Very rarely does a gentleman ask of my interests, nor am I supposed to speak of such things. Everything, the whole world, is centered around men. If I were to marry, my entire life would be centered around my husband. I would cease to exist. Well, I have no desire to do so. I have my own interests, my own mind and thoughts, and I would not like to have to change them to conform to those of some man."

Lady Preston thought about this for a moment. "It is true that a woman has no legal standing once she is married, but neither do you have one now. You are your brother's responsibility. Anything you do reflects on him."

"Yes, but once I come of age, I shall inherit my own competence and will be able to live on my own. Or if I want, I can continue to live with my brother. You see, it's my choice."

Lady Preston nodded. "But would you be happy alone?"

"I would. I would be able to write, paint, and do whatever I wanted."

"So, you would like to be just as self-centered as you accuse men of being."

Emilie pursed her lips together. "I plan on being the most adoring of aunts to my nieces and nephews. I also plan on volunteering with some organization to help other women. I haven't explored the possibilities as yet, but I'm certain they abound."

"I see. How very generous of you."

Emilie nodded.

"And what of your mother's happiness? And your brother's? Do you not care for them?"

"Of course I do!"

"Well, in that case, give me a chance. Allow me to find your soulmate and if, at the end of the Season either I have not located him or you still cannot see yourself marrying, I will ask your mother to consider allowing you to remain unwed. How is that for a compromise?"

Emilie thought about it. "Do you really think my mother will go along with this? She will allow me to stop looking for a husband if you cannot find one for me—one who I would be willing to marry—by the end of the Season?"

"I cannot honestly say, but I will strongly suggest it." She paused then added, "You do know your mother will insist you make an effort, whether we come to this agreement or not. It would simply be so much easier if you were to be open to the idea as well."

Emilie frowned. "Well, it doesn't look like I actually have a choice in the matter."

"No, but I do assure you, the man I find for you *will* be your soulmate. If you open up your mind and your heart to him, you will both be happier for it."

"Do you know who this man might be?"

"No, not at the moment. But, have no fear, I will find him." She smiled at Emilie with such confidence there really was nothing for her to do but agree to this outrageous scheme. And it would make her mother happy and perhaps get her to stop hounding her with men.

"So, you will introduce me to one man, is that correct?" Emilie asked, to make sure she understood this.

"Yes, that's right."

"Just one?" Emilie confirmed.

"One."

"And he will be my soulmate?"

"I will not introduce you to anyone who isn't... or, well, I will certainly do my utmost to ensure the man I introduce you to will be the one," the lady conceded.

"So, I won't need to dance with many gentlemen, or go for promenades with a different gentleman every day or anything like that?"

"No. I will do all the meeting of men until I find the right one for you. I will then introduce the two of you, and that will be that. You will get to know him, then he will get to know you, and you will have till the end of the Season to decide whether you want to marry."

Emilie could only shake her head. "It almost seems too good to be true."

Lady Preston laughed. "Well, let's see how I do." She got up and rang the bell. When the butler came back in, she requested he bring Lady Tremelling back into the room.

Emilie's mother came in a little hesitantly. She stood just inside the door looking from Lady Preston to Emilie. "Well?"

"I think I've got all the information I need, my lady," Lady Preston said brightly. "There's only one more thing which I need from you."

"And that is?" Lady Tremelling asked.

"Lady Emilie's date and time of birth," the lady said.

Emilie's mother looked at her curiously and then gave a little shake of her head as if she couldn't fathom why the lady would need such information. "She was born on the 5th of May. I don't know precisely what time it was, but it was definitely in the evening."

"Would you say before or after seven?"

"Before. The older children had had their dinner, but my husband had not yet eaten, I remember that."

"Excellent! So approximately between five and seven."

"Yes, that's right."

"Why do you need to know?" Emilie asked.

"Oh, it will help me find the right gentleman for you to marry," she answered cryptically.

Emilie shared a look with her mother. "Well, if it will help," Lady Tremelling said, finally.

"Yes, thank you. And thank you, Lady Emilie, for keeping an open mind."

# CHAPTER FIVE

Rebecca walked her guests to the door and then headed toward the back of her house.

"I beg your pardon, my lady," Connor said, stopping her. "But would you happen to be heading to your study?"

"Yes, why?" she asked.

He nodded gravely. "Then I shall see to it that your dinner is served to you there."

She gave a little laugh. "Afraid I'll forget to eat again, Connor?"

He shook his head sadly. "You do have a habit of doing so, my lady."

"Thank you for looking after me so well." She gave him a little smile and then continued toward her study. She was very lucky to have such caring servants. And he was absolutely right. When she got involved in her work, she did have a tendency to completely forget everything else.

Two of the walls in her study were lined from floor to ceiling in shelves packed with books. There were so many that she'd had to resort to laying some sideways on top of others, but she simply could not bear to get rid of any, no more could she stop herself from buying more when one caught her eye. Why only last week, her favorite antiquarian bookseller had gotten a shipment from Jerusalem of ancient Hebrew and Aramaic texts. She had purchased six of them and had no idea where she was going to put the books once she was finished translating them.

She paused here and there, pulling the books she would need for today's work from the shelves and piling them on the large worktable in the center of the room. At one point, she had had a desk placed in front of the window overlooking her tiny little garden in the back of the house, but she discovered she would spend too much time just staring out the window daydreaming instead of actually getting her work done. After that, she'd had the desk taken away, and a table moved into the center of the room, where she could still see out the window if she wished to daydream, or she could sit on the opposite side with her back to the window if she truly needed to get work done.

Today she sat with her back to the window. She pulled forth a piece of paper, sharpened her pencil, and opened her books of calendars, star charts, and interpretations of each and got to work creating a horoscope for Lady Emilie Pelham.

Before she knew it, there was a light tap on the door, and Connor entered carrying a tray for her. He placed it at the other end of the table, well away from her precious books.

"Has it been three hours already?" she asked, looking up at him.

"It has been three and a half. I peeked in thirty minutes ago but judging by the expression on your face decided to leave you for a little while longer. Now, however, it is time you took a break and ate," he informed her.

She gave him a grateful smile. "I don't know what I would do without you, Connor."

"Probably starve, my lady."

She laughed. "Indeed, I'm certain I would. Someone would find my lifeless, emaciated body and know I had worked myself to death."

The butler gave a delicate shudder. "I promised Lord Preston before he passed I would care for you, and I shall keep that promise until I am no longer physically able."

At the mention of her dead husband, Rebecca glanced up at his portrait above the mantel and felt a heaviness flow through her soul. "You are a good man, Connor."

He bowed and left her to her repast.

Brian Preston had been the best of men. Rebecca had known they were meant for each other the moment they'd met. It was then Rebecca truly began to believe in soulmates. The thought had her thinking about her conversation with Lady Emilie.

"This is truly going to be a challenging job," Rebecca said to the portrait hanging above the fireplace. Her husband's loving gaze looked down at her with understanding. "Not only does Lady Emilie not believe in soulmates, but she also has a convoluted idea of men *and* she's a Taurus. We both know when a Taurus makes up their mind about something, it is nearly impossible to tear the idea out." Rebecca shook her head sadly before continuing to eat her meal. "I cannot imagine how she came to view men so poorly. Clearly, she has not had a great deal of experience with them if she is basing her entire concept of the gender on what they speak of when at a ball. Poor thing." She took a drink from her wine glass.

"I will have to find someone strong, passionate, and caring in order to change her mind. A Cancer is just the sort she'll need." As she ate, Rebecca ran through all the available men of her acquaintance. There were a few who were the right sun sign, but none who she thought would be right for Lady Emilie.

No, she had yet to meet the man for her newest client, but she was certain he would show up sooner rather than later. "He will, won't he, Preston?" she asked the portrait. "Please, tell me he will. The girl isn't giving me a great deal of time to find him, and he's going to have quite a lot of work cut out for him once I do. No, this is not going to be as easy as last time. I can still do it, but it's *not* going to be easy."

The following evening Gabriel had just popped his hat onto his head when his grandmother's voice stopped him. "You are not going to Lady Sorrell's soiree dressed like that," she said as she made her way slowly down the stairs.

"No, I am going to my club dressed like this," he answered.

She shook her head. "Willington, you told me you wanted to find a wife. I can assure you, there won't be any eligible young ladies at your club, whereas there will be quite a few at Lady Sorrell's soiree."

He smiled at her as she reached the floor. She was dressed in a beautiful deep-plum silk with a white lace stretch of fabric covering her from her neckline to her slender throat. He bowed and took her hand, placing a kiss on her purple leather-clad fingers. "You are looking exceptionally lovely this evening, Gran."

"Do not think you can charm your way out of this one, Grandson." He could see a slight twitch of her lips, so he knew she was pleased despite her harsh words.

"I would never even attempt to get anything past you, Gran. You are much too wily."

"It is true. Now go upstairs and change. I shall wait for you in the formal drawing room." She began to make her way in that direction not even waiting for him to assent to her schemes.

"Gran, I told you I wanted to marry and I would be happy with whoever *you* chose for me."

She turned, letting out an exasperated sound. "I am not going to choose your bride for you. Have you no thought of love? How could I possibly know if a girl is destined for you?"

He let out a laugh. "Destined for me? Really, Gran, you are getting fanciful in your old age."

"I may be old, but I assure you I haven't lost it yet. I firmly believe in destiny—your grandfather and I were destined for each other. We knew it very soon after we met, and we had a very happy marriage for over thirty years." She turned around and continued her way to the drawing room, saying as she did so, "Now, go upstairs and get changed."

"Gran, just because you and Grandfather loved each other doesn't mean—"

"Gabriel, you are going to Lady Sorrell's. I shall await you in the drawing room," she snapped in a voice that would brook no arguments.

"You would think she was the marquess for all the say I get," he grumbled as he headed up the stairs to change for the evening.

Rebecca loved a good party, and it was a good thing since attending society events was essential for her budding business as a matchmaker. How else could she match people if she didn't know them? Luckily, from the time she and Brian had moved to London, when he'd been elected one of the representatives from Ireland in the House of Lords, she had been an active member of society. At first, she had done all she could to support her husband's political agenda, and then it simply became something she did for the joy of it.

Now, she did so with a particular eye out for eligible gentlemen.

She stood near the door watching who arrived at Lady Sorrell's soiree and who they were accompanied by. Lord Wickford escorted his lovely wife, followed by his stunningly beautiful mother, Lady Keppel, who, if rumors were to be believed, was born a princess in Africa. There was Lord Stenford. He came in alone and was eligible. Poor as a mouse, but certainly eligible. He was followed by Lord Willington. Was that his grandmother he was escorting? Yes, it must be.

Rebecca's interest was piqued. She followed the two farther into the room, watching as he found his grandmother a chair and made sure she was as comfortable as possible.

"I am fine, Willington," the lady exclaimed loud enough to be heard above the rumble of other voices. "Now I want you to go off and meet some nice young ladies. You certainly won't meet any hanging about with an old lady."

"Gran, I..." he started.

"You want to find a wife? Go meet young ladies," she said again, shooing him off.

He sighed before giving her a little bow, then went off to do as his grandmother told him. What a biddable man! And he was looking for a wife? Now that *was* interesting. He was kind, considerate, and amenable. A tingle made its way into Rebecca's hands—a tingle of *knowing*.

Rebecca immediately scanned the room, searching for her hostess. She spied her not too far off speaking with a footman. Rebecca hurried over to her before she disappeared.

"Good evening, Lady Sorrell. I was wondering if I might trouble you for an introduction?" Rebecca asked as the footman stepped away.

"Of course! I am so glad to hear you are considering remarrying, Lady Preston," Lady Sorrell said. She gave Rebecca an encouraging smile.

"Oh, no," Rebecca gave a little laugh. "Actually, I was wondering if you might introduce me to Lady Willington."

"Oh! You haven't met her?"

"Well, I don't believe we have been introduced. Of course, I know who she is, but I am not sure she knows me."

"Well, let's remedy that right away," Lady Sorrell said, heading straight for Lady Willington. "My lady," she said, as she reached the older woman's side. "May I introduce the Countess of Preston?"

The gray-haired woman looked up at Rebecca with a faint smile on her lips. "Of course, Lady Sorrell. It is a pleasure to meet you, Lady Preston."

"Thank you, ma'am. The honor is mine," Rebecca replied, giving the older woman a curtsy.

"If you will excuse me, I see someone motioning for me," Lady Sorrell said, giving them both a smile.

"I assume you know who I am?" the older woman asked.

"How could I not know one of the most well-known ladies of *ton*?" Rebecca said. "Truly, I asked Lady Sorrell to introduce us for two reasons, the first of which was because I have seen you so often and heard so much about you and yet never had the opportunity to be introduced."

"I see. So, you've been in London for some time?"

"Yes, ma'am. I moved here about seven years ago with my husband. Sadly, he passed a few years ago, but I chose to stay here in London," Rebecca explained.

"Rather than return to Ireland?" the woman asked, astute as Rebecca was certain she would be.

Rebecca smiled. "My accent gives me away every time, I'm afraid."

Lady Willington smiled. "I had a close friend who was Irish many, many years ago. Do you know the Viscount Gormanston?"

"Yes, we had the pleasure of meeting once, soon after I was married, before we moved here," Rebecca said, fondly remembering the vibrant man.

Lady Willington nodded. "His wife was a wonderful woman."

"She drowned, did she not?" Rebecca asked, recalling there was something unusual about her death.

"She did. Such a terrible tragedy," the older lady said with a sad shake of her head. She was silent for a moment, and Rebecca respected her privacy while she remembered her dear friend. A moment later, however, an inquisitive smile returned to the lady's face. "And what was the other reason why you wanted to meet me, Lady Preston?"

"Oh! I couldn't help but overhear your grandson is looking for a bride."

"He is, but I believe he would be too young for you, my lady."

Rebecca burst out laughing. "No, no, I am not interested for myself. But I happen to know of a young lady in search of a husband. You see, I am a matchmaker."

"As in, you find matches for young people in exchange for... compensation?" the woman asked with some surprise.

"It is mostly for the fun of it, but, yes, I am paid for the work I do, as well."

"I see. And you think my grandson might be a match for your client."

"I have a feeling..." She never knew how to phrase this without sounding as if she should be put into Bedlam. "If you think he might be amenable, I would appreciate it if he could visit with me so I might see if he is a match."

"Hmm..." The lady seemed to consider the idea.

"Do you believe in soulmates, my lady?" Rebecca asked.

The woman looked up at her, startled. "Why yes! Yes, I do. My husband and I were soulmates. We barely knew each other, but we were certain we meant to be together."

Rebecca nodded, understanding immediately. "With my husband and I, it was the very same."

Lady Willington nodded, not at all surprised.

"I cannot tell you how I know this, but I have a feeling your grandson might very well be the soulmate for my client."

"And my grandson need only pay you a visit and you'll know?" the woman asked.

"It would also help if I knew when his birthday was." Rebecca smiled.

Lady Willington gave a little laugh. "And from that you will know."

"From a combination of both," Rebecca agreed. "He wouldn't happen to have been born in June or perhaps the beginning of July?"

The woman's mouth dropped open a touch. "The second of July. But how did you know?"

The tingling in Rebecca's hands grew stronger and she could not hold back the smile from her face. "His zodiac sign is Cancer and from all I've seen of him, he is quite typical of the sign. He is kind, considerate, and caring."

"Yes! He is. Clearly, however, you have not heard of his reputation," the woman responded.

"Oh, that he is cold, rude, and quite possibly a calculating sort? Of course I have. But I look at a man's actions rather than what other people have said about him."

"You are clearly an intelligent woman, Lady Preston. Very well, you have convinced me. I shall send Gabriel to meet you. And if you do manage to match him with your client and they decide to marry, I shall make your name known throughout society."

"And you will make sure everyone knows if I do not as well?" Rebecca asked with a little laugh.

"I can make you, or I can destroy you," the woman agreed.

"Well, then, I shall do my utmost to ensure only the former occurs. And if Lord Willington is not right for this particular client, I will be happy to see if I can't find another young lady who is right for him."

"Excellent."

# Chapter Six

Emilie found her sister on the floor of the nursery in her home the following afternoon.

Eliza looked up when she entered the room. "Did Hawkins not offer to announce you?" her sister asked as she handed over the stuffed bear in her hands to her daughter, Georgiana.

"No, Mama, you must do *all* the buttons," Georgianna protested, handing the bear back.

"Oh, yes, of course. I was distracted by Auntie Emilie," Eliza said, taking the bear and buttoning up the little dress it had on.

"He did, but I told him it was unnecessary," Emilie said, joining them on the floor. "That's an adorable little dress Miss Bearina is wearing," she said to her niece.

"Mama just finished making it," Georgie informed her seriously. "But she made the buttons too small. I can't get them through the holes."

"Oh, yes, I see," Emilie said, taking a closer look at the dress. Her niece's adorable little chubby fingers were as yet too clumsy to grasp the dainty little buttons her mother had sewn onto the dress. "Well, perhaps I shall make her another with much larger buttons so you can do them up yourself."

"Oh, yes, Auntie Em, do! And make it prettier than the one Mama made with lace or ruffles," the little six-year-old insisted. It was incredible. The older Georgie got, the more she looked like a little feminine version of her father with his straight, blond hair and hazel eyes. The shape of her face was still too round with baby fat, but Emilie was certain she would thin out to have the well-sculpted face of her father. She already had his chin. Her little brother, on the other hand, was sure to look like a Pelham through and through.

"Indeed, I will. And shall it be yellow like this one or would you prefer pink?"

"I would like it to be blue," the girl insisted.

"Very well, blue it shall be." Emilie looked around for her nephew. "Where is Nathan?"

"He's out in the garden with Nanny," Eliza told her.

"They're collecting bugs," Georgie said with obvious disgust.

"Not collecting, just investigating. I've expressly asked Nanny not to allow Nathan to bring any inside the house," Eliza said.

"Good! The last time he did, I found a spider in with the blocks," Georgie said with a delicate little shudder.

Emilie had to suppress a laugh at her niece's theatrics.

"I heard Lord Willington was seen at Lady Orford's the other night," Eliza said in an offhand way.

Her sister knew Emilie's history with man because their younger sister, Amelia, hadn't been able to keep it to herself, and she had been witness to the entire episode.

"He was," Emilie said, reaching out and smoothing down the bear's dress. She mentally estimated the measurements of the stuffed animal so she could do as promised and make another dress for it.

"And I heard you gave him the cut direct," Eliza continued. She gave Emilie a sidelong glance as if asking whether it was true.

"Goodness, how gossip does spread!" Emilie couldn't help exclaim.

Her sister turned to her fully. "So, it's true?" She sounded shocked.

"I'm afraid it is." Emilie gave a little shrug as if it was nothing of import.

"Emilie! First of all, you cannot do that, no matter how awful the man," Eliza protested. "And secondly, I can't believe you had the nerve to do so!

You have always been the shyest of all of us when in public. Where did you get the courage?"

Emilie kept her eyes on the bear in her niece's hands. "Anger, I suppose."

"Well, you should channel that more often. I mean, you've made huge strides since you made your come-out last year, but still…"

Emilie gave an embarrassed little laugh. "It is all thanks to Amelia, I think."

Eliza put her hand on Emilie's arm. "I know. It can't have been easy growing up in your little sister's shadow. To be honest, I would have been there too if I weren't seven years older than her."

"She is a… vibrant person." Emilie gave a little laugh, thinking of her domineering younger sister who was so bright, talkative, and charming that she always stole the spotlight, no matter what the occasion.

"Thank goodness she never had a Season. Every young woman in the *ton* would have hated her for stealing all the attention."

"She certainly would have been considered the diamond of the Season."

"Yes. We have much to thank Sommets for," Eliza said with a laugh.

"I like Uncle Sommets," Georgie piped up.

"So do we all," Eliza agreed, giving her daughter's little nose a loving tap.

"I think Auntie Amelia likes him best of all," the little girl said, thoughtfully.

"Well, since she's his wife, I should hope so!" Emilie said.

Eliza turned back to Emilie. "So, tell me more about Lord Willington."

"There's nothing more to tell," she said with a shrug. "Mother tried to introduce him to me. I had no desire to even speak with him, so I simply turned my back and walked off to the ladies' retiring room."

Eliza shook her head in wonder. "And what of Mother?"

"I apologized to her before I did so," Emilie conceded.

"I'm certain it wasn't enough to console her."

"No, she is still furious with me and insists I tell her why I did it. I just... I just cannot tell her," Emilie admitted, keeping her gaze lowered.

"Well, I can understand that. So, what did you say?"

"I told her I needed to use the retiring room urgently," she said with a shrug.

"Surely, she didn't believe you."

"No, but she left the matter alone."

"Thank goodness for that. And I don't suppose she'll try to introduce him to you again." Eliza said, moving to get up.

Georgie hopped to her feet and took her mother's hand to assist her. Eliza was a wonderful mother and pretended the little girl actually did help as she regained her feet.

"You aren't increasing again?" Emilie asked, also standing. It was the only reason why she could imagine Georgie would feel the need to help her mother to stand. She must have seen her father do so.

Eliza gave an embarrassed little shrug and a smile. "It's early days yet, but yes, I am."

Her sister led the way down to her private sitting room, requesting tea from a passing maid along the way. Both Emilie and Georgie followed her down and made themselves comfortable on the settee with Georgie's little bear sitting properly in between them.

"Well, Mother got her own back for my rude behavior," Emilie told Eliza as they waited for their tea.

"Oh?"

"She took me to meet a matchmaker. Have you ever met Lady Preston?"

"Yes. She's Irish, isn't she?" Eliza asked, turning as a maid came in bearing a tea tray.

"She is." Emilie scooted forward to pour out.

"She's a matchmaker?" her sister asked.

"Apparently so. She spouted all sorts of nonsense to me about soulmates," Emilie told her as she handed over a cup of tea. She poured half a cup for Georgie and added a biscuit onto the side of the saucer.

After carefully placing it on her niece's lap, she turned to pour a cup for herself.

"Do you not believe in soulmates?" Eliza asked, reaching forward for a biscuit for herself.

Emilie just gave her sister a skeptical look. "Don't tell me you do?"

"I do! I'm not entirely certain his lordship is mine, but I'm happy nonetheless."

"Really?" This was news to Emilie. She hadn't realized her sister didn't love her husband.

Eliza just gave a little shrug. "I've seen some people who are just so madly in love and are just so... right for each other. Look at Amelia and Sommets. The way they look at each other? And they've always known they would marry."

Emilie couldn't help but agree. Their youngest sister was clearly head over heels in love with her husband and always had been. "Do you wish you had that?"

"As I said, I'm perfectly happy with what I've got. I would, however, be extremely happy if you could find the right man for you. Perhaps Lady Preston will be able to find him."

Emilie just frowned. She had no great confidence in the woman, but she would attempt to keep an open mind—if only to make her mother happy until the end of the Season when she would finally be allowed to fade into blissful spinsterhood.

Gabriel was breakfasting the following morning when he received a surprise visit from his grandmother. "Forgive me, Gran, but I have to admit to being rather surprised to see you up so early." He resumed his seat at the head of the table as Lady Willington chuckled and settled herself into the seat at his right hand.

"I do have to admit I rose early today in order to catch you before you went off to..." she waved a hand in the air, "wherever it is you go."

He smiled before taking a sip of his coffee. "I actually have an appointment with my solicitor this morning."

"Yes, well..." she paused as the footman placed a cup and a pot of tea before her. "I have another errand I'm afraid I must ask you to make. It doesn't have to be until this afternoon, however."

"Oh?"

"Yes, I met a woman last night. Have you ever heard of Lady Preston?" his gran asked as she poured herself a cup of tea.

"No. Who is she?"

"She's an Irish woman and apparently a matchmaker."

Gabriel nearly choked on the bite of ham he was just swallowing. He took another drink from his cup to clear his airway. "I beg your pardon? Did you say matchmaker?"

"Yes. She claims to be very good at it, naturally."

He gave a little laugh. "Well, I suppose many women consider themselves as such."

"Yes, well, she does this as a sort of employment. She apparently has a female client who she thinks might be a very good match for you. You did say you didn't care who you married, so I thought this might be a good way to find someone. I'm certain she'll do a much better job of it than I would."

Gabriel considered this and had to agree it wasn't a bad idea. "All right. What do I need to do? Does she want me to present myself to her client or—"

"No. She wants to meet you first." Lady Willington fished a card out from somewhere and handed it over to him. "Here is her direction. She is expecting you this afternoon."

And so it was that Gabriel found himself on Lady Preston's doorstep that afternoon and soon thereafter being admitted to her drawing room.

A handsome woman with dark hair and brilliant green eyes greeted him with her hand outstretched. "Lord Willington, thank you so much for coming to see me."

He bowed over her hand. "Of course. My grandmother tells me you are a matchmaker."

"Indeed. And she told me that you are looking for a match."

He smiled as he took the offered seat. "I am."

"I have spoken with your grandmother, now I would like to hear from you what sort of young lady you are looking for," she said, giving him an inquisitive look.

"I am not overly particular," he started.

"Yes, so I understand from Lady Willington."

He nodded. "I am honestly surprised my grandmother couldn't find someone for me herself. She knows most of the beau monde. I'm certain there are plenty of eligible young ladies—"

"So very many," Lady Preston agreed, cutting him off. "However, your grandmother doesn't want you to marry just anyone. She is hoping I will be able to discover your soulmate. That, after all, is my business."

"Soulmate, destiny," he sighed. "You sound just like her. I am sorry, Lady Preston, but I am not looking for some great love. In fact, I would prefer not to have one. I am looking for a practical young woman to bear my children, and I would rather there not be any of this love nonsense involved in the business." He paused. "It is quite common among the *ton*, what I am looking for. I don't see why you and my grandmother must muddy things up with... with..."

"Emotions?" Lady Preston suggested with a broad smile on her face.

Gabriel wondered if she was laughing at him. He shoved the thought aside and said, "Yes, precisely."

"Do you not believe emotions—love—should be a part of marriage, my lord?"

"It is fine and good for others but not for myself. I'm certain you have heard of my reputation?"

"As a cold-hearted man? Yes, of course. But I don't believe it for a moment."

"Well, you should because it is true. I have no interest in love. I do not want to shower some young lady with flowers, sweets, and—God forbid—poetry. I am looking for a different type of relationship altogether. And I am beginning to think it was a mistake to leave this up to my grandmother. It may be something I will need to arrange on my own in conjunction with another level-headed gentleman, a father looking to see his daughter married."

Lady Preston nodded her understanding. "That would certainly be one way to go about attaining a marriage such as the one you say you are looking for. However, I would ask your indulgence for a short while. As your grandmother may have told you, I have a client who I think you would suit perfectly. In fact, I am nearly certain of it."

"Nearly?"

"I only need one small piece of information in order to make my calculations to see if my hunch is correct."

Gabriel sat back surprised at this sudden mention of information and calculations. "And what is that, my lady?"

She smiled at him. "Your time of birth. Your grandmother has already shared the date with me, but I'm afraid I forgot to ask her what time of day you were born. You wouldn't happen to know, would you?"

He looked at her strangely. "I have to admit, er, while I was presumably present at my own birth, I can't say I looked at the time."

Lady Preston burst out laughing. "No, I don't suppose you did. Nor would you have been able to read the clock if you had happened to look in that direction. But perhaps your mother mentioned it to you at some point when you were older?"

"I don't believe..." He paused and thought about it, a memory nagging at him. "You know, I do believe she did. I remember her once commenting on how exasperated she was when her time came. She'd had plans to go out for the evening and instead spent the entire night laboring to bring me into the world instead."

"Ah, so you were born late at night?"

"Er, no, early in the morning, I believe," he told her.

"Excellent!" Lady Preston said, jumping to her feet. "Well, then, my lord, I appreciate your time a great deal and I shall be in touch. Perhaps early next week?"

He stood as well. "To meet my prospective bride?"

"Exactly. I will send 'round a note with all the pertinent information."

Later that evening, Gabriel was enjoying a drink at his favorite club, Powell's. They had the finest rum in all of London—made exclusively for the club on the owner's own plantation in the West Indies. The whole reading room smelled like the rum so many were drinking—of course, mixed in with the less enticing smell of men and too much cologne.

"Ah, there he is," a large man said as he approached.

Gabriel looked around to see who the man was speaking to, but found the fellow had stopped directly in front of him. He recognized the man from having seen him about Town, but he didn't think they'd ever met. The fellow looked like he should be working for Gentleman Jackson at his pugilistic saloon, but he was dressed as a gentleman and, clearly, was a member of Powell's exclusive club.

Gabriel stopped. "Are you looking for me?" he asked.

"You are Lord Willington, are you not?"

"I am," Gabriel acknowledged.

The man smiled broadly. "Then, indeed, you are the one I was looking for."

"I'm afraid you have me at an advantage, sir."

The man hesitantly held out a beefy hand, as if he wasn't certain it would be accepted. It was so enormous, as was the arm attached to it, that Gabriel thought the man could easily fell him in a single blow, and Gabriel was no delicate flower himself. "Uxbridge, er, Earl of," he corrected himself. "My friends call me Ox, however."

Gabriel couldn't help the smile that twitched onto his lips as he shook the offered hand.

"Yes, I know," the man said with a chuckle. "It's a little too apt. I tend to stay away from Gentleman Jackson's. Everyone wants to take me on and see if they can't fell the giant." He shook his blond head, still smiling. He then indicated the two empty chairs. "Mind?"

"No, not at all." Gabriel nodded and then took a seat.

"Heard through the grapevine that you might be meeting with Lady Preston soon," the man said, leaning toward Gabriel so he might speak more quietly without being overheard.

Gabriel frowned. "That's a mighty fast grapevine. Were there spies hanging about the lady's door?"

"Oh, you've already seen her?"

"This afternoon," Gabriel admitted.

"Well, I have to admit the grapevine is a very short one. My fiancée happened to be standing nearby last night at Lady Sorrell's soiree when your grandmother was having a chat with the matchmaker. She mentioned it to me."

"Ah. That's a bit of a relief. I'm afraid the chatter of the *ton* is something I have not missed in my time away."

"Yes, er, condolences by the way. I heard your mother passed."

"My father as well—both from influenza," Gabriel told him. "Although, I suppose it is my mother who will be... er, missed more."

Ox nodded. "She was quite active in society."

"At least with the gentlemen," Gabriel said with a slight sneer.

"Er, ah, um, yes," Ox said, shifting in his chair.

"You weren't... you didn't..."

"Oh, no! Goodness, no! I never..." Ox cleared his throat. "Not my sort."

Gabriel nodded. He never knew how many of his mother's former lovers he ran into in a day, but he had a horrible suspicion there were a good number of them. He had no desire to find out, however.

"Er, anyway... Lady Preston..." Ox said, bringing the conversation back to safer grounds.

"Yes, what do you know of her?" Gabriel asked, curious.

"I know she is one very persistent woman," Ox said with a laugh. "Doesn't take no for an answer. When she thinks she's found your soulmate, she will keep driving the two of you together until you finally give in. The darndest thing is, she's right. I recommend you listen to her."

"You sound as if you speak from experience."

Ox's smile turned inward as if he were thinking of something. "I am. I had absolutely no intention of marrying and then Lady Preston introduced herself to me and then me to Miss Ellison."

"Your fiancée?"

Ox gave a little nod and then chuckled again. "I truly had no desire to wed, and neither did Clarissa, er, Miss Ellison. Lady Preston didn't give up, though, not until we agreed to a walk in the park. I'm afraid I was lost after that."

"Lost? You got lost in the park?" Gabriel asked, wondering if perhaps this fellow had had too much rum.

"No, no!" the man let out a bold laugh that turned a few heads in their direction. "My heart was lost to Clarissa. She is... perfect. Beautiful, fascinating, and a great deal more intelligent than I could ever aspire to."

"I'm very happy for you," Gabriel said, lifting his glass to this clearly besotted fool. "However, I'm not looking for that sort of marriage. I am looking for a practical girl who would be willing to marry me with the full understanding there will be no emotional attachments. In short, I'm looking for your usual society marriage."

Ox shook his head. "Then Lady Preston is not the right matchmaker for you. She is all about soulmates."

Gabriel frowned again. "Yes, I know. She was spouting all that nonsense at me this afternoon."

"And she's right."

"I'm afraid I don't believe—"

"In soulmates? Neither did I," Ox said.

Gabriel could only sigh.

"Give her a chance, Willington," Ox urged him. "And give the lady she pairs you with a chance. You may be surprised." The man gave a meaningful lift of his eyebrows before getting up and sauntering off.

"What nonsense," Gabriel said to himself. And even if it wasn't, he had no desire for a soulmate. He wanted nothing to do with emotion, passion, or love. He was done with all that. He'd learned his lesson and had no desire to repeat the mistake.

# Chapter Seven

Emilie was just rising from her dressing table when there was a brief knock on her chamber door before her mother walked in.

"Let me see," Lady Tremelling demanded.

Emilie presented herself to her mother, even turning in a slow circle so she could see every angle of her.

Her mother nodded approvingly. "That is an excellent choice of gown. The pale green with the pink embroidered flowers is very spring-like while also bringing out the green of your eyes and the pink in your cheeks." She turned to Emilie's maid. "Well done."

The girl flushed and dipped into a curtsy. "It was Lady Emilie's choice, my lady."

"Really?" Emilie's mother turned toward her with surprise. "Well, I am especially impressed. You've never shown such good taste before."

"Why, thank you—I think?" Emilie said, confused as to whether she was being praised or insulted. Possibly a bit of both, but she decided to look at the positive side of the comment.

Her mother gave a little laugh but didn't indicate whether she'd meant her words as a compliment or not.

"So, you truly know nothing at all about this gentleman we are hosting this evening?" Emilie said, as she followed her mother out of the room and down the stairs to the drawing room.

"Nothing! I declare, it is infuriating! All I know is we are to expect two people for dinner in addition to Lady Preston—a gentleman and a lady."

"Well, presumably this would be the match and his mother?" Emilie asked.

Lady Tremelling lifted one shoulder. "I assume so, but we won't know until they get here." Clearly, her mother was feeling as nervous as Emilie for she headed straight toward the drinks and poured them both glasses of Madeira.

Emilie had just been handed hers when her brother, Evan, strode into the room looking very handsome. His light-brown hair was tousled just so, and he wore a deep-blue coat and matching breeches.

"Oh, thank goodness," Lady Tremelling said with a sigh. "I was worried you might be late. Browning said you were out when I asked earlier."

Evan came over and gave his mother a buss on her cheek. "As you see, I have returned and even changed for the occasion."

She smiled up at him. "Yes. Thank you for being—"

Her words were interrupted by the sound of the knocker on the front door, sending Emilie's heart into her throat.

"Oh, that's them!" her mother said, in a moment of panic.

"Mother! This is not *your* intended, but Emilie's. You really must calm yourself," Evan said with a laugh.

She smiled. "Yes, yes, you're right." She turned toward Emilie now that she'd been reminded of her presence. "How are you doing?" her mother asked.

Emilie opened her mouth to say she was rather nervous, but a tap on the door followed by Browning's entrance stayed her words.

"The Countess of Preston, my lady," the butler intoned.

"Oh! Lady Preston, how delightful it is to see you again," Lady Tremelling said, coming over to greet the matchmaker. "You remember my daughter, of course," she said, indicating Emilie. "And may I make you known to my son, Lord Tremelling?"

Lady Preston smiled and gave Evan a curtsy. "I am very pleased to meet you, my lord."

"And I am pleased to meet you, Lady Preston," Evan said with a bow. "And I am especially glad that you have arrived before our other guests. Perhaps you will have the ability to calm my mother before they arrive?"

Lady Preston gave a little laugh and turned toward her hostess. "It is *you* with nerves, Lady Tremelling. I would have thought it would be Lady Emilie."

"Well..." Emilie began again, but this time it was her mother who cut her off.

"Please, Lady Preston, can you tell us anything at all about the gentleman? His name? Who will be accompanying him?"

The lady gave a little laugh. "Well, I don't believe I shall divulge his name, if you don't mind. It's entirely likely that you may have already met him, and I'd like for you both to see him with new and open eyes this evening." She gave Emilie a meaningful look. "No matter what you may know about the gentleman or have heard about him, I want you to approach him this evening as if he were an entirely new-to-you person."

"But if we already know him..." Lady Tremelling started.

"You *may* know of him from society, but today he comes to you as a suitor for your daughter's hand, which is an entirely different sort of person, don't you agree?" the lady said, looking between Emilie and her mother.

Lady Tremelling sighed. "I suppose so."

"Lady Emilie?" Lady Preston lifted a querying eyebrow.

"I shall reserve judgment," Emilie said. She wasn't ready to forget whatever she might or might not know about the man. "To be honest, I don't know a great many eligible men in society, so it is unlikely I even know this man," she admitted.

"Good enough, I suppose." Lady Preston turned back toward Emilie's mother. "And as for who his companion is—." She paused as the sound of the knocker was heard down in the hall. Instead of finishing her sentence, she just smiled and said, "Well, I think you'll be finding out momentarily. They are right on time."

"There you are!" Gabriel said with some exasperation. He swallowed the rest of his whiskey and put the glass down on the table with a distinct *tink*.

"I beg your pardon, am I late?" his grandmother asked with a lift of her eyebrows.

"Nearly so. And I don't want to be late," he told her, ushering her out the drawing-room door. He offered her his arm going down the stairs.

"Goodness, I didn't realize you were so looking forward to this evening."

"I'm not. In fact, I would like nothing better than for it to be over with," he told her.

"Ah, so the sooner you get there, the sooner you can leave, is that it?"

"Something of the sort."

"And here I was thinking you were anxious to meet this mystery girl Lady Preston has determined is your soulmate," Lady Willington chuckled.

Gabriel sighed but decided they'd debated the concept of soulmates enough lately. His grandmother clearly believed in them; he clearly did not. There was no changing either one of their minds.

"Do we at least know where we are going?" Gabriel asked as he handed his grandmother up into the carriage.

"The footman has been given the direction by Lady Preston," she answered as she settled herself on the seat.

"So even you do not know?"

"No."

Wherever it was, it didn't take them long to get there. But the moment he stepped down from the coach, he was ready to step right back up again. "No..." it came out more as a groan.

"A hand if you please, Willington," his gran said from just inside the carriage. He, of course, was standing in the way of either her descending by herself or the footman approaching to assist her.

"No. It's no use. I think we should just turn around right now. This isn't going to work," he said, moving to get back into the vehicle.

"What? Absolutely not! Joseph, go knock on the door," Lady Willington said, attempting to get down by herself.

Gabriel had no choice but to assist her. "But Gran, do you see whose house this is?"

"No, I do not. I don't know where everyone in the *ton* lives. Whose house is it?" she asked, looking up at the façade of the stately townhome with its navy-blue door at the top of three marble steps.

The door opened to reveal a butler in a demur black suit.

"This is the home of Lady Emilie Pelham," Gabriel groaned. Already Gabriel could feel the excitement bubbling up inside of him, his emotions preparing for action, getting ready to tear past the wall he'd built in his mind to keep all that nonsense at bay. And warring with all of it was the intense feeling of embarrassment and fury he'd had when he'd actually faced her the other night.

His grandmother stopped and turned to him. "The girl who gave you the cut direct the other night?"

"The very same."

"Oh dear." She looked up at the waiting butler. "Well, I'm afraid there is nothing we can do about this now. Come along. It's time to show what the Willingtons are made of." With a lift of her chin, she began to climb the steps.

Emilie had time before their guests made it up the stairs to finish the glass of Madeira in her hand.

Her brother was an excellent host and offered a glass to Lady Preston and then refilled Emilie's glass and their mother's.

She was about to take another sip when the scratch at the door signaled the arrival of the butler escorting their guests. She thought it best to put down her glass instead of gulping down the wine despite her sudden desire to do so.

"The Marquess of Willington and the Dowager Marchioness of Willington," Browning intoned.

For a moment, Emilie was shocked into silence. It was a good thing she'd put down that glass a faint voice said in the back of her mind, otherwise she might have dropped it.

"Ah, Lord Willington, Lady Willington, how lovely to see you this evening," Lady Preston said when none of the residents of the house said a word.

"Lord Willington," Emilie's mother managed to whisper.

"No! Absolutely not!" Evan nearly shouted.

"I couldn't agree more," Emilie said, turning to look at her brother, wondering what he was objecting to. He had been Lord Gabriel's friend. He was the one who had brought him into their home.

"Please, my lord, Lady Emilie," Lady Preston said, turning toward them both. "What did I say earlier about forgetting anything you might have heard or known—"

"He... he defiled my sister," Evan growled, pointing at Willington.

"What?" Emilie's mother nearly shrieked.

"He didn't defile me," Emilie conceded. "That's coming on a bit too strong. He kissed me." She spun around to glare at Lord Willington. "And then never wrote to me, or visited, or said a word to me ever again, the odious rotter, thoughtless, despicable..."

"Thank you, Lady Emilie, I think we all get your meaning," Lord Willington interrupted.

"Gabriel!" his grandmother said, clearly as shocked as anyone else in the room. "Why would you do such a thing?"

"Why would I kiss her, or why would I never contact her afterward?" he asked blandly.

Emilie was spitting mad, and he just stood there as if this were all some joke. How dare he look so calm!

"Well, both," Lady Willington clarified.

"I should think it obvious why I kissed her. She's sweet, charming, and beautiful," he said, his eyes softening as he looked at her. "Well," he quickly amended, "not so sweet and charming at the moment."

Emilie burst out laughing. She couldn't help it. Oh, her anger was still boiling within her, keeping her heart rate up and, most likely, her color high, but no, she was certainly not sweet nor charming at the moment. "How kind of you to mention the fact, my lord."

Lord Willington's lips twitched, but he managed to keep a straight face as he acknowledged her words. His grandmother frowned at both of them.

"And as for why I never contacted her again—" Lord Willington continued.

"I think we've had enough of this," Evan said, interrupting him. "Thank you very much for coming, Lord Willington, Lady Willington. Lady Preston, find another match for my sister."

"But Lord Willington is the perfect match for her," the lady protested. "Clearly, both he and Lady Emilie thought so earlier—whenever this, er, kiss occurred." The woman had the nerve to smile at them all.

"It was a very long time ago," Lord Willington said.

"And yet, somehow completely unforgettable—and I don't mean that in a good way," Emilie said.

His lordship had the grace to turn his gaze to the floor.

"I still believe it proves I am right," the woman persisted.

"Surely, madam, you can't think Lady Emilie and I could possibly make a match of it with this history behind us?" Lord Willington asked incredulously.

"Oh, but I do! I think you will make a wonderful match." She smiled at them both, but Emilie just could not find it within herself to return the smile and clearly neither could Lord Willington. In fact, she was nearly certain everyone in the room was looking at Lady Preston as if she should soon be on her way to Bedlam. "However," she conceded, "I do believe they would most likely do better getting reacquainted in a more, er, private setting—but not too private," she added quickly to appease anything Evan might have said in response to her suggestion. "Perhaps a drive in the park?"

Lord Willington seemed to agree to the idea, much to Emilie's surprise. Why would he want to have anything more to do with her? She had given him the cut direct in public. She couldn't fathom what might be going through his mind. Surely, he wasn't actually considering marrying her. No, that was preposterous.

On the other hand, he *had* kissed her so many years ago. Could he possibly still hold a tendre for her? She couldn't see how. No, this was all too confusing.

He gave them all a sharp nod. "Lady Emilie, I shall pick you up..." he considered for a moment, "the day after tomorrow at two o'clock. That will give us both time to recover from our shock of this evening. Does this suit you?"

Emilie clenched her teeth together to keep her mouth from falling open. "You actually want to take me for a drive? Why?"

"Well, if nothing else, to stop the tongues from wagging about the fact that you gave him the cut direct," Lady Willington answered before his lordship could.

"There is that, but truly I am unconcerned about being the subject of gossip. No, actually, I would like the opportunity to get reacquainted with Lady Emilie."

"Might you be persuaded to explain your earlier behavior?" she asked, not even trying to keep the sharpness from her voice for all she tried to say the words as sweetly as possible.

His lips twitched again. "I might," he conceded.

"In that case—" Emilie started.

"We will think about it," Evan interrupted before she could accept his invitation.

She looked at him curiously.

"I *am* your guardian, and I don't know I like the idea of you going anywhere with Willington, even for a drive in Hyde Park," Evan said, explaining himself.

"He couldn't possibly do anything improper," Lady Tremelling said.

"I still don't like it," Evan folded his arms across his chest as well as he could in his tight coat.

"I will contact you, my lord, once my brother and I have conferred," Emilie told him. She gave her brother a look as if to ask if that satisfied him.

He gave a nod.

"Very well. I shall look forward to hearing from you."

Browning saw all three of their guests out.

# CHAPTER EIGHT

"Well, that was a complete failure," Lady Willington said after they'd said their goodnights to Lady Preston. They had seen her off in her own coach and now watched as their own pulled up next to them. "On the other hand, I do see her point about you and Lady Emilie having a connection. If you hadn't, presumably you wouldn't have kissed her all those years ago."

"Gran, if you please, can we not talk about Lady Emilie just now? I think I'd like to simply put the girl out of my mind for a little while," Gabriel said, opening the door and assisting his grandmother inside. "In fact, I believe I'm going to drop you at home and go to my club to unwind."

"You will get some dinner there?" she asked. He couldn't see her in the dark, but he heard the concern in her voice.

"Yes. And I'm sure the cook will be able to put something together for you."

"Oh, don't you worry about me."

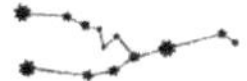

After they left, Emilie, Evan, and their mother sat down to eat the excellent meal that had been prepared, rather than see it all go to waste.

Emilie found she didn't have much of an appetite, and judging by the way her brother was just moving the food around on his plate, he didn't either. Only Lady Tremelling consumed an ordinary amount.

"You aren't really going to go out for a drive with him," Evan finally burst out after pudding had been served.

"I don't know. I have no idea if I'll even be able to bear sitting so close to him," Emilie replied, finishing the wine in her glass. She wasn't certain she should have another glass. She'd already drunk a great deal more than usual.

"He kissed you!" Evan reminded her unnecessarily.

"How do you know this?" her mother asked.

"I caught them," he told her.

"Emilie?" Lady Tremelling looked to her daughter.

"He kissed me," she agreed with a deliberately negligent lift of her shoulders.

"And did you try to stop him? Did he force himself upon you?" her mother asked, looking worried.

Emilie swallowed down her shame. "No," she whispered. "I... I welcomed it." She glanced at her brother who was staring at her incredulously. "He is handsome and kind!" she nearly shouted.

"And four years older than you, and should have known better," he snapped.

"Only four?" Lady Tremelling asked. When both Emilie and her brother looked at her, she said, "Your father was six years my senior."

"Willington clearly took advantage of a girl too young to know her own mind," Evan stated. "He was nineteen, and she was fifteen. Fifteen, Mother!"

"That is entirely too young to even be thinking of boys, I agree," Lady Tremelling conceded. "Emilie, why did you not stop him?"

Emilie opened her mouth to answer but her brother spoke first. "She didn't know any better, clearly."

"Thank you, Evan, but I *did* know better. I wanted to kiss him, which is why it hurt so very much when he never wrote to me after you both left. He didn't even say goodbye!" All the hurt from those weeks after her brother and his friend had returned to school so precipitously came back, filling her throat. "Now, if you will excuse me, I am going to bed. It's been an extremely difficult evening." She left the dining room before anyone could object.

Gabriel bypassed the glass and went straight to the bottle, ordering it the moment he'd crossed Powell's threshold.

"Very good, my lord, I shall see one is delivered to you in...?" the footman asked, as he took Gabriel's hat and gloves.

"In the reading room," Gabriel said, giving the man a nod and a coin from his pocket.

"Thank you, my lord," the man said to Gabriel's retreating back.

One of the only empty chairs was just across from the door. Gabriel wasn't thrilled with the location, but Powell's had become increasingly popular. Perhaps Wickford should be more discriminating who he allowed to join, Gabriel thought, looking around the room. There was, naturally, only the most reputable gentlemen, but maybe he shouldn't have allowed quite so many to become members. Gabriel's bottle of rum was delivered to him, the footman pouring his first glass.

"Ha! Willington!" a voice said just as he was taking his first sip. Ox threw his enormous bulk into the chair next to Gabriel. "So—"

"If you are here to discuss Lady Preston, matchmaking, or how extremely happy you are with your fiancée, you can get yourself right up again, Ox," Gabriel growled.

The jovial fellow immediately lost his smile. "Oh dear, did you—"

"I do not want to talk about it!" Gabriel interrupted him again. "That is why I am here—to *not* talk about it."

Ox nodded. "Understood." He took in a deep breath and then said, "So, what do you think of Warwick's latest proposal in Lords?"

That Gabriel *would* discuss. The Duke of Warwick was an intelligent man, and Gabriel generally agreed with him, but this time he was proposing something even too radical for Gabriel's way of thinking. He spent a very pleasant hour with Ox debating the topic and even branching off into the economic implications of Warwick's proposal, which of course led to discussing the economy in general.

Gabriel was truly enjoying himself and his opinion of Ox had grown immeasurably when they were interrupted by Lord Tremelling. Without even a word of apology or a proper greeting, he stopped directly in front of Ox. "I need to have a word with Willington."

Gabriel's new friend looked at him in askance. Gabriel had the greatest desire to tell Tremelling to go away and leave him alone, but he was certain that would be a bad idea. He gave a slight nod to Ox who shrugged and got up. "We'll talk again later."

"Do you want to take this with you?" he asked, picking up the now mostly empty bottle of rum. He meant it as a peace offering and clearly Ox saw this.

He gave Gabriel a little half smile. "No, mate, I have a feeling you're going to need that." He took his glass and wandered off with only a nod of acknowledgement to Tremelling.

His lordship took the chair Ox had been in, but he just sat and looked at Gabriel for a long minute. Gabriel was not going to fidget like a schoolboy if that's what Tremelling was waiting for. Finally, Gabriel said, "I can assure you that it wasn't my idea. In fact, I had as much knowledge as to who the lady had chosen for me as you and your sister did."

"You knew the moment you entered the door, possibly even before."

"As soon as my grandmother and I got down from the coach, but there was nothing I could do at that point, and Gran was already marching up to the door. You may not know it, but the woman is impossible to stop once she's got something in her head."

Tremelling nodded. "Emilie is the same way. Stubborn."

"Yes, well..."

"Why did you ask to take my sister out for a drive? You know very well how I feel—"

"Evan, it's been six years. We've all grown up since then," Gabriel said in exasperation. He certainly wasn't going to let on that, the moment he saw her again, all he wanted to do was explore her lovely mouth, those sweet, full lips, run his hands down—Gabriel sat forward in his chair to hide his growing interest in the girl. And yet, despite his physical attraction to her and his absolute knowledge that he should not be feeling this way, it was Emilie herself with whom he wanted so much to become reacquainted. It was her quick wit, her endearing sense of humor, her intelligence that had attracted his nineteen-year-old self to her as much as her beauty had. And it was what he wanted, even now, to have an opportunity to experience once more. "Can you not let the past—"

"You kissed my sister!" Tremelling growled.

"Yes, and she kissed me back," Gabriel said, working hard to keep his voice down when really he wanted to shout.

Tremelling's face turned an unpleasant pink making Gabriel think he'd just said the absolute wrong thing. "Listen, I know you were angry with me then, and you had every right to be. I was nineteen, your sister fifteen. I should not have taken advantage of her. I agree completely. I let my passions take control, and I am sorry, but I've done as you asked. I stayed away from her. You heard her this evening—I never contacted her, never wrote, nothing. I have kept my distance despite the fact that it hurt her." *Hurt me*, he thought, but didn't say. He shoved aside the feeling. It was irrelevant.

"Better to be hurt that way than..."

"Yes, well, I wouldn't have hurt her in any manner if I'd had a choice."

"You didn't and you don't. Leave her alone."

"I cannot. Lady Preston is going to continue pushing us together no matter what. You saw her this evening. She is convinced Lady Emilie and I are soulmates." Immediately, Gabriel held up a hand to stop Evan from interrupting, as he looked ready to do. "Don't say it. I agree completely. It's ridiculous. I don't believe in this nonsense any more than you."

"I *do* believe in soulmates, but in this case, I think Lady Preston has it wrong," Tremelling said, surprising Gabriel. "My parents were especially close. I could see the love they shared. My eldest sister, on the other hand—while I'm sure she likes her husband well-enough and he likes her, I can see the difference in their relationship. They were probably not meant to be together."

Gabriel just blinked at him for a moment. "Then how do you know Lady Emilie and I are not destined to be together? We did have rather an instant connection all those years ago."

Tremelling blew out an exasperated breath and looked away. "I don't," he said softly after a moment. He looked down at his hands clasped in his lap and then back up at Gabriel. "Six years ago, I beat you to a bloody pulp for touching Emilie."

"I remember it well, I assure you," Gabriel acknowledged.

"You were bigger than I was."

"I was a year older," Gabriel pointed out.

"You're still bigger than me, although I may have more muscle—I go to Gentleman Jackson's regularly. But that's not the point. The point is you *let* me beat you. Why?"

"Because you had the right to do so," Gabriel answered simply. "I should never have kissed your sister—not good form."

Evan nodded. "I figured as much. But if you knew you shouldn't have done so, why did you?"

Gabriel gave a little shrug. "I was nineteen and couldn't help myself. She was beautiful, funny—"

"Do you still feel that way?" Evan asked, interrupting him.

"I should hope I have more self-control now, but yes."

"For your sake, I should hope so as well. With your current reputation, can I assume you learned from that experience?"

"I have."

"So, tell me, why should I allow you to court my sister now?" Evan's eyes bore into Gabriel's.

Gabriel didn't hesitate for a moment. "Because those feelings I had for her then have not diminished over the years, no matter how hard I've tried to rid myself of them. She is still a beautiful woman—quite possibly even more lovely now. And I would like to discover if she is still as clever and charming as she was then."

"Even more so," Evan said. "But she's... quieter now, I believe. I mean, she's always stood in Amelia's shadow, but... I worry she doesn't have the confidence she should, especially when it comes to finding a husband." He paused and then sighed. "I want to see her happy and to be honest, I think the last time I saw her truly happy was those few weeks you stayed with us six years ago."

They were both silent for a minute digesting this, then it occurred to Gabriel just what Evan was saying. "Then I have your permission to court Lady Emilie?"

"If I allow this, promise me one thing," he paused, and Gabriel nodded for him to go on. "Don't tell her that it was because of me that you never contacted her. She would... she would probably never forgive me."

"So, you'd rather she continue to think me a horrible person?" Gabriel asked incredulously.

"You *are* a horrible person." And with that, Tremelling got up and walked away.

Gabriel could only laugh as he watched him go.

# Chapter Nine

"So, then he said, 'I think we should get a divorce,' and I just laughed," Eliza said to Emilie as she leaned forward to pour her another cup of tea.

Emilie gave a quick shake of her head. "I'm sorry, what did you say?"

Eliza laughed. "Nothing, actually, I just wanted to see if you were listening."

"No, did I hear the word divorce?" Emilie asked, lowering her eyebrows and wondering if she had actually missed something terribly important.

"You did, but I only said it to gain your attention. No one is getting a divorce, I assure you." Eliza helped herself to another piece of cake. "So, what has scattered your mind?

"Lady Preston asked Mother to host a dinner last night, so we could meet the man she chose for me," Emilie told her sister.

"Oh, yes! My goodness! Mother told me about this, but I'd forgotten it was to be last night. Remind me why I wasn't invited?" Eliza asked.

"Lady Preston asked we keep it as small as possible," Emilie explained. "I suppose so as to not overwhelm the gentleman."

"Ah, I suppose that makes sense." Eliza leaned forward. "So, how was he? *Who* was he?"

"You would not believe!"

Eliza widened her eyes. "Lord Easton?" her sister guessed.

"No. Try again."

Eliza thought for a moment. "Lord Cumberland? Not Lord Humphrey, he's already married," she thought aloud.

"Who is the person I would least like it to be?"

"No!" Eliza exclaimed.

"Yes."

"Not..."

"Lord Willington," Emilie said with a nod.

"Oh. My. Word! What did you do?"

Emilie gave a little laugh. "Actually, I wasn't the first one to object. Evan had that honor. He accused Lord Willington of defiling me."

"What?" The word came out as a breath of disbelief.

"I said he had done no such a thing, but I did tell everyone assembled that he had kissed me—and then never contacted me again." She placed her now empty teacup on the table in front of her. "You should have seen his grandmother's expression," she said with a chuckle.

"Lady Willington was there?" Eliza's eyes widened again.

Emilie nodded.

"So, will Lady Preston find another match for you?"

"No! She still thinks Lord Willington is my soulmate, if you can believe it!"

Eliza's mouth fell open for a moment, but then she went back to looking thoughtful. "Well, he did kiss you—and you let him."

"It *was* pointed out," Emilie reluctantly acknowledged. "But that means nothing. And besides, he clearly didn't mean to, or wasn't impressed after he did since he never spoke to me ever again." She hated the look her sister gave her, as if she felt sorry for her. "Please, Eliza, it's fine. I am very happy—now—that he never did so. He's clearly a thoughtless, self-centered man, just like the rest of them."

"But, Emilie..."

"No, really, I am not interested in him, or anyone. You know this!"

"Em..."

"Eliza."

Her sister just looked at her sadly for a moment or two, then she asked, "So, what are you going to do?"

"He asked me to go driving with him tomorrow. Evan said he wasn't sure he was going to allow it," Emilie said with a shrug.

"Do you want to go driving with him?"

"No! After what he did to me?"

"It would give you a chance to rail at him," Eliza said with a giggle.

Emilie smiled. "But what good would it do? It's been so many years. I'm really not interested in him anymore."

"Are you sure you wouldn't like to yell at him, just a little? Maybe get a bit of retribution?"

Emilie straightened her head and stared at her sister. "Retribution? As in... kiss him and then never speak to him again?"

"Well, no, obviously not that," Eliza said with a wave of her hand.

"But make him feel as bad as I felt when I never heard from him?" Emilie asked slowly, thinking about this. The idea did sound... enticing.

Eliza gave a little shrug and then shook her head. "Forget it. It's a silly, childish idea. Go out for a drive with him. Maybe he is a nice sort, after all. I mean, you liked him enough to kiss him once."

"Yes," Emilie said, not really paying attention to her sister anymore. No, now she was thinking about retribution. Revenge. How could she do it? She was certain she could think of something. She gave her sister a little smile. "You know, you really are the best sister one could ever have."

Eliza looked a little startled. "Oh, well, er, thank you?"

The following afternoon Lord Willington was exactly on time in picking up Emilie for their drive in the park. Sadly, Emilie wasn't as precise and had to make the gentleman wait for over five minutes as she donned her coat, hat, and gloves.

"I do so apologize, my lord," she said, as he handed her up into a smart phaeton. Thankfully, it wasn't one of those extremely high-perched phaetons which some gentlemen liked to drive, although it did have bright yellow wheels.

"No worries, Lady Emilie. I can be annoyingly prompt," he said, giving her a cheery smile. He loosened the reins, giving the horses the go-ahead as his tiger let them go to run and take up his perch behind.

She stayed quiet as he negotiated London traffic and headed into the park. The weather was typical for London in the spring. It wasn't too cold and there was a warm breeze in the air, but the sky was overcast. Despite that, the park was packed with members of the beau monde out to see and be seen. As they headed down Rotten Row, Emilie was made quite uncomfortable when quite a few looks of interest turned in their direction.

"It looks as if we are being noted," she said. She did not like being the object of so many stares.

"Yes, I was worried that might happen. Considering all the talk after you gave me the cut direct, I don't think we should be at all surprised."

"I am sorry. I was... taken aback at your sudden arrival," she said. It wasn't much of an excuse, but it was the best she could come up with on short notice. She supposed she should have realized he would say something and thought of something better.

"I do understand," he said kindly.

"Thank you." She did her best to sit up straight and ignore the stares of those they passed. "And if there was any harm to your reputation as a result, I'm certain it will be forgotten after today."

He gave a little laugh. "Oh, do not worry on that head. I care very little for what others think of me. And, besides, I'm not certain I had a very good reputation to begin with."

"Really?" she asked.

He glanced at her, amusement dancing in his deep-blue eyes. "Have you not heard what others say about me?"

"Er, no, I don't believe I've heard anyone speak of you—oh! Except for Lady Winbourne. She spoke of you the other night before you approached me," she said, suddenly remembering the lady's comments about him. She then immediately realized she may have just opened herself up to revealing something uncomplimentary, which she was certain would be rude to even acknowledge, let alone inform him. She was searching about for a way to change the subject when he laughed.

"I suppose she told you I was a cold fish."

Emilie's mouth dropped open a touch, and she turned to stare at him. "Yes! Those were her precise words."

He nodded. "That is what they say—and by 'they,' I mean everyone."

"But why? You are not cold," Emilie said in confusion.

He turned and gave her another smile, this one even warmer than the last. She was certain her face was flushing with such attention. "You do not think so because you don't really know me."

"Oh, come now. I know you well enough. We did spend nearly two weeks together…"

"Six years ago. I think we've both changed since then, Lady Emilie," he said.

It didn't take a great deal of thought to know he was right.

"So, now that we have established you barely know me, I think now is an excellent time to mention your brother did give me leave to pay you court," he told her. He kept his eyes straight ahead as he said this, so she couldn't see if he was teasing her or not.

"You… you are joking, are you not?" she asked hesitantly. She couldn't imagine her brother doing anything of the sort. He'd objected as strenuously as she had, if not more so, when Lord Willington had walked into their drawing room the other night.

"No, actually, I'm not," he said, turning toward her so she could see the sincerity in his face.

"But, why? I mean, he didn't like the idea of me even going out for this drive with you, at first."

"I suppose he thought about it and decided to allow us to see where this goes."

Emilie wasn't certain she was as amenable as her brother in this regard. She was still toying with the idea Eliza had suggested—getting revenge on his lordship for what he'd done to her so many years ago. Emilie had never before been so grateful to be interrupted in their conversation. A handsome, blond gentleman on a dappled horse approached them calling out Lord Willington's name.

"I say, Willington!" he said, as he pulled aside their conveyance.

Lord Willington drew the horses to a stop. "Brice. Good afternoon."

"It is, indeed, a good afternoon," the man said, doffing his hat at Emilie. "Quite lovely."

She ducked her head a little, uncertain whether he was speaking of the day or her. She was certain her cheeks were flaming once again.

"Say, did you hear Warwick's speech in Parliament the other day?" Lord Willington asked, reclaiming the gentleman's attention.

"Eh? Warwick? Yes, yes, of course."

"I look forward to hearing your thoughts on it," Lord Willington said, completely ignoring his friend's pointed looks at Emilie. Why wasn't Lord

Willington introducing her? It was as if the moment he saw his friend he completely forgot she even existed!

"Er, of course. Happy to discuss it with you," his friend said, giving Lord Willington a slightly confused look. At least it wasn't only her who was confused by his lordship's rude behavior.

"Will you be at Powell's later this evening?" Lord Willington asked, ignoring his friend's odd looks.

The man's dark eyes shifted back to Lord Willington. "What? Oh, er, yes, of course. You'll be there?"

"I will. I'll look forward to seeing you, then," Lord Willington said, giving the horses leave to move once again.

"But you haven't introduced me to your beautiful companion," the man exclaimed, sounding quite offended.

"Who? Oh, yes, of course. I do beg your pardon." Lord Willington's eyes flitted over to Emilie.

How could he possibly have forgotten from one moment to the next that she was even there? Clearly, she meant absolutely nothing to the man. And now she was beginning to understand why he'd never written to her. He'd probably forgotten about her the moment he'd left their house. What a lovely way to make a girl feel good about herself, she thought, trying to keep a little growl of irritation from escaping.

"Lady Emilie Pelham, may I make you known to the Viscount Brice?" Lord Willington asked.

"Of course. Any friend of yours is a friend of mine," Emilie said, deliberately giving his friend a bright smile, hoping it would annoy Willington greatly.

"It is an honor, Lady Emilie," Lord Brice said, giving her a slight bow.

"Yes, well, we must continue on before we cause even more problems than we already have. I will see you later, Brice," Lord Willington said, giving the reins a harder slap than necessary. The horses jumped forward and Lord Brice was quickly left behind.

Of all the men they could possibly run into in the park, Brice was the one Gabriel would have least wanted to meet. Oh, it wasn't that he didn't like the fellow. He was nice enough, but he was a well-known rake, a ladies' man—definitely not the sort he wanted Lady Emilie exposed to.

Sadly, there hadn't been a thing Gabriel could have done to avoid him. He'd ignored Brice when his friend had first called out to them, but when he actually came up and stopped his carriage, there was nothing he could do but be polite. And then he'd thought he'd fobbed him off by mentioning Warwick's speech in Parliament, but the fellow didn't get the hint and insisted on an introduction. Gabriel really hoped Brice didn't seek Lady Emilie out at the next party now they'd been introduced. He was certain no good could come of that—and he really didn't want to have to call the man out.

Gabriel gave a little start as he realized he wouldn't hesitate to do just that if Brice bothered Lady Emilie, even if he stole one tiny smile from the girl, or made her lower her shapely eyebrows in that way she did when she was annoyed. Gabriel wasn't a violent man, but when it came to Lady Emilie and her honor, he would fight to the death—which was a great deal more disturbing than any other thought he could possibly have had about the girl.

He dared a glance at her. Indeed, just as he suspected—those eyebrows were down, and she was frowning. Damnation!

"Ha! Do you see the pair attached to Lady Ayre's barouche?" he said, nodding across the way to the carriage in question as it started to pass them.

Lady Emilie jumped slightly as she startled out of her thoughts. "What? Oh, yes. What about them?"

"They used to belong to Lord Bowlette. I remember how he used to complain about those horses—could hardly walk at a pace, he would say. I do hope Lord Ayres got a good price for them." Gabriel couldn't believe he was talking horseflesh with Lady Emilie, but he had to take her mind off Brice and Gabriel's own rude behavior.

"I don't know either Lord Bowlette or Lord Ayres, so I couldn't say if one would be likely to take advantage of the other," she commented.

"Ah, yes, well, you see, Bowlette has a tendency to spend a bit more than what's in his pocket, so I'm not surprised he needed to sell the horses," Gabriel said, searching his mind frantically for something—anything—else to talk about.

"Oh, dear. Well then, I do hope Lord Ayres got a good deal on them." She sounded as distracted as she had a right to be. A more boring conversation for a young lady there never was.

"So... er, what is next on your social calendar, Lady Emilie?" he asked, finally hitting upon another topic.

She gave him a suspicious look as if trying to figure out just what he was up to. "I'm not certain. My mother makes those decisions."

"Well, then, if you could find out whether you are free tomorrow night, I would love to escort you both to the opera," he said, wondering where this idea had come from. It was true, his grandmother was speaking of wanting to attend the opera a few days ago, but he'd done nothing to procure a box as yet. He wasn't particularly fond of listening to a group of people caterwauling on stage while the other occupants of the theater stared at you—you either have to look interested in the singing or stare right back. It was not Gabriel's idea of a most pleasant evening out.

"Oh! That would be lovely. I've never been to the opera before. My brother has taken me to the theater but never the opera," she said, her expression lightening immediately.

"Really? My grandmother is particularly fond of attending opera. At her request, I've gotten a box for tomorrow night's performance," he said, smiling over at her.

"I would enjoy that immensely, my lord, thank you."

He gave a nod, as if it were all settled. Of course, now he'd have to hope a box was still available.

# Chapter Ten

"Oh, Willington, how did you ever convince Warwick to lend you his box?" Lady Willington exclaimed as she walked through the deep-red curtain into the opera box.

"Quite easy, actually, Gran," Lord Willington said, holding open the curtain for Emilie and her mother. "I asked."

"I've heard His Grace is a very kind and considerate gentleman," Lady Tremelling said as she took a seat next to Lady Willington in the front of the box. That left the two seats behind the ladies for Emilie and his lordship. Emilie wondered if this was deliberate or merely an oversight by both of the older ladies.

She shared a curious look with Lord Willington, who also stood there looking a little nonplussed at the choice of seating arrangements.

"What is it, Willington?" his grandmother asked, turning around in her chair.

"Er, nothing, Gran," he said, giving her a little smile. He indicated the chair behind her to Emilie.

"Oh, you think it odd that Lady Tremelling and I are taking the front seats?" the astute woman asked with a little chuckle. "Well, it is because we are the only two actually interested in seeing the performance. I'm certain neither you nor Lady Emilie care very much for opera. Young people don't," she added in an aside to Emilie's mother who nodded her agreement.

"A good number of younger people do," Lord Willington protested.

"Just not us," Emilie added with a laugh of her own.

"Well, no," his lordship agreed, giving her a conspiratorial smile.

"Therefore, you two can sit in the back and chat or look about as Lady Willington and I enjoy the program," Emilie's mother said. As soon as she'd said this, however, she raised her opera glasses to see who else was seated in the boxes about the theater.

"I think it's not just the music that she's most interested in," Emilie said quietly to Lord Willington.

"Nor is my grandmother," he agreed, giving a nod to Lady Willington who was now leaning toward Emilie's mother and whispering as she nodded toward someone in the box across from them.

Emilie laughed behind her hand to hide the sound.

It did have to be said the two ladies did actually pay some attention to what was happening on the stage during the performance—but only once in a while and for very short periods of time. Emilie and her companion carried on an interesting quiet conversation about the Duke of Warwick's latest proposal in Parliament, which Emilie had deliberately read up on. She had been curious as to what could have distracted Lord Willington so much that he forgot she was next to him when they'd been speaking to Lord Brice in the park.

As the curtain closed for the intermission, Lord Willington stood and stretched. He then held out a hand to Emilie. "Would you care to go for a walk?"

"I would very much, thank you."

"I shall go with you if you don't mind, Lady Willington," Lady Tremelling said.

"Oh, no, not at all. I believe some friends of mine will be stopping by momentarily. You all go on." The older lady shooed them on their way.

The lobby was packed with audience members so one had to squeeze in between people to move anywhere.

"Goodness! This is worse than Lady Sorrell's soirees," Emilie commented with a laugh.

Lord Willington turned to give her a smile as he attempted to make a path for them to get through.

"My word!" a woman exclaimed from nearby. "Is that Lord Willington with Lady Emilie?"

"I saw them together at the park the other day," another woman replied.

"Truly? What does Lady Emilie think she's about? She gives him the cut direct and then turns around and allows him to escort her about Town?" the first asked.

"Well, what can you expect from a wallflower who has no idea how to go on?" the second said. Then she added, "Perhaps she only cut him to gain his interest."

"Well, it's certainly an unusual way to do so," the first commented, her voice growing softer as they moved away.

"It worked," the second said.

Emilie could feel her face heat with embarrassment.

"Lady Emilie, please do not let the comments of others disturb you," Lord Willington said softly in her ear. She looked up at him. He was so close she could feel the heat of him and even smell his cologne amongst the press of other scents and bodies in the crowded room. She could only nod before she turned back to see if her mother had overheard the two women as well. From the glare in the lady's eyes, it was clear that she had. Unfortunately, the glare was directed at Emilie, not the other women.

Emilie could only hope she wouldn't be hearing about this later.

The second half of the opera passed in much the same way as the first, and Emilie thanked the stars that her mother was not given an opportunity to speak with her privately.

At the end of the performance, Lady Willington turned around to face her grandson and Emilie. "Would you mind very much sitting here a little while until the crowds have thinned? I find it difficult to maneuver with so many people about."

"No, not at all," Emilie said immediately, and returned to her seat, which she'd just stood up from.

"I think it's an excellent idea, Gran," Lord Willington said.

They sat for another twenty minutes discussing who was seen with whom and even managed to touch on the actual performance in their conversation. When they finally made their way down the stairs and out to Lord Willington's coach, most of the crowds had gone.

Lord Willington was walking ahead of Emilie and her mother, assisting his grandmother down the front steps of the theater when a laughing couple walking arm in arm caught Emilie's attention. She stopped and did a double take, looking closely at the man in particular.

She grabbed onto her mother's shoulder, two steps down from her. "Mama, look," she whispered.

Lady Tremelling, too, stopped walking, glancing back to see what Emilie was looking at before turning her head toward the couple in front of them. For a moment Emilie thought her mother was going to accost Lord Sommets, but instead her mouth just pinched into a thin line. "Come along, Emilie," she said quietly and continued toward Lord Willington's coach.

"But, Mama," Emilie said, catching up to her.

"*Sh*! I can see with my own eyes."

Emilie stopped and stared at her brother-in-law, Lord Sommets. He giggled and pulled the opera singer he was walking with closer so she was pressed right up against his side.

Emilie's arm was suddenly pulled sharply, and she had to stifle a cry of pain. "What Sommets does is none of your business, Emilie Ann Pelham," her mother whispered fiercely.

"Do you think Amelia knows?" Emilie asked.

"I am certain she does not, and you are not to say a word to her either. It is none of your business," her mother repeated.

"But—"

"Look, here is his lordship's coach," her mother said, unnecessarily as the vehicle was directly in front of them and Lord Willington was handing his grandmother up into it.

Emilie couldn't help but watch her brother-in-law and his opera singer continue down the street as they passed, completely oblivious to anyone else around them. She was seething with anger. Her sister was madly in love with that reprehensible profligate! How dare he have a mistress!

She suppressed a growl of anger and frustration. Men were absolutely the worst!

Her gaze slipped over to Lord Willington sitting next to his grandmother. He was no better than any of them.

No, Eliza was right. She needed to get her revenge on this man. He most definitely deserved to feel what it was like to have his heart broken the way he'd broken Emilie's... the way Amelia would feel if she ever found out her husband had a mistress.

# CHAPTER ELEVEN

The Reading Room at Powell's the following evening was emptier than usual when Gabriel sauntered in. He had just taken a seat and ordered a glass of rum when Easton bounded into the room with three other younger men all talking and laughing loudly. An older gentleman near the fireplace, who was reading a newspaper, shushed them with a *tsch*! and a glare.

Easton received pats on his back from his friend and fell into the chair next to Gabriel. "Oh, you missed a good one, Willington," he said quietly with a chuckle.

Gabriel gave the man a little smile. "What did I miss?"

"Foxworthy had a run of seven—seven!—hands of vingt-et-un. Can you believe it? Even Wickford stopped and made him take off his coat to be sure he wasn't hiding cards up his sleeves," the man said laughing.

Gabriel, too, laughed. "But that's remarkable!"

"I know it!" Easton shook his head. "And then at the end of it, he'd only won a monkey."

"The other men with him didn't dare risk too much money on such a winning streak?" Gabriel guessed.

Easton nodded before taking a sip from the glass he'd brought with him from the gaming room.

"Still, quite impressive," Gabriel said with a little chuckle.

"So, is it true that you escorted Lady Emilie to the theater last night?" Easton said, changing the subject rather abruptly as he cocked his head in curiosity.

"The opera," Gabriel acknowledged. He wasn't at all surprised that Easton was asking about it. He had only been more surprised that other men hadn't already done so. On the other hand, he could see a number of men sitting nearby lean a little toward them to hear the conversation better.

"And took her out for a drive two days prior?" his companion confirmed.

"Indeed."

"But... how? How did you manage it? I took her for a stroll at a ball one evening and could barely make it around the room in her presence."

Now it was Gabriel's turn to look with curiosity.

"The girl doesn't talk!" Easton explained. "I felt as if I was being interrogated. She asked me question after question, not giving me a chance to reciprocate—I couldn't even ask what she thought of the blasted weather," the man said with a chuckle.

"Really?"

"A more awkward young lady I have never met. How do you stand being in her company?"

"I suppose she's just more comfortable in my presence than yours. We have quite fascinating conversations. Why, the other night at the opera—neither one of us had any interest in actually listening to the music—we had a fascinating conversation about the bill Warwick put up in Parliament. She was very informed and had a solid opinion."

"That her brother fed to her, no doubt," Easton said into his glass.

"No, actually, I've spoken with Tremelling about it as well, and he holds a very different opinion than she did," Gabriel told him.

Easton lowered his glass in awe. "You must be joking."

"No." Gabriel smiled as he remembered the discussion he'd had with Lady Emilie about her opinions—not all so well founded in fact, but more so in emotion, but then she only had the account written up in the newspaper informing it. "I find her quite charming and intelligent to converse with." Gabriel sat back in his chair feeling quite pleased with himself. "I suppose you just don't interest the girl," he said as blandly as he could.

Easton *harrumphed* then sat there in silence for a minute. Gabriel started when the man suddenly sat up. "I say," he started, "what happened to Thetford? Don't believe I've seen him around lately."

"In the country with his wife. She has gone into confinement—expecting a joyful event any time now."

"Ahh..." Easton nodded his understanding. He then shook his head. "Poor sod." And with that, he got up and sauntered away.

For the next few days, Gabriel couldn't seem to stop from smiling every chance he could. He was going to ruin his reputation as a cold fish at a very fast rate if he went on like this. He was just so tickled that Lady Emilie only spoke comfortably with him. He'd even confirmed what Easton had said by speaking with a couple of other men who he knew had been introduced to the girl. All of them had said exactly the same thing. They had been unable to hold even an ordinary conversation with her. Either she didn't say anything or she would grill them with question after question, never once answering one of theirs.

It was no wonder she spent all her time at parties as a wallflower. Men had no interest in even attempting to converse with her.

This was going through Gabriel's mind as he escorted his grandmother into Lady Farnsworth's soiree a few evenings later. As usual, he was abandoned almost immediately as his grandmother sought out her friends.

He began to scan the edges of the drawing room for Lady Emilie, but his view was suddenly blocked by an enormous man. Gabriel looked up to find Ox smiling at him. "Oh, good evening," Gabriel said.

"Good evening." He stepped slightly aside to introduce the tallest woman Gabriel had ever seen. She was practically as tall as he, and he was above average at six feet. "Lord Willington, may I present my fiancée?"

"I would be honored," Gabriel said, smiling at the woman. She was, indeed, very pretty, just as Ox had told him. Everything about her was long and slender. Her hair was a lovely deep mahogany, and her eyes were a very pretty blue matching her gown.

"Gabriel, Lord Willington, Miss Ellison," Ox said, introducing them.

Gabriel took the lady's hand and bowed over it, keenly aware of his friend's eyes on him.

"It is so nice to finally meet you, my lord. Jonathan has told me so much about you," the woman said after executing her curtsy.

"Jonathan?" Gabriel asked, momentarily confused.

"Oh, perhaps you call him Ox?" she said with a giggle as she looked up at her fiancé. He gave a nod.

"I didn't know your Christian name was Jonathan," Gabriel said.

"Very few people call me by my given name. In fact, I think Miss Ellison and my mother are the only ones, and even then, Mother usually just calls me Uxbridge."

Gabriel nodded. "I can always tell something is wrong if my grandmother calls me Gabriel."

They all laughed, but just then, Gabriel saw Lady Emilie as a couple standing near her moved out of his line of sight.

Ox raised his eyebrows. "Did you just catch sight of Lady Emilie?"

Gabriel was certain his cheeks had turned pink. "Am I so obvious?"

Miss Ellison giggled. "Your eyes suddenly grew very wide."

He could only shake his head. "How embarrassing."

"Think nothing of it, my man. Go on and speak with her. We are going to join the next set if my lovely fiancée would care to dance?" Ox said, giving a slight bow toward Miss Ellison and holding out one very large hand. She just laughed and placed her hand in his.

Gabriel didn't even watch them go. He was already on his way across the room.

♉

# CHAPTER TWELVE

Emilie was standing across from the door into Lady Farnsworth's drawing room with Miss Merrill when she noticed Lord Willington come in with his grandmother.

"What is it?" Miss Merrill said, turning and looking in the same direction as she.

"Oh, nothing, why?" Emilie asked, turning toward her friend and pasting an innocuous smile onto her lips.

"You started as if you saw someone."

"Did I? No, there is no one in particular," Emilie told her. Goodness, she had to get better at not giving herself away! She continued to watch Lord Willington out of the corner of her eye, though. She wondered whether tonight was the night she should begin her campaign.

She had decided to make the man fall madly in love with her—and then reject him. It was the easiest and most direct way she could think to get back at him for breaking her heart so many years ago. Yes, she would lavish attention on him, flirt, and charm him until he didn't know if he was coming or going and then she would turn her back on him and never speak another word to him. That would teach him a lesson!

And just as she'd hoped, as she glanced in his direction, she could see he'd spotted her and was coming over. She placed a warm, welcoming smile onto her lips as he approached.

"Good evening, Lady Emilie," he said, with a bow.

She curtsied in response. "Good evening, my lord. May I make you known to my friend, Miss Merrill?"

He turned and bowed, giving Miss Merrill a polite smile. "It would be an honor."

Miss Merrill curtsied after giving Emilie a wide-eyed look. She was clearly remembering how Emilie had treated him not too long ago. Emilie forgot she hadn't told her friend that she'd decided to let the past go.

"Lord Willington and I have decided to make a fresh start on our relationship," Emilie told her friend.

"Oh!" Miss Merrill said. She gave his lordship an uneasy smile.

"If I'm not being too bold, I might even venture to say we're becoming friends," he said, giving Emilie a warm smile.

"Indeed, you might say that," Emilie agreed.

"And in such a spirit, might I ask for this dance?" he asked, holding out his arm for her to take.

Emilie took in a deep breath. She had carefully cultivated her persona as a wallflower. It was easy, comfortable, and most importantly, it kept men away from her. But now… how was she going to do this? How was she going to be the bright, witty, and charming young that Lord Willington would fall for?

An idea popped into her mind. The first person she thought of when she imagined a girl like the one she needed to be now was her younger sister, Amelia. She knew how to be all those things—and she was beautiful too. Emilie had been beyond relieved when her sister had decided to marry their neighbor, Lord Sommets, rather than have a Season. She would have most certainly been labeled a diamond of the first water.

With her sister firmly in mind, Emilie turned a bright smile onto Lord Willington. "I would enjoy that a great deal. Thank you, my lord." She turned to her friend. "If you will excuse us, Miss Merrill?"

"Of course," the young lady said, still looking rather confused.

"I do hope we are becoming more than just friends, Lady Emilie, or am I getting ahead of myself?" he asked soon after the dance had begun.

This was the perfect opportunity, Emilie thought. She couldn't have planned for her seduction to begin in a better way than this. Strangely, her throat tightened ever so slightly as she nodded. "I do hope so, my lord," she answered, forcing the words around the constriction. What was this? Was she just a bad liar? She never had been before. On the other hand, she hadn't had very many occasions when she'd had to lie so boldly.

It certainly could be because she was putting her plan into action. She was quite determined on getting her revenge. After what Willington had done to her, she wanted nothing more than to see him hurt. Of course, even then, he probably wouldn't feel it as acutely as she had—she had been merely fifteen when he'd broken her heart, and he was now a grown man. Still, it would be worth it.

He was saying something, she suddenly realized, and she hadn't been paying any attention. "I do beg your pardon, my lord, I didn't catch what you said. The music is quite loud," she said, giving him a look of supreme interest.

"I just said I had a most enlightening conversation last night at my club."

"Oh? On the Duke of Warwick's bill?" she asked.

"No, although one might think as much. Actually, the topic under discussion was you," he said before turning away with the movement of the dance.

"Me?" she said, missing a step. She quickly caught up with the dance and moved behind and around the girl to her right before meeting up with Lord Willington again. "Me?" she asked again, only this time without quite so much surprise in her voice.

"Indeed. Other gentlemen were asking me how I managed to hold a conversation with you. Apparently, you have made it quite difficult for other men to do so, questioning them instead of answering kindly intended questions to you. They said they felt like they were being interrogated rather than having a conversation."

Emilie burst out laughing but quickly hid it behind her hand. Luckily, she was forced to move away from his lordship for a moment, giving her a breath to regain her composure. "I'm afraid they were right," she admitted.

He looked at her curiously. "But why would you do that? You haven't done so with me. We've had delightful conversations."

She just gave a little shrug. "I suppose it was just my way of keeping them at arm's length. I wasn't interested in them."

"Ah, but you are interested in me?" he asked, giving her a happy little smile.

She moved away with the dance but looked back over her shoulder as she turned about, keeping her eyes on him. He was doing the same but looked curious and not a little pleased with himself.

"And how are you finding the weather, my lord?" she asked, when they came together again.

He burst out laughing. "So, you are not going to answer my question?"

"Have you seen Lord Pentworth's new curricle? I heard he paid much too much for it. It had bright yellow wheels, but I heard he had them painted red."

Lord Willington just smiled at her for a beat before he said, "I have heard he'd gotten taken on that purchase, although I had not heard he'd painted the wheels. I must say, I much prefer yellow for wheels, don't you?"

She barely held back a laugh, and they enjoyed a meaningless, yet somehow very flirtatious conversation for the rest of the dance.

Gabriel had never enjoyed a dance more. He felt a strange buoyancy in his chest, a lightness he hadn't felt in far too many years. It was as if something had been pressing down on him and suddenly it had been lifted.

As he returned Lady Emilie to her friend, the girl was standing there all alone, looking about her. Her large brown eyes were wide, watching all the people dancing and chatting. Idly she twisted a piece of colorless blonde hair that had come free of its pins. He wasn't certain, but he thought he heard the slightest sigh coming from Lady Emilie. Suddenly, he knew exactly what he needed to do, what would make her happy.

After bowing to Lady Emilie and thanking her for the dance, he shifted his attention to her friend who was now looking much happier with Lady Emilie by her side. "Miss Merrill, might you be willing to stand up with me for the next dance?"

"Me? Oh! I... er..." Her cheeks pinkened as she turned and looked to Lady Emilie as if for permission. The expression of surprise on the girl's face was overshadowed by the broad smile on Lady Emilie's as she pushed her friend forward toward him. "Oh, do go, Miss Merrill. Lord Willington is a wonderful dancer. He didn't step on my toes even once," she said with a laugh and a knowing look at Gabriel. Was it possible for his heart to expand even more?

He laughed and held out his arm for the girl to take. He was a little tired from the last dance, but he was certain he could manage two dances in a row, especially seeing how happy this made Lady Emilie.

He was soon hopping and moving with the dance—this one a quadrille. "Miss Merrill, I do not know why you are shy about dancing," he said, as he took her hand to turn her about. "You are a very graceful dancer."

"Oh, thank you, my lord," the girl said, keeping her eyes on the ground. "It is not dancing that has me quaking, but..." She stopped speaking, and it wasn't because they were forced to move apart, although they were a moment later.

Once they came back together, he prodded her. "But what, Miss Merrill. You can tell me. I won't share it with a soul, on my word."

She shifted with the dance, and he was able to see over her shoulder to the other quartet of people dancing nearby. He was so surprised to see Lady Emilie there he completely missed Miss Merrill's answer to his question.

"I do beg your pardon? Er, the music," he said, using the same excuse Lady Emilie had used when she'd gone somewhere else in her own mind for a moment as they'd been dancing earlier.

She smiled shyly up at him. "Well, seeing as you are truly not interested in courting me, but only dancing with me to get in Lady Emilie's good graces... it's that some gentlemen frighten me. They have so much energy," she admitted.

Goodness, had his motives been so very obvious? He felt momentarily ashamed. "It is true that a good number of gentlemen have a lot of energy," he agreed, ignoring the first part of what she'd said. "On the other hand, if perhaps, you were to show a little more yourself, a gentleman would not feel as if he needed to be energetic enough for the both of you."

Luckily, the movement of the dance had them change places in the square, so his back was now to Lady Emilie's.

"So, you think it is because I'm quiet and shy that men feel they need to be brighter and louder?" Miss Merrill asked, frowning at him.

He wondered if she could tell his attention was elsewhere. He simply couldn't help it. He needed to see who Lady Emilie was dancing with, but the man had his back to Gabriel.

He returned his attention to Miss Merrill and nodded. "Yes, that's it precisely."

"Hmm, I hadn't thought of it that way. I suppose I could try to be a little more energetic myself."

"Try it, perhaps it will work. At the very least, you will attract more gentlemen to your side. Men are always more attracted to brighter, livelier girls."

"Thank you, my lord, I shall try it."

Miss Merrill had said something again and Gabriel knew he had to stop watching Lady Emilie and start paying attention to his own partner. This lasted for approximately three movements until he switched places with his partner once again. This time, he distinctly heard Lady Emilie say, "Doing it too brown, Lord Brice, truly," with a laugh.

Brice! What the hell was Brice doing dancing with Lady Emilie? Damnation, but he had known he should never have introduced the rake to her!

"Was it something I said?" Gabriel heard as he grasped hands with Miss Merrill in the center of the square.

"What?" He redirected his attention back to the girl.

"You are looking... well, furious," she told him, her large eyes looking worried and a little watery.

"Oh! No, no, I just, er, I just saw my grandmother standing by herself, that's all, and I, er, I was worried for her," he said, making something up on the spot.

"I am so sorry. Do you need to go to her?" Miss Merrill asked, turning to see if she could spy Lady Willington.

"No, thank you. I'm certain she'll be fine. You are very kind," he said, forcing a smile onto his lips. He really had to pay more attention to this girl and not Lady Emilie and Brice. But just the thought of… no, no… he had to stop this. Brice had every right to ask Lady Emilie to dance. She wasn't Gabriel's yet.

That thought nearly threw him off his steps. His? She *wasn't* his. And she probably never would be. He shouldn't want her to be! He would have thought he'd learned that lesson six years ago. Despite the fact that her brother had said he could court Lady Emilie, he wasn't so sure the man wouldn't change his mind. No, it would be much safer to just remain friends with the girl and nothing more despite Lady Preston's insistence they were destined for each other, or whatever the nonsense she'd spouted was.

He redoubled his efforts to put Lady Emilie straight out of his mind and focus his attention on her friend, the now very worried-looking Miss Merrill. Damnation! That was his fault.

He managed to make it through the rest of the dance only looking toward Lady Emilie twice more before telling himself firmly that he would speak with her after the dance and warn her off Brice. He only hoped she heeded his words and didn't think him jealous—because he most certainly was not!

He bowed to Miss Merrill at the end of the dance and then held out his arm to escort her back to her wall. There was an older lady standing there looking about when they arrived, but he looked to see if Lady Emilie and Brice were just behind him. Oddly enough, they weren't. Where could they have gone?

"... my mother, Viscountess Merrill," Miss Merrill was saying.

Gabriel turned back to the lady in time to bow to her. "It is a pleasure to meet you, my lady." He took a step to his left, forcing her to turn slightly so he could look over her shoulder toward the dance floor. Where had—oh no, no, no, no!

His gaze happened to look beyond the couples assembling for the next dance and saw Brice leading Lady Emilie outside onto the balcony. He couldn't let her go out there! Goodness only knew what that rake would try with a sweet, innocent like Lady Emilie.

# Chapter Thirteen

"Lord Willington?" Lady Merrill's voice cut through his thoughts.

"I do beg your pardon. I was, er, checking on my grandmother. Just making sure she was all right. What did you say, my lady?" he said, redirecting his attention to her.

"Oh! Lady Willington is just fine," the lady said, putting a comforting hand on his arm. "She's right over there. I was speaking to her just a little while ago. It's so hard to believe she is still as energetic as ever." The woman chuckled.

Gabriel forced his lips up into a smile. "Yes, indeed. She quite wears me out at times," he said politely. How was he going to get out of this? His grandmother, unfortunately, was perfectly fine and speaking with some friends on the other side of the drawing room. But Lady Emilie was still outside on the balcony with Brice. Where was Lady Tremelling? Surely the woman should be keeping a closer eye on her daughter. Or Lord Tremelling. Was he even here?

Gabriel's stomach tightened into a knot at the thought of Lady Emilie, Emilie, out there all alone with that rake. Who knew what he might be trying to do! He was ready to stop being polite and simply run out there and put his fist right into Brice's face, preferably his nose, preferably hard enough to break the damned perfect appendage so badly the man would never be able to attract another innocent young woman into such a situation ever again.

And then Gabriel realized what an idiot he was being. This was none of his business. Lady Emilie was none of his business. She wasn't his. He had absolutely no claim on her whatsoever—hadn't her brother informed him of this again and again as he'd smashed his fist into Gabriel's face when they'd arrived back at school after that fateful Easter holiday?

Gabriel could still remember it as clear as day. That, along with looks of disgust from all the friends he'd shared with Tremelling. Once their friends had returned to school, Evan had informed them that Gabriel had tried to take liberties with Lady Emilie but he'd been stopped just in time—the little bending of the truth was to keep Emilie's reputation intact. Gabriel had been intelligent enough, even then, not to correct him. Gabriel sighed. Hadn't he learned his lesson then? Surely, he had.

His heart leapt into his throat as he saw Lady Emilie come back through the door from the balcony—without Lord Brice. That was odd. He also caught the words of the woman standing directly in front of him. "... clearly not interested in speaking with us," Lady Merrill said, turning on her heel and walking away from him, dragging her daughter with her.

Oh, goodness. He'd been completely ignoring the woman, hadn't he? He groaned inwardly. He'd been extremely rude, but he just couldn't help it. Nor could he help noticing right at this moment the anger on Lady Emilie's face. What had that randy lecher done to her? And where was he? Was there a reason he hadn't escorted her back into the ballroom?

Gabriel's curiosity won out, and he made his way behind other couples to be sure Lady Emilie didn't see him heading for the French doors and then slipped outside. He first looked left, but the balcony was empty, then he glanced to his right. There, in the pale light from the drawing room, Brice was standing, bent at the waist, his hands on his knees.

Gabriel walked over. "All right, there, Brice?" he asked, as blandly as he could.

"That little... girl kneed me in the..." Brice ground out.

A laugh bubbled up inside of Gabriel. She had kneed him in the groin? "Well done, Lady Emilie!" The words spilled from his lips before he could catch them.

Brice glared up at him. "You think this is funny?"

"I think you got what you deserved." He paused and then considered the man. "Actually," he added, "you should consider yourself lucky that you are currently incapacitated because otherwise my fist would be becoming much better acquainted with your nose just about now."

Brice straightened himself as best as he could. "What do you mean?"

"Let me put it into plain English. If you weren't obviously in pain, I would be planting you a facer," Gabriel explained slowly and deliberately.

"For what?" the man protested.

"For whatever you did to Lady Emilie that caused her to have to defend herself."

"All I did was—" The man wisely stopped speaking. His eyes darted around Gabriel's face and no doubt he could tell whatever he had been about to say would not be taken well. Brice swallowed. "It, er, doesn't matter," he said softly.

"The only thing which matters at this moment is that you will be paying Lady Emilie a visit tomorrow to apologize for your behavior," Gabriel told him. "Unless you do wish to have that pretty nose of yours altered?"

Brice shook his head briefly.

"Excellent. I'm so glad we understand each other. Have a good evening." Gabriel turned and started to walk away. "Oh, and once your apology has been accepted, you will never bother the young lady ever again. Is that understood?"

Brice sighed. "You can be sure I won't. I happen to prefer being, er, in good working order."

Gabriel nodded and continued back into the drawing room with a little chuckle.

He caught a glimpse of Lady Emilie. She was standing back against the wall with Miss Merrill, right where she should be. His heart gave a funny little leap when he saw her standing there. She was fine, clearly unharmed by her little escapade with Brice. He was impressed, but he supposed he shouldn't be. She was a remarkable woman.

But she was not for him, he reminded himself. He should not even be approaching her as he was. He was to marry someone with whom he would share no affection. He must.

He forced himself to turn away from Lady Emilie, annoyed with himself for so quickly forgetting his own decision. He would do better. He had to. He couldn't afford to allow his passions free rein once again.

Emilie looked around the room for Lord Willington as she made her way back to Miss Merrill by the wall. Her chest was still heaving in fury at that lout, Lord Brice. She hadn't exactly expected Lord Willington to come to her rescue, and she hadn't needed him to do so—she was perfectly capable of defending her own honor thanks to a short but effective lesson from her brother the summer after that fateful Easter holiday. But still, it might have been nice if he'd even noticed she'd been gone from the ballroom.

But no, what was she thinking? Lord Willington was probably off charming some other innocent into thinking she was worth his time. Emilie knew better. No one was worth his time. No one was more important than himself. The only person who he truly doted upon, truly looked after was his grandmother. She did have to acknowledge that— Lord Willington loved his grandmother and took excellent care of the lady.

Emilie searched around the room for Lady Willington and found her sitting in a chair like a queen, surrounded by admirers and friends. But her grandson was nowhere to be seen. What had happened to the man? Oh well, she shouldn't be thinking of him anyway, although she was as determined as ever to see her plan through.

"Who are you looking about for?" Miss Merrill's voice cut into Emilie's thoughts.

"Hmm? Oh, no one. Did you enjoy your dance with Lord Willington?" she asked her friend.

"Oh, yes. He's a very good dancer. Although, he was rather distracted by you dancing just behind me."

"Oh! I didn't even notice," Emilie said, lying through her teeth.

"Who was it you were dancing with?" Miss Merrill asked with a little smile that told Emilie she knew a lie when she heard one.

"Lord Brice. And I advise you very strongly to stay away from the man. I agreed to dance with him because he's a friend of Lord Willington's. I assumed that he was a gentleman. I thought that anyone who was a friend of Lord Willington's would be a safe, upstanding—I never thought Lord Willington would introduce me to someone who wasn't.

"He... he wasn't a gentleman?" Miss Merrill asked, worry pulling the pitch of her voice higher.

"He took me onto the balcony after our dance for some air and attempted some inappropriate behavior. I put a stop to it, but I wouldn't want to give him a second chance."

"Oh, no! I am so sorry." Miss Merrill's voice held true concern.

"Thank you."

"I'm certain your warning won't be necessary as I've never even met the man, but if I am introduced to him, I shall be polite and nothing else."

Emilie nodded and then noticed Lord Willington coming toward her. The man looked disgusted as if he'd just seen something grotesque. But he was looking straight at her!

Had she done something? Was her dress askew? Her hair falling down? Surely, Miss Merrill would have said something if that were the case.

She was just about to turn toward her friend to ask when Lord Willington suddenly stopped and changed directions. Where was he going? Was he not going to come and speak with her? Well, she supposed, with that expression on his face, she probably didn't want him to. If only she knew what she had done.

A horrible thought occurred to her. Had he seen her go out on the balcony with Lord Brice? Was that why he was angry? She might have just destroyed her entire plan before it even fully began. She needed to be in his good graces in order to make him fall in love with her and it now looked as if she was most certainly not. Oh, what had she done?

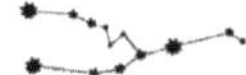

"You are looking very peaked this morning, Emilie," Lady Tremelling said as she sat down at the breakfast table the following morning.

Emilie put down her teacup, which she'd been about to take a sip from. "I'm afraid I didn't sleep very well last night."

"Is there anything bothering you, Sister?" Evan asked from the head of the table, peering over his newspaper.

"No, not really... I mean... I don't know why but Lord Willington looked rather annoyed with me last evening," she admitted. In fact, the look on the man's face as he'd turned away from her had haunted her all night long—that, and her plans to get her revenge. She still wasn't one hundred percent certain the plan was a good idea. She understood what her sister had told her about deserving respect, but she didn't know how to make a man fall in love with her. She didn't know if she would have the strength of will to turn him down if he professed his love. No, she had not slept well at all.

"I noticed you danced with him. Could you, perhaps, have said something to annoy him?" her mother asked, looking concerned.

"I don't think so. He seemed quite happy when he took me back to Miss Merrill. He even asked her to dance with him afterward," Emilie said.

"Did you speak with him after? When he returned after that dance?" her mother prodded.

"No. Actually, I wasn't there. I had been dancing with Lord Brice, and he took me out onto the balcony for a breath of fresh air." No need to tell her mother and brother that he had attempted to stop her from getting the breath by trying to plant his lips on top of her own.

"Perhaps that's why," Evan commented from behind his paper. He lowered a corner to look at her. His eyebrows were drawn down in the most menacing way. "You really shouldn't go alone onto a balcony with a gentleman. You know this."

"I do. He was introduced to me as a friend of Lord Willington's." She tried to think of a nice way of saying this so as not to worry her family. "I was mistaken in the gentleman's character."

Evan frowned at her. "Brice?" His eyes drifted away, but finally he came back to her with a shake of his head. "I have to admit, I don't know the fellow. He didn't misbehave in any way, did he?" The words came out low and menacing.

"Don't worry, dear Brother, thanks to you I am quite capable of defending myself should the need arise," she said, giving him a little smile. She wouldn't mention it had, and she had. He didn't need to know that.

He just nodded and went back to his paper.

"Well, we can only hope, in that case, Lord Willington comes to call this afternoon. You can then have a chat with him, although you'll have to be careful not to disparage his friend. Maybe you can give him a gentle hint. I'm certain he will have a word with Lord Brice if necessary," her mother suggested. "It couldn't be because you danced with the gentleman that he's angry, could it?"

"I doubt very much that he is jealous if that's what you are hinting at, Mother. But should he call, I will try to discover what is bothering him. I'm sure it's something completely unrelated to me," she said with a great deal more certainty than she felt.

It turned out Emilie never had to make such a decision as to where to walk with Lord Willington because he never showed up. It was nearly four, and Emilie was about to go up to her room to lay down for a rest before the events of the evening when Lord Brice was announced, however.

She shared a brief look of surprise with her mother that the gentleman would call so late. "What a... a surprise, my lord," Emilie said, hoping it wouldn't be too obvious that she'd left out the word "pleasant."

He paused to bow just inside the door. "My lady. Lady Emilie, I do hope you will forgive my intrusion into your afternoon."

"Of course. Please, do come and sit down," Emilie said, deliberately moving to a chair rather than the sofa where she'd been sitting when he'd come in. She didn't want to even give him the option of sitting directly next to her.

"I shall order a fresh pot of tea," Lady Tremelling said, moving to the door to call to a footman rather than simply ringing the bell.

Emilie wondered why her mother was giving them a moment of privacy, and she wasn't thrilled with it. At least she hadn't left the room altogether. She was still standing by the door having a word with the footman but looking back at Emilie every so often.

"Lady Emilie," Lord Brice said quietly so only she could hear. "I actually came to apologize for my atrocious behavior last night."

"Oh!" Now that was unexpected.

"Yes. I'm afraid I'm simply not used to... er... the company of innocent, young ladies such as yourself," he admitted. "I usually limit my attentions to, er, more worldly ladies."

"I see," she said, although she wasn't entirely certain she did. Did having more experience in the world mean these ladies welcomed his advances?

Surely, if they were widowed, they might, but if they were married? She gave herself a mental shake. It was none of her business.

"Yes, so…" he glanced up and Emilie did as well as her mother rejoined them. "It was such a pleasure to dance with you last evening, I just felt the need to come and pay my respects," he said, increasing the volume of his voice.

"Er… yes. I appreciate that, my lord."

"Do you attend Lady Morton's soiree this evening, my lord?" Lady Tremelling asked.

"No, I'm afraid I have another engagement," he said, giving her a polite smile.

He stayed for the requisite quarter of an hour and then made a hasty exit just as Eliza breezed into the room with little Georgie on her hip.

Emilie's mother jumped to her feet to take the little girl, all smiles and giggles. "You brought me a present!" Lady Tremelling exclaimed. "Oh, come here, my sweet." She took the little girl into her arms and gave her a squeeze and a kiss, receiving a very wet sounding one in return.

Emilie and Eliza just laughed and left their mother to dote on her granddaughter.

# CHAPTER FOURTEEN

"So?" Eliza asked Emilie as they took a turn about St. James Square.

Emilie turned toward her older sister. "So what?"

Eliza gave an exasperated huff. "How goes your plan of revenge? I saw you dancing last night with Lord Willington. He looked to be enjoying himself a great deal."

"Oh, er, yes," Emilie replied. She watched a little girl, on the green in the center of the square, run after a ball her older brother had kicked toward her.

"And Lord Brice called upon you today. Could you be playing a double-headed game?" Eliza asked, giving Emilie a sly little smile.

Emilie continued to watch the little girl kick the ball back to her brother.

Her sister continued, "Attracting Lord Willington by charming him to his toes, making him want you, and then you are charming another gentleman as well in order to make Willington jealous is brilliant, Em. Honestly, I hadn't thought you so devious." Eliza gave a little laugh.

Emilie turned back toward her sister. "Wh-oh! Yes, er, I just want to be sure, you know."

"Of course. I don't think I could have come up with a better plan myself."

"But do you think it really is a good plan?" Emilie asked, voicing her concerns. "I mean, is this really going to work? Do you think Lord Willington will understand the point of it all when I rebuff him?"

"Oh, he'll understand all right! And so will everyone else once it's explained he did the very same thing to you when you were merely five and ten. I can assure you women will be outraged at his callous treatment of you, and gentlemen will most certainly think twice of getting involved with women that they have no intention of actually courting."

"But we can't let it be known that he kissed me!" Emilie objected.

"No, no! Of course not." Eliza said immediately. "We will merely let it be known that he was kind to you, paying significant attention before leaving and never contacting you again."

Emilie let out a breath of relief.

"But *he* will understand. And you will be doing a service to the ladies of society." Eliza seemed to be so very certain that Emilie had no choice but to believe her.

Emilie merely had to set aside her worry that what she was doing wasn't actually a good thing. That hurting him in this way would be good for all women. She had to stop worrying about Lord Willington himself and broaden her thinking—like Eliza had.

"Well, then, I may have to work a bit harder at this. Last night he did not look happy with me for some reason, and I have absolutely no idea why," Emilie admitted to Eliza.

Eliza stopped walking. "What do you mean? When was this?"

"After my dance with Lord Brice. I saw him coming toward me. He saw me and there was such an expression of disgust on his face, and then he just turned around and walked away. I'm afraid the dance with Lord Brice took it too far. You may have thought it brilliant, but clearly Lord Willington did not."

"Are you sure it was disgust? Perhaps it was just jealousy?" Eliza asked, sounding a little uncertain herself.

"It looked that way to me." Emilie took her sister's arm and propelled her forward to continue their walk. It was too strange to simply stand in the middle of the walkway and talk. People would think something was wrong.

"Hmm, well, then. You may need to work a little harder at attracting the man."

"I don't know how. If he avoids me, then how can I charm him?"

Eliza was quiet for a few minutes as she thought about this.

"I was wondering if I shouldn't say something to Lady Preston," Emilie admitted.

Eliza stopped walking again. "But of course you should! She is the one who is determined the two of you make a match. She will, naturally, do anything and everything she can to bring the two of you together."

Emilie nodded and took Eliza's arm once again. "I'll seek her out tomorrow night at Lady Loughton's soiree."

"First, ascertain Lord Willington is indeed avoiding you for whatever reason," her sister warned.

"Yes, of course, I will."

Twenty-four hours had not improved Gabriel's mood. If anything, he was feeling even more annoyed than he had been the previous night. The most frustrating thing, of course, was it was himself who he was annoyed with. There was absolutely no one else on whom he could blame this. He'd thought he could pin it on Brice, but the man had merely behaved the way he usually did and Lady Emilie had defended herself—quite appropriately, he might add.

No, these feelings churning inside of him were his own doing. He should never have accepted Lady Preston's suggestion that he make an attempt to get to know Lady Emilie again. He should never have agreed to spend so much time with her. He should have realized his baser emotions would become involved and with that... well, there was no telling where it might lead.

He was ashamed. How could he even think to claim the title of gentleman when such thoughts ran through his mind, such as those that had done so last night as he'd attempted to sleep? It would have been one thing if they had been merely lustful fantasies of having Lady Emilie in his bed, but no, they were not only that—although, of course, there were some of those as well. Instead, it was not only sleeping with her that he'd fantasized about, but waking up with her in the morning, laughing with her over breakfast, gazing adoringly at her over dinner, and then climbing into bed with her again at the end of the day, every day. What nonsense! What utter ridiculousness. He was not going to marry Lady Emilie. He was not going to allow his passions to rule his head.

To prove as much, he strode into his club that evening determined to have a sharp, intelligent debate. He didn't care what the debate would be about, but he would debate another gentleman, and he would do so calmly and from a place of reason using his intellect only. There would be no feelings, no passion, nothing of the sort. He would reinforce his reputation as a cold, unfeeling fellow and be done with these blasted emotions.

♉

# CHAPTER FIFTEEN

True to her word, as soon as Emilie entered Lady Loughton's soiree, she began looking about for Lady Preston.

"What in the world are you doing, Emilie?" her mother whispered, giving her a sidelong glance.

"Looking for Lady Preston. Do you see her?"

Her mother seemed a bit taken aback at the idea that Emilie would actually seek the woman out, but she looked about anyway, only not quite as obviously as Emilie had been. "No, I don't see her. But I'm certain she'll be here. She always attends the most sought after invitations."

Emilie supposed she had to be satisfied with that. "Well, then, I suppose I'll join my friends. I see Miss Merrill over by the—"

"Wall?" her mother interrupted. "Absolutely not. I would like you to stay by me this evening."

"But why?" Her mother never insisted they stay together at parties, and certainly not soirees where there would be no dancing, only people milling about exchanging gossip.

"Because I think it would be better for your reputation if you weren't always seen with the wallflowers. If you are going to marry Lord Willington—"

"There is no reason to think that will happen, Mother," Emilie interrupted.

Her mother scowled at her. "Your brother has given the gentleman permission to court you. Where else might you believe that is to lead? To him going off into the country to oversee his estate?"

Emilie frowned at her mother. "Honestly, I don't believe it's going to lead anywhere. I think the man has been avoiding me. It doesn't matter what Evan has given him permission to do or not do."

"Since when?" her mother said, now truly turning toward her.

"Since Lady Farnsworth's party," Emilie said, deliberately lifting one shoulder and letting it drop as if she didn't care.

"What did you do?"

"I didn't do anything. Mother, we've already discussed this the other day," Emilie reminded her.

Her mother thought for a moment. "Oh, yes. You did say he'd looked annoyed with you. But I hadn't realized he had begun actively avoiding you."

Emilie just sighed, but as she did so, she caught sight of Lady Preston entering the drawing room just behind her mother. "Oh! There she is. Excuse me, I'm going to discuss this with her and see if she has any suggestion as to what I can do about Lord Willington."

If her mother could have looked any more surprised, Emilie had never seen it. It was with a great deal of satisfaction that she went over to the lady who was surveying the company. As soon as her eyes lit on Emilie coming toward her, she smiled a welcome to her. "Lady Emilie, how lovely to see you this evening," she said.

"And you, my lady. I was wondering if I might have a word?" Emilie asked, giving the lady a curtsy.

Lady Preston inclined her head and took Emilie's arm, leading her into a slightly less crowded area of the room. "How are things with Lord Willington?"

"Well, not very good, I'm sorry to say," Emilie said, rather surprised to truly feel as upset about this as she knew was expected of her.

"Oh dear!"

Emilie explained everything that had happened at the party the other night—dancing with Lord Willington and then Lord Brice—and, just as she did with her mother, she left out the part of him attempting to kiss her.

Lady Preston, however, was much more astute than Lady Tremelling. She narrowed her eyes at

Emilie and asked, "Did he take you out onto the balcony after your dance, by any chance?"

Emilie found the hem of the lady's dress suddenly very interesting.

"I see," Lady Preston said before Emilie could even say anything. "Well, there you have your answer. Lord Willington saw Lord Brice take you out onto the balcony and, knowing the gentleman's reputation, assumed you'd gone with him willingly."

"But I didn't know of Lord Brice's reputation! If I had, I wouldn't have even danced with him, let alone allowed him to take me outside," Emilie protested. "And it was Lord Willington who introduced me to him."

"He did?" Lady Preston looked surprised.

"Well, he wasn't given much of a choice. The man specifically asked for an introduction," Emilie admitted.

Lady Preston just pursed her lips together as if to say, *I figured as much.* "Well, knowing all this, I'm not surprised Lord Willington has come to a wrong conclusion—that you were a willing participant in whatever Lord Brice might have attempted. Er, I assume he *did* attempt something?"

"He did," Emilie admitted. "But my brother has taught me how to effectively repel such unwanted behavior. I left him doubled over in pain when I returned to the party."

Lady Preston's lips twitched, but she managed to keep from laughing outright. "I don't suppose Lord Willington was aware of this. He probably only saw you go out, not when you came back in."

Emilie sighed. "But then, what am I to do? Should I explain to him exactly what happened?"

"Well, you should, but not, I think here or tonight..." The lady was clearly thinking, trying to come up with some sort of plan. "Do not say anything to him if you see him again. Unfortunately, it might not be as difficult as you might think. It's possible that he may continue to avoid you. If he does not, be warm and charming, but don't mention Lady Farnsworth's party or what happened there. I will come up with an appropriate place and time for you to speak with him about what really happened." She patted Emilie's arm. "Have no fear, Lady Emilie, I've got some excellent ideas running about in my mind. It shall all work out well."

As it turned out, Emilie needn't have worried about what she would say to Lord Willington because he never came to Lady Loughton's soiree. That in itself was worrisome—and made Emilie's life a great deal easier at the same time.

She randomly stabbed a needle into her embroidery. Her mother was sitting across from her with her own stitching but somehow managed to execute it in a much more calm and measured fashion.

Never in her life had Emilie felt so conflicted. On the one hand, she truly wanted to get her revenge on the man. On the other, she felt bad for doing so. She would much rather just leave him alone and have him continue to ignore her. If he did so, she wouldn't have to come up with any sort of excuse as to why she couldn't marry him at the end of the Season. It wouldn't even be a possibility, and her life would be so very much easier. She could only wish he would.

On the other hand, she missed him. She had no idea why or how, but she just felt... hollow. And sad.

She gave herself a good shake. She was being ridiculous! She did not miss him. She had avoided a bad situation. Then why had she spoken with Lady Preston? She could have just left well enough alone. Perhaps she should have. But just the thought had made her feel so low she knew she could not have.

And now it was too late.

As if to prove her right, the footman came in just then with a note on a tray. "This was just delivered for you, Miss."

She set aside the mess that was her embroidery to take the note. Could this be from Lady Preston? Had she, in fact, come up with a plan for getting Emilie and Lord Willington back together.

"Well? Aren't you going to open it?" her mother asked, sounding exasperated. "It is addressed to you. I could very well have opened it for you, but you always become so upset when I do so."

"I appreciate you did not, Mother," Emilie said, taking a seat at the edge of a chair. Taking in a deep breath, she opened the letter and scanned it. She looked up at her mother, who was watching her avidly.

"It is an invitation from Lady Preston to go on a picnic to Greenwich."

"Greenwich? That's rather far," her mother exclaimed.

"I've never been there, but I've heard it's very pretty," Emilie said.

"It is. Very rural, but there are lovely areas for picnics along the riverbank. When does she say it will be? I'll have to see if we're available or change around—"

"The invitation specifically states you are not included—with her most sincere apologies," Emilie added quickly.

At her mother's surprised expression, Emilie hastened to explain. "She says there isn't enough room in her coach for a large party and doesn't believe it would be wise to make it one. She's invited me and Lord Willington only and will be our chaperone."

"Only you and his lordship?" her mother asked.

"Yes." Emilie handed over the note.

Her mother quickly read it through and then lowered it to her lap. "Well, I suppose she feels this would be a good way to get the two of you back on good terms. I suppose I must trust in her intuition that this is the right way of going about it."

"You did hire her," Emilie said, with a little satisfaction at being able to throw that back at her mother.

The lady just frowned. "Very well. You may write back to Lady Preston, thanking her for the invitation and telling her you will be expecting her tomorrow morning."

# CHAPTER SIXTEEN

Rebecca sat back in her traveling carriage trying not to look too satisfied with herself. Lady Emilie and Lord Willington sat across from her in awkward silence. They had hardly said a word to each other beyond their polite greetings.

Lord Willington was deliberately keeping his gaze out the window, watching the city go by. Lady Emilie looked meaningfully at Rebecca, probably wondering when she was going to start the conversation. What the poor girl didn't know was she wouldn't be doing so. She was going to leave that up to her.

When the girl had come to Rebecca to tell her of her worries concerning his lordship's interest, she'd been thrilled that not only had Lady Emilie come around to accepting Lord Willington as her soulmate, but she clearly trusted Rebecca enough to bring her troubles with the gentleman to Rebecca's attention. As she lay in bed that night, thinking over the events of the evening, she realized she'd been a fool. Lady Emilie was a Taurus. She wouldn't change her mind and accept the inevitability of marriage to Lord Willington so easily. She wouldn't accept the fact that she was going to get married at all since she'd already decided she would not.

No, there had to be something that Rebecca didn't know about—some scheme or trick the girl was planning. She had no idea what it was, but she was nearly certain Lady Emilie had absolutely no intention of marrying Lord Willington. There had to be another reason why she was concerned with how he felt about her. Rebecca could only hope Lord Willington's sensitive emotions wouldn't get hurt anymore than they already clearly were.

Still, that didn't mean Rebecca wasn't going to do her utmost to give the two of them the opportunity to discuss whatever it was that was bothering him. She had gone through with her idea of inviting the two of them on this picnic and could only hope by the time they returned to the city this evening that they would have resolved their differences, and Lady Emilie could continue on with whatever she was planning. It was the only way Rebecca would be able to learn what the girl was up to.

Lady Emilie sighed softly. "It certainly is a lovely day for a picnic," she said, finally realizing Rebecca wasn't going to do her work for her.

Rebecca looked to Lord Willington. He was still staring out the window.

After a moment, he realized Lady Emilie wasn't speaking to Rebecca and reluctantly turned toward the girl next to him. "Er, yes, it is."

"It's practically warm enough to think it was summer," Lady Emilie continued.

"Indeed," was his lordship's uninspired response. He began to turn back to the window, but Lady Emilie stopped him.

"Have you ever been to Greenwich, my lord?"

"Er, yes. It's quite pretty."

"Do you think there will be boats for us to take a journey on the river? Or is there a wood to walk through?" she asked. Rebecca had to applaud her polite, meaningless conversation. It was clear the girl was trying hard.

"Er, no. I don't believe there are boats, nor a wood. Usually, one simply sits by the riverbank in the shade of a tree and enjoys the lovely surroundings."

"Oh."

"There are paths along the riverbank," he added, at least giving some effort to furthering the conversation.

"That sounds nice." Lady Emilie could not possibly sound any less enthusiastic. She frowned at Rebecca as if to ask why she'd thought Greenwich would be a good place for them to go.

"It is nice," Rebecca said. "It's open and on a sunny day like today, a perfect place for a picnic." She gave Lady Emilie a reassuring look.

They lapsed into silence again and, unfortunately, stayed that way until they reached their destination. Clearly, Lady Emilie was saving up her polite conversation for later. Rebecca sincerely hoped she would not need it.

When they arrived at the spot she had chosen for their picnic—prearranged with Ned, her driver. They all got out, stretching their legs after being cooped up for the past two hours. Her traveling coach was quite comfortable for a vehicle of its sort, but it still felt good to move about after sitting still for so long.

Ned unstrapped the trunk from the back of the coach and began setting up the chairs and table she'd brought. The small man had unexpected strength in those slender arms. Once he'd placed the dishes and cutlery on the table, she pulled out the two large picnic baskets and began setting out the delicious meal her cook had prepared for them.

"May I help you with that, ma'am?" Lady Emilie asked, coming up next to her.

"Thank you, Lady Emilie, it's very kind of you," Rebecca said, shifting a little to her left so the girl could reach into the basket she was emptying.

"Goodness, it looks like you brought enough food to feed a great many more than just the three of us," Lady Emilie commented.

Rebecca chuckled. "Yes, my cook does tend to overdo it just a bit. It's all right. Whatever we don't eat, we'll just bring back with us."

"And I suppose your driver will assist us in consuming it all too," she said, almost as a question.

"No, I believe he's got a basket of his own." Rebecca looked back toward the coach where Ned had settled himself on the ground, his back against one of the wheels as he dug into his own picnic.

"Oh, yes."

Lord Willington had wandered closer to the river and stood with his back to them, gazing downstream. As Rebecca watched, his shoulders seemed to come down a touch as he relaxed. That was a good sign. Perhaps he would be more amenable to opening up about what was bothering him. A glass of the fine cider cook had included wouldn't hurt either.

"My lord, would you care to join us?" Rebecca called out, as she poured out cider for all three of them.

He turned and smiled politely as he made his way back to the table in the shade of the large oak tree. "This looks wonderful, Lady Preston, thank you."

"Of course. It's my pleasure."

They all took their seats and helped themselves to the sandwiches and salads provided.

"So, tell me, how do you both think this is progressing?" Rebecca asked after they'd satisfied their initial hunger.

"Progressing?" Lord Willington asked, drawing his eyebrows down.

"Yes. The courtship," Rebecca clarified.

"That's a rather direct question, don't you think, my lady?" he retorted.

"Oh, well, yes, it is. On the other hand, I thought the direct approach would be more likely to be appreciated by you both. Was I wrong? Would you like me instead to comment on how lovely the weather has been these past few days and ask if you've had a chance to go out to the park to enjoy the sunshine?" She lifted one side of her mouth into a sly little smile.

In answer to her question, he took a large bite of his sandwich so his mouth would be too full to speak. Rebecca turned to Lady Emilie. "How do you believe it's going, Lady Emilie?"

"I think it's going remarkably well," the girl said a little too brightly. "We had a lovely dance the other night at Lady Farnsworth's party, and then his lordship even asked my friend, Miss Merrill, to dance. I thought that was extremely kind and considerate of him." She turned and presented the gentleman with a brilliant smile.

He merely inclined his head, his mouth still too full to speak.

"Why, that's excellent!" Rebecca said. "I can't tell you how happy I am to hear this. Although, I have to admit, I have heard that you were seen in your club the other night engaging in some rather heated debates." She turned an inquisitive look on Lord Willington.

He took a drink of his cider. "I wouldn't say it was heated, ma'am. Your source must have been mistaken. And it is not uncommon for gentlemen to engage in debates at the club. Some even consider Powell's an extension of Parliament."

"Oh, yes, I have heard as much. However, it seems you are not usually one of those who join in such debates," she countered.

He lifted one shoulder and gave her a forced smile. "What can I say, I was interested in engaging in some intellectual conversation that evening."

Rebecca nodded her acceptance of his answer but didn't believe it for a minute. He had been out to pick a fight, probably in order to relieve himself of some of the emotions he'd been suppressing. "The friend who I had been speaking to also said he's never seen you at Gentleman Jackson's. Do you not enjoy pugilism, my lord?" It was a well-known fact that fist fighting was another excellent method gentlemen used for relieving tension.

"No, I've never enjoyed hitting other men or being hit by them. Would you enjoy such a thing, Lady Preston?" he asked with a lift of his always expressive eyebrows.

"I can't think why anyone would want to do such a thing," Lady Emilie answered before Rebecca had a chance.

"Precisely so," Lord Willington said with an approving nod.

"And yet so many gentlemen do enjoy it or at least pretend to do so in the name of exercise, I suppose," Rebecca commented.

His lordship nodded as he speared another bite of his sandwich with his fork. "I prefer fencing as a form of exercise. And riding, of course."

"Really? How fascinating," Rebecca said as she watched him fill his mouth once more. This wasn't getting her anywhere. "And what of you, Lady Emilie? Is dancing your preferred method of getting exercise?"

The girl nearly choked on the cider she had been in the act of drinking when Rebecca posed her question. She coughed into her handkerchief and then cleared her throat. "Er, no. I don't dance very often. I prefer to walk—daily."

"But you danced with Lord Willington the other night and then, I understand, you danced the very next set with Lord Brice," Rebecca said, looking at Lord Willington out of the corner of her eye to see his reaction.

Lady Emilie wiped her mouth again and then said, "Er, yes, that is true. And I'm afraid I was so warm from the unusual amount of exercise that I allowed the gentleman to lead me out onto the balcony for a breath of fresh air."

"Oh! I do hope you were not alone out there," Rebecca said, pretending concern.

"Only for the briefest of moments. As soon as I realized my mistake, I immediately turned around and returned to the drawing room," Lady Emilie explained, to her credit. Rebecca was happy to note that she left out the part where Lord Brice might have attempted to take advantage of the girl.

"His lordship was even so kind as to come and apologize to me the following day," Lady Emilie said, turning toward Lord Willington. "Clearly, he, too, realized the inappropriateness of his actions and said it would never happen again. Wasn't that kind of him, my lord?" She gave the gentleman a reassuring look.

Lord Willington lifted his lips ever so slightly, looking rather satisfied. "Indeed, it was. I am glad to hear of it."

"I thought it was a little odd, but I appreciated it," the girl said, turning back to her own food.

For some reason, Lord Willington looked more relaxed now. Perhaps knowing Lord Brice had behaved appropriately eased his mind. Rebecca could only hope it was merely that which had been bothering the man.

Once they had all finished with their lunch, Rebecca sat back in her chair. "Oh, my I am quite satisfied. But you young people must go for a walk along the riverbank."

"We could not possibly leave you all alone, ma'am," Lord Willington protested.

"Certainly, you could! Please don't give it another thought," she said.

"I would be terribly remiss were I to do so. I am sorry. Lady Emilie, if you'd like to—"

"I couldn't go for a walk by myself," she protested immediately.

"No, she could not. Lord Willington, Ned is nearby, and I shall be perfectly fine on my own," Rebecca reassured him.

The man would not be persuaded, much to her annoyance. Instead, he poured himself another glass of cider and turned his chair in order to stretch out his legs toward the river. "It is absolutely lovely right here."

Rebecca gave Lady Emilie an apologetic look. The girl shrugged. Clearly, there was nothing either one of them could do.

# Chapter Seventeen

Emilie wasn't certain what to make of Lord Willington's insistence that they not leave Lady Preston alone while they went for a walk along the lovely bank of the river after their picnic. She really wanted a chance to speak with him and find out if it was, in fact, her time alone on the balcony with Lord Brice that had caused him to be annoyed with her. If it had been, she sincerely hoped she'd allayed his concerns. It's just there was no way to tell if he wouldn't speak with her—and she was certain he wouldn't say anything more in front of Lady Preston.

After a short period of awkward conversation and even more uncomfortable silence, Lady Preston finally agreed to join them on a walk. Their time doing so also gave Ned a chance to put away the table and chairs after Emilie and Lady Preston had put away the remainders of their luncheon.

Once they returned, they all climbed up into Lady Preston's rather ponderous traveling coach and headed back to London. Emilie was glad of it. She was exhausted from the outing—more so emotionally than physically. She wanted nothing more than to curl up in the window seat of her bedchamber with a novel and relax. She knew it was a happy fantasy, sadly, because the moment she returned home her mother would be wanting to know every detail of the outing and probably wouldn't allow her a moment to herself for some time.

As the coach traveled back toward London, Emilie adopted the same position as Lord Willington—simply sitting and staring out the window at the passing scenery. She was jolted out of her little reverie by the thunderous sound of another vehicle approaching. By the sound of it, it either had to be another large traveling coach like the one they were in or one being pulled by at least two horses—at a full gallop. The sound was coming from behind them and got louder as the other vehicle got closer. Emilie sat back and turned to exchange a look with Lord Willington, who was looking as curious as she. Lady Preston had fallen asleep on the opposite seat, her head gently lolling on her chest. But at the sound of the approaching carriage, she too jolted awake.

A moment later the other vehicle came alongside of Lady Preston's coach so close the wheels practically scraped against each other. There was a shout from Ned, some intense jostling and suddenly the coach was in a ditch along the side of the road, nearly on its side.

Emilie had grabbed onto the strap with all her might, managing to keep herself from falling into Lord Willington. Lady Preston wasn't so lucky since she'd been sitting in the center of the backward facing seat. She was jolted forward and into Lord Willington, who was now near the ground.

"Oh! I beg your pardon, my lord," Lady Preston said. She tried to shift away from the man, but with the odd angle, she was having difficulty.

"It's perfectly all right," he said, assisting her, but it seemed neither one of them knew where she might sit in the tilted cabin. She opted for what was now the bottom and had been the side wall next to where she had been sitting. "Lady Emilie, are you all right?" he asked, after helping the lady situate herself.

"Er, yes? No. I'm not sure," Emilie said. She was still hanging onto the strap, partially dangling from it in order to keep from falling into Lord Willington as Lady Preston had.

"Oh, dear. Er, let me..." He took hold of her waist. "Let go of the strap. I've got you."

"But if I do, I'll fall on top of you," Emilie said. One terrible part of her mind asked whether that would be such a bad thing after all. He was rather large and well built. It might be quite nice to be in his strong arms, cuddled up against his broad chest. But she would not be cuddled up against him, she would more likely be sprawled across him in a very unladylike position.

"It's all right. I'm holding you. You won't fall."

Tentatively, she released her grip on the strap. He did seem to have a good hold of her. She was rather impressed he could hold all her weight from his awkward angle. He had to be very strong indeed.

He very gently lowered her toward him until she was, in fact, snuggled against his body. For a moment her mind and body rejoiced, but she very quickly tamped that down. He made some odd grunting sounds as he extricated himself slowly from under her, making sure she didn't fall hard onto the side of the coach now nearly against the bottom of the ditch.

He managed to get himself nearly standing with his feet on the bottom door. "I'm going to see about Ned and the horses. Are you both all right for the moment?"

"Yes, yes, please do. We're fine," Lady Preston said with urgency. She'd turned herself so her back was to the wall and one knee was on the seat. It looked like a rather comfortable position despite the awkward angle of the coach, so Emilie turned herself to sit likewise.

While she was doing so, a voice called from outside of the coach. "Haloo? Are you all right in there?"

"Yes. Can you open this door?" Lord Willington banged his fist against what was now the top door.

There was no handle on the inside of the coach as Lady Preston always relied on a footman to open the door for her.

"Er, uh, yes, yes, of course," the man outside said. "Just... just a moment." There was a bit of a scrambling sound as the man tried to reach them. After some more strange sounds, there was finally a thump on the side of the coach and then the door was lifted up and flipped open. Some more grunts and groans, a word or two that Emilie would never repeat and then the fellow called back, "There you are."

In the meantime, Lord Willington placed a hand on either side of the door frame and, then with a jump, pulled himself out of the coach. Emilie could hear him stand on the side of the coach and then saw him jump from there to the roadside next to the ditch. After that, there was merely the muffled sound of men's voices—Lord Willington's being the loudest as he yelled at the man who had caused the accident. Their voices withdrew as they moved away from the coach, presumably to see about the horses and Ned.

"Oh, dear," Lady Preston said. "I do hope they'll be able to get the coach out of this ditch without too much damage to the vehicle."

"Well, the gentleman who caused the accident should certainly pay for whatever damage there is," Emilie reassured her.

"Yes," Lady Preston said on a sigh. "Yes, I do hope so."

"I'm more worried about Ned and the horses," Emilie admitted.

Lady Preston turned worried eyes toward her. "And how we are going to get out of here as well."

"Yes." Emilie stood up and managed to peek out of the open door, but there wasn't much she could see beyond the top of the ditch and the road beyond.

Lord Willington appeared about five minutes later.

As soon as Emilie saw him, she called out. "How is Ned? Will we be able to get out of here?"

The gentleman came toward her and crouched down so he could speak to her without her having to crane her neck to look up at him. "Ned is extremely lucky. He was thrown from the coach and suffered nothing more than a broken arm."

"Oh no!" Lady Preston said from below Emilie. She moved slightly out of the way, so the lady could join her at the door.

"He'll be fine," Lord Willington assured her.

"And the horses?" she asked.

"I'm afraid one is lame. The other should be all right, aside from being a bit upset," he informed her. "The man who ran us off the road acted quickly and got the traces and harnesses off before there could be any further harm."

"Oh, good."

"We've had words," his lordship told her. "He will be compensating you for all the damage."

"That is very good of you, my lord. I do have to admit to having worried about the cost," the lady said with some embarrassment.

"Of course. Now, if the two of you wouldn't mind very much staying right where you are, I will go with Mr. Stanley to the closest town to get some help in extricating both you and the coach from this ditch. And I want to get Ned to a surgeon as quickly as possible. He's in a good deal of pain, as you can imagine."

"Oh, yes, of course," Lady Preston said.

"But wait, can you not help us out of here before you go?" Emilie asked.

"Are you certain you wouldn't be more comfortable remaining inside the coach?" he asked.

"I am absolutely certain. Lady Preston?" Emilie asked, turning to the older lady.

"I, er, don't mind either way. The coach isn't too uncomfortable, considering..."

"There really is no place for you to sit out here, aside from the ground," Lord Willington pointed out.

Emilie resigned herself to being stuck in this vehicle for some time until his lordship returned with help. "Very well."

"Do try to hurry back, my lord," Lady Preston said.

"Of course. Mr. Stanley is going to drive us to the closest village, and I shall return presently, I assure you."

With that, the man disappeared. As they settled themselves back inside the sideways coach, Emilie could hear the other vehicle leave them.

She heaved a sigh and stared up, out of the door. "I wonder how long he'll take."

"He shouldn't be too long, I imagine, since this Mr. Stanley is driving him to the village. If he had to walk, it would be a great deal longer," Lady Preston said, as she arranged her skirts so she was sitting comfortably while staying properly covered.

After about five minutes that seemed more like fifty, Lady Preston turned to Emilie. "Well, now it's just the two of us here, would you mind my asking a rather impertinent question?"

"My lady? What sort of question from you could be impertinent?" Emilie asked.

"Well, I'm afraid it rather assumes the worst of you—which, I assure you, I would never do ordinarily. However, knowing you are a Taurus and understanding the characteristics of people born under that sign, I'd say there is an alternative reason as to why you were so concerned about Lord Willington's feelings toward you."

"I am a what?" Emilie asked, suddenly feeling extremely worried Lady Preston had seen through to her real plans.

"Taurus. It is the constellation that was most prominent in the sky when you were born. Your astrological sign."

"Oh. While I have heard of astrology, I have to admit I know nothing about it. I am a Taurus, you say? And what does that mean?" Emilie asked, hoping the lady would forget her previous question.

"It means you are an extremely stubborn person. It is most difficult to change your mind once you have decided upon something. As you have told me yourself, you had decided not to marry, so I was surprised to hear you were worried about Lord Willington's feelings toward you. Why is that?"

Drat! Emilie's attempt to change the subject had failed spectacularly. The question was, could she trust Lady Preston? Dare she actually tell her the truth? Emilie thought about it for a good minute and then finally decided since she, herself, was wavering in her conviction about carrying out this plan of revenge, it couldn't truly do any harm to admit as much to her. And even if she did so, it didn't mean she wouldn't be able to continue with the scheme if she chose to—despite the lady's knowledge of it. And, Emilie thought, being completely honest with herself, it might not be bad to get another opinion.

"Very well, my lady, I will admit I have... an alternate plan in mind," Emilie said slowly.

"Hmmm... and what might that be, Lady Emilie?" The lady looked over at her suspiciously but still with a little tug of a smile on her lips.

Emilie sighed. "Well, as you are fully aware by now, Lord Willington and I knew each other for a brief time when I was fifteen and he was nineteen."

"Yes, so I understood from when the two of you met at your home. It seems he kissed you at that time?"

"He did. We had a wonderful two weeks together where we got to know each other quite well and enjoyed each other's company immensely."

"But?"

"But then he kissed me... and Evan—my brother—witnessed it. He and Lord Willington, as he was called then, were gone by the time I woke up the following morning. They didn't say goodbye to anyone, although Lord Willington did leave a note thanking my parents for their hospitality, from what I understand."

"But there was no mention of you in the note, I presume," the lady said. It wasn't a question, but a statement.

"No. None. And I never heard from him again. I asked Evan about him, and he said he and Lord Willington were no longer part of the same circles at school," Emilie told her.

"And you, in your adolescence, were devastated," Lady Preston said, astutely.

"Yes," Emilie admitted, her voice much quieter than she had intended.

"And now?"

"Now I want nothing more than for Lord Willington to know what that felt like. I want him to hurt the way I hurt. I want him to feel—" she broke off, her voice getting louder as her anger grew. It would not do to show such emotion to Lady Preston. Emilie clamped her mouth shut.

"I see," Lady Preston said after a moment. "So, you want to make Lord Willington fall in love with you, so you may spurn him the way he did you, is that right?"

"Yes," Emilie whispered.

The lady was quiet for a moment.

Emilie could not withhold her misgivings, however. "I know it is a horrible thing to do to someone. I know it because I was devastated when he did that to me. I... I'm not certain I want to make Lord Willington feel the same way. I don't think I want anyone to feel that way. It would be... cruel," she ended slowly.

"I do agree, but I also see why you might be tempted to get your revenge on the gentleman."

# Chapter Eighteen

"You do?" Emilie was stunned.

"Of course. We are so vulnerable at fifteen—young girls, especially. You must have been extremely upset at the time."

"I was!"

"And so, naturally, you want him to have a taste—even if it might be a smaller one due to the fact that he is, after all, an adult when you were not," Lady Preston said, clearly thinking this through.

"Yes, precisely! I don't know how much hurt he would feel were I to do this, but dare I...?"

The lady sighed. "There is one thing you should understand, Lady Emilie. Just as you are a Taurus and ruled by your constellation, Lord Willington is a Cancer and ruled by his."

"And what does that mean? What characteristics are common in people under that sign?"

"They are very passionate people and feel their emotions intensely—much more so than others. So, if you were to go through with your plan of revenge, you can be sure that Lord Willington, despite the fact that he is a grown man, would feel the pain of your rejection most acutely."

"Oh." Emilie sat back and thought about this. She truly didn't want to cause Lord Willington such distress. Yes, she had felt it herself when she was younger, but was it right to cause such pain in another merely so he would understand what she had gone through? Could she do that to him? Somehow, just the thought of doing so left a bad taste in her mouth.

"I cannot say whether you should continue with your scheme, Lady Emilie," Lady Preston said after a moment of silence. "Naturally, I hope you do not as it is my job to see the two of you are wed."

"Yes, of course. I do hope your fee is not dependent upon our getting married," Emilie asked, feeling awkward mentioning the lady's fee at all.

The woman waved the thought away. "Have no fear, Lady Emilie. I am not in such straits that I would suffer in any way if I was not paid for my services. My husband left me a very comfortable annuity. I charge for my service more so people will take me seriously than because I am in need of funds."

"Oh! I am glad to hear that, ma'am."

"I am more concerned about what the repercussions would be were you to carry out your plan. Is it only Lord Willington who would be hurt by it? Or might you also feel something other than satisfaction at getting back at someone who hurt you?"

Emilie hadn't considered that she might get hurt by her own revenge. She was pretty certain she would feel bad if Lord Willington was very badly hurt, as Lady Preston had implied he might be.

"Or perhaps," the lady continued, "you might, instead, fall in love with him and decide not to carry through with your scheme, in which case your attempts at making him fall in love with you would not have to lead to a bad end."

"That is what I worry about," Emilie admitted quietly.

"I am not surprised. You're an intelligent girl and you did develop a tendre for him when you were young. There is no reason to think you might not do so again."

"So, what am I to do? I am still furious and hurting from what he did to me."

"Of course you are. I think it would be best if you were simply open and honest with him. Tell him how you feel. Perhaps even tell him that you were thinking of getting your revenge on him. See what he says. I have a feeling he will be regretful for how he behaved in his younger days and understanding of how you feel now."

"You think I should tell him?" Emilie was stunned.

"I do. It will establish a level of trust that is so very essential in a strong relationship."

Emilie sat back and thought about that for a moment, but as she was doing so, the sound of carriage wheels approaching made her jump. "That must be his lordship, returning to rescue us." She stood up on the seat and popped her head out of the door to the coach, but the vehicle approaching didn't even slow. It barreled straight past leaving them alone once more. Emilie sagged with disappointment.

"Where is that man?" she said, stamping her foot on the seat. She ducked back down into the coach. "If he has left us here... No! I am certain he has. He is probably halfway to London by now."

"Oh, no, he would not..." Lady Preston objected weakly, clearly wondering whether it might be true.

"I cannot sit here another minute. Which way do you think it was to the village?"

"I, er, I don't know. I'm nearly certain it is in the direction we were heading. There is a turn off not too far from here that I believe leads to a small village."

"Excellent. Then I shall go there and then hurry back with the help Lord Willington promised."

"But how..." Her words petered off as Emilie grabbed the sides of the doorway and pulled herself up, pushing on the seat with her feet. In a minute she was out and sitting on the side of the vehicle.

"Have no fear, ma'am, I shall return as soon as possible," she called back into the coach—just before she jumped from the coach to the side of the road in the same way she'd seen Lord Willington do earlier.

Gabriel let out a frustrated sigh. Was there no way to get this pony to move any faster? It was a stubborn thing which absolutely refused to go any faster than a slow trot. Gabriel had spent the past hour seeing to Ned, the horses, and trying to find enough men to help pull the carriage from the ditch. It had been incredibly frustrating when all he'd wanted to do was to return to the ladies to rescue them from the coach.

He wondered if the pony would respond to pleading. He'd already tried slapping the reins. He didn't have a whip. But the thing simply would not—

Gabriel stopped thinking about the blasted animal and watched as a figure came closer. Who in their right mind would be walking along this road when dusk was coming on?

No... it couldn't be. He blinked, shook his head and then pulled the cart to a stop. "What in all that is holy are you doing?" he called out.

Lady Emilie stopped just in front of the pony, her hands on her hips. "I got tired of waiting for you!"

"Oh, well, I am terribly sorry to have taken so long. I only had half a dozen things I needed to do including going from house to house begging the men within to come and help get the damned coach out of the ditch!" He knew it wasn't Lady Emilie's fault he'd had such a difficult time and immediately felt bad about yelling at her and worse for using such language. That diminished the moment she raised her own voice, however.

"Well, how was I to know? You don't have the greatest record of getting back to people, you know!"

"What is that supposed to mean?" he asked hotly.

"Oh, I don't know... because you once might have kissed me, told me you cared, and then disappeared *never* to be heard from again," she snapped.

His mouth dropped open. "That is not—" He bit off his words and then ground out, "I was nineteen years old."

"And I was fifteen. I expected more."

"I am no longer nineteen. When I say I am going to return to rescue you, I mean what I say," he told her in no uncertain terms. He was shocked to realize he was quickly losing his anger. She had every right not to trust him. He had never done anything to prove to her that he *could* be trusted.

And he had taken an inordinately long time returning. She couldn't have known it would take him so long.

She just stood there glaring at him with her arms crossed over her chest.

"Get in Lady Emilie, or… don't if you prefer. Walk back to the coach. You won't get there much after me. This…" He withheld the curse at the tip of his tongue. "…pony refuses to go much faster than a walking pace." She hadn't said anything about his language so far, but it still wasn't right to use such terms in the company of a young lady.

He was surprised to see her lips twitch. Her hand flew to cover her mouth as she began to giggle. "So that's what took you so long? You can't get the pony to gallop? Why do you have a pony and cart anyway?"

"It's an extremely small village. No one had a carriage I could borrow. This was the best I could do," he admitted, allowing his mouth to quirk up on one side.

"Oh dear. I am sorry." She moved to the pony's head and stroked his nose. "You poor thing. You're not used to being asked to go any faster, are you? Well, let's see if I can coax you into doing so, shall I?" She looked into the animal's eyes and smiled. "It's all right. I won't let the bad man hurt you anymore." She gave the pony another little caress and then climbed into the cart next to Gabriel, who was having the hardest time not rolling his eyes.

"Give me the reins, my lord," she demanded, holding out her hand.

"What? Why?" he protested.

She gave him a look that said *just do as I ask* and waited, her hand held out expectantly.

He sighed and passed over the reins.

"Thank you. Do you know the pony's name?" she asked.

He frowned. The woman who'd lent him the pony and cart had told him, but he couldn't remember.

"You don't know its name?" Lady Emilie asked.

"Mr. Brown!" he said with a snap of his fingers as the name suddenly came to him.

Lady Emilie's lips twitched, but she just nodded and turned forward again. "All right, Mr. Brown. Let's be off."

To Gabriel's incredulous surprise, the pony immediately moved forward and quickly attained a speedy little trot.

"You can close your mouth now, my lord. If you don't, an insect might fly in," Lady Emilie said with a laugh.

Gabriel had already done so, so instead he turned and doffed his hat to her. "I applaud your skill with animals, Lady Emilie."

"Thank you." She gave him a regal nod of her head.

At this pace, it didn't take them long to reach the coach. Lady Preston was standing inside with the top of her head peeking out of the door. "Oh, thank goodness!" she exclaimed as Gabriel jumped from the still moving cart even as Lady Emilie was pulling it to a stop.

"My most sincere apologies, ma'am. It was a great deal more difficult to complete my tasks than I had anticipated," Gabriel said, approaching her. "Now, let's see to freeing you from your coach."

"Oh, yes, please!" she said with feeling. "And have you found some men to come and get it out of the ditch?"

"We will discuss that as we return to the Duck Pond," he said as he grabbed a hold of both of her arms and lifted her out of the vehicle.

Once she was safely on the side of the road, she turned to him. "The Duck Pond? Why are we going to a duck pond?"

He smiled. "It's the name of the tavern. I am hoping to get a tall glass of ale for myself, and we'll see if they have some passable wine for you two ladies."

"I'd be happy with anything at this point," Lady Emilie said from the pony's head where she had been holding on to his bridle and stroking his nose.

"Oh, yes, do let's go to this tavern. It's clear we won't be able to get very far in this cart," Lady Preston said, giving Gabriel a pat on his arm before climbing onto the rear-facing seat, allowing him to take the forward-facing one.

"I'm afraid it was all that was available," he told her.

Lady Emilie walked the pony around so they could return the way they'd come, and then she climbed back onto the bench next to Gabriel. He was still impressed when she managed to coax the animal into a trot even with the added weight of all three of them in the cart.

"We were extremely lucky," he told them as they headed toward the village. "The surgeon happened to be in town to tend to a local woman. I got him to see Ned."

"Oh good! And how is he?" Lady Preston asked, partially turning around.

"His arm is, in fact, broken as we suspected. And the surgeon said he had a concussion as well. He recommended he not move for the next twelve hours or more."

"Oh, dear!" Lady Emilie exclaimed.

Lady Preston, too, looked upset at the news.

"The one horse is lame, as we figured, but the other is fine. And I think I managed to get enough men to pull the coach out of the ditch, but none of them wanted to do so this evening. It was too late, they said, and the sun will be setting soon." To punctuate his words, he looked toward the west where the sun was, indeed, sinking quickly.

"So, we'll need to spend the night?" Lady Emilie asked, not sounding happy about this at all.

"I'm afraid so. The Duck Pond has two guest rooms, and luckily, no other guests. So, I've reserved them for us. I'm afraid you ladies will have to share," he added.

"Not a problem at all," Lady Preston said quickly.

"My mother is going to be beside herself with worry," Lady Emilie said.

"No, I'm happy to say she won't. I've sent Mr. Stanley on his way back to Town with notes for Lady Tremelling and your household, ma'am," he said, turning to look at Lady Preston. "And my grandmother. And I've asked Lady Willington to send my carriage to fetch us first thing in the morning. As soon as I see your coach freed from the ditch, we'll be able to return to London."

"Oh, how very clever you are, my lord," Lady Preston said with a little clap of her hands. "It seems as if you've thought of everything."

"Indeed, thank you, sir," Lady Emilie said, keeping her eyes on the road. Had her voice held a touch of disapproval? He would have expected relief.

"Is everything all right, Lady Emilie?" he asked.

"What? Oh, yes! I'm just... well, I've never actually spent a night away from my family," she said.

"Oh! Have no fear. I will make sure you are well taken care of," he told her. He gave her a reassuring smile. "And, of course, Lady Preston will as well."

"Naturally," the lady said. "There is absolutely nothing to worry about. Think of it as a little adventure."

# Chapter Nineteen

It wasn't only that she'd never spent a night away which bothered Emilie, she admitted to herself, although she supposed that was part of it. No, it was Lord Willington.

She wanted to hit the man for being so thoughtful. She wanted to rage at him for thinking of all the little details to set her mind at ease. She wanted to scream at him—*why had he not behaved in this way when he was younger?* Was it age that had taught him these lessons? Had something else happened in his life in the intervening six years which made him realize the importance of thinking of others?

Emilie didn't know, and she wasn't certain she cared. All she knew was he had no right being so wonderful now when he'd been so thoughtless before. How was she to act when he behaved this way? How was she to maintain her anger and believe all men were self-centered oafs?

This just wasn't fair. It wasn't right. And she hated having her assumptions called into question in this way. It made her feel... off balance. Indecisive. And therefore furious.

After watching Lady Emilie follow the landlord up to her room, Gabriel led Lady Preston into the private dining room he had asked to be set aside for them.

"I'm surprised a tavern this small has another dining room," the lady commented as they entered.

"I don't believe it's meant to be a private dining room but merely a second dining room," he said, indicating the five tables scattered about the room.

"Oh, yes, I see. Well, it will do for us." The lady gave a little chuckle before pulling a chair from one of the tables closer to the fireplace and seating herself. She let out a sigh. "I don't know why I feel so tired. I've been doing nothing but sitting in that carriage for the past few hours."

He went behind the smaller bar, which probably backed up to the larger one in the main room, and found a bottle of wine on a lower shelf. He poured her a glass and came around to hand it to her.

She smiled at him. "Are you certain the landlord won't mind you helping yourself?"

He shook his head. "I don't think so, so long as we pay for it later." He then returned to the bar and tried the taps. Just as he'd hoped, there were two different types of ale. He chose the lighter one and filled a glass for himself. He then pulled up a chair next to Lady Preston and relaxed into it.

"You must be exhausted. You accomplished quite a lot in a relatively short time," she commented.

"I am, rather. Although to hear it from Lady Emilie, I took entirely too long to do what needed to be done."

"Well, you can't blame the girl for worrying." She paused and then added more softly, "I'm afraid you have not done anything to make her believe you would return."

Gabriel winced but had to acknowledge he deserved that. "I hope after today she will have more confidence in my word."

"I do as well, but..." she paused. She turned toward him, her face more serious than he'd ever seen it. "You need to do something, my lord, something to not only make her trust you, but to make her... like you."

He sat up straighter. "Do you think she doesn't like me?"

"I'm certain she doesn't trust you, and even she is uncertain whether she is attracted to you or not—she admitted as much to me when we were waiting for your return."

Gabriel leaned back against his chair again, thinking about this. "She has seemed to be interested. We've danced, and she was constantly smiling. We've gone for drives in the park and to the opera where we talked. I had the impression she was comfortable in my company."

"Oh, I'm certain she is comfortable with you, but does comfort lead to one wanting to marry? I'm not so certain."

Gabriel took a long drink of his ale, wishing he could drown away this whole day and especially this very conversation. "It is precisely what I was looking for in a marriage," he told her.

"You were not looking for love?"

He scoffed. "Most definitely not."

"Do you fear your passions?"

His head whipped toward her, and he nearly spilled his drink. "What?"

"You heard me. You are a Cancer, sir, the most passionate of all the astrological signs. You have already proven yourself to be an emotional sort of man despite the reputation you have carefully crafted amongst the *ton*." She looked so calm as she laid him bare, stripping him of the face he showed to the world.

He didn't know what to say.

She reached out and touched his arm. "It is all right, my lord. There is nothing wrong with being passionate, with having emotions—just so long as you do not allow them to rule over you and your actions." She paused and tilted her head a little as she considered him. "Is it that which got you into so much trouble when you were nineteen? You allowed your passions to get the better of you and you kissed Lady Emilie when you probably knew in your mind that it was—if not a bad idea—one that could possibly get you into trouble with her brother and your friend."

He said nothing, but did allow his head to nod ever so slightly in acknowledgement of the truth of her words.

"You are not a boy any longer, Lord Willington," she said deliberately. "You are a man and you, presumably, have learned to control your actions. You are no longer ruled by your passions. That doesn't make them any less potent, but I have every faith that you are able to behave properly."

She allowed him a few moments to digest her words, then she said, "If you wish to gain the trust and affection of Lady Emilie then you need to be open and honest with her, my lord. While I fully believe the two of you are meant for each other, it doesn't mean you do not have to try to engage her feelings."

"And you think the best way to do that would be to be honest with her?" He gave a little laugh which held no humor in it at all. "I would think that would be the surest way to scare her off."

Lady Preston smiled. "Think about it," she said briefly as the door opened to reveal a refreshed-looking Lady Emilie.

Both Lady Preston and Gabriel stood at her entrance.

"Oh, this looks, er, pleasant," she said, looking about the room.

"It's the best we could do, I'm afraid," Gabriel told her.

She came farther into the room. "It's quite nice. And the room upstairs is clean."

"Excellent. I shall go up and avail myself of it. I'd like to wash up and perhaps rest for a little before we dine." Lady Preston gave Gabriel and Lady Emilie a nod and then left them entirely alone, closing the door behind her.

Lady Emilie seemed to be as surprised as Gabriel. "Er, but she is supposed to be chaperoning us, isn't she?" she asked, turning back to Gabriel.

"I had thought so. Clearly, she doesn't feel the need."

"But if someone were to come in... I would be ruined."

Gabriel thought about that for a moment and then just shook his head as he smiled. "It might be part of her plan to force us to marry."

"Oh no! She wouldn't!"

"No, I'm certain she didn't even think it. She is too kind a lady to do anything so underhanded. I'm sure she simply trusts that we will be left alone." Gabriel moved behind the bar once more and poured another glass of wine.

"Thank you," Lady Emilie said, accepting it.

"I've just had a most interesting conversation with Lady Preston," Gabriel began, not at all certain where he was going with the statement. He still had no idea whether he was going to follow the lady's advice.

"Oh?"

"She is quite a fascinating lady. I'm not entirely certain what to make of her strong belief in astrology," he said, deliberately turning the conversation away from the dangerous waters his first statement had started toward.

"I am the same way! We were talking while waiting for you to return and... well, what she said about me was uncannily accurate."

"Yes! I just had the very same experience," he said, taking a step closer to her.

"So, perhaps there is something to this zodiac?"

He shrugged. "I would never have believed as much if someone had simply told me about it. But she has proven its accuracy."

"It is odd."

They fell into an awkward silence until Gabriel dredged up the courage to ask, "So, what was it she said? About you, I mean."

"Oh, er, just that I am quite stubborn. I am sorry to say it is entirely true. When I put my mind to something, I will see it through. When I believe something, it is difficult to change my mind. What about you?" she asked, tilting her head in curiosity.

He had been afraid she would ask that. Well, he'd already dipped his toe in, he might as well submerge himself and see if he drowned or swam.

"She pointed out that I, er, feel things very strongly."

Lady Emilie slowly nodded her head. "She told me as much as well."

"Did she?"

"Yes. She said you were a man of passion." She immediately began to turn red with embarrassment. "Er, I'm certain she didn't mean—"

"No," he interrupted her. "It is true." He took in a deep breath. "When I was younger, I allowed my passions to rule my head. It is... well... it is how I came to kiss you six years ago even though I knew very well it wasn't the right thing to do."

Her eyes stayed glued to his, but she said nothing so he continued on, wading into deeper waters. "I... I should not have done that. It wasn't right, and it wasn't fair—to either of us, honestly. I should have known—and I imagine I probably did and simply didn't care in the moment—I could do nothing to further our relationship at that time."

"So, you knew you weren't going to contact me again?" she asked. "And you kissed me anyway."

He lowered his gaze to the floor. "It was shameful of me, but... as I said, I was young and allowed my passions to rule."

"And now?" she asked, putting her now empty wine glass down on a nearby table.

He looked up again. "Now I am a man and I have no problems controlling myself, I assure you."

"You are certain?"

Was she asking him to kiss her? The idea flashed into his head, but he immediately dismissed it as ridiculous. Why would she... unless she was testing him. "Yes, I am. Absolutely certain." He took a step closer to her. "Do you not believe me?"

"I... I don't know what to believe anymore." Somehow, that seemed like the most honest thing she'd ever said to him. And it also made him want to prove himself.

He took another step closer so he was now standing only inches from her. "I would be more than happy to—"

"Show me?" she asked, looking up at him. She looked uncertain, as if she hadn't actually meant to challenge him.

"Yes." He moved closer and brushed his thumb down her soft cheek.

"But what if you can't control yourself?" she said, taking a small step back.

"You may stomp on my foot. But I would appreciate it if you were not to do to me what you did to Lord Brice." He grinned.

Her mouth dropped open. "You... you know about that?"

He nodded. "I went out onto the balcony to make sure you were all right, but you'd already left. I found him doubled over in pain."

Her cheeks colored once again. "My... my brother told me to do that if any man should try to take advantage of me."

Gabriel nodded. "It's a good thing to teach your sister. If I'd had one, I would have done the same. However..." He moved closer again. "I would appreciate it if you would not do that. As I said, you may step on my foot should I get carried away." He placed his hand on her cheek, holding her head in place, and slowly bent himself toward her. Deliberately, he moved with a slowness even he couldn't believe, but he wanted to be sure she had time to retreat should she want to.

She didn't.

She merely looked up at him, her beautiful green eyes growing wider the closer he came, until just a breath before his lips descended upon hers when they closed. He saw her dark lashes flutter against her cheek before he redirected his gaze to her enticing full lips. His own eyes closed with ecstasy at the feel of her lips against his own. He started slowly with gentle, featherlight kisses. When she didn't pull away, he pressed his lips more firmly against hers and then dared to run his tongue along the seam of her lips. She was as delicious as he'd expected—sweet like honey, but with a slight tang from the wine she'd just been drinking.

Hesitantly, she allowed him entrance to the heat of her mouth. He swept his tongue inside even as he pulled her closer, fitting her soft curves against him. Without a doubt, this was what heaven felt like. He could imagine slowly undressing her. Exploring her with his hands, his eyes, and his mouth, but he knew it was a pleasure that was to come. He would wait patiently for her. He would wait until they were joined in marriage, and it would be all the sweeter for having waited. Still, he could enjoy this for the moment. He deepened his kiss before pulling back again because he knew despite his desires, he *could* do so, and he was here to prove it.

With one last gentle kiss, he slowly lifted his head to look at her. Her beauty awed him as she stood there with her head tilted up and her eyes closed.

Suddenly, she seemed to remember she needed to breathe and opened her mouth ever so slightly as her eyes opened to look up at him. "You stopped." She sounded almost sad.

He just smiled. "I told you I could."

She nodded. "Yes. Yes, you did."

"And now you believe me." He took a step away. He truly did not want to. "I want to continue kissing you," he told her softly. "I would forgo food, wine, and everything else to kiss you all night long, but it wouldn't be right."

"Oh," she breathed. She cleared her throat. "No. No, it would not be right." She turned away and picked up her wine glass. "Is there more wine?" she asked as she turned back to him.

He could only smile. "Yes, there is." He went to fetch the bottle.

# CHAPTER TWENTY

When Rebecca deemed Lord Willington and Lady Emilie had had enough time alone, she returned to the dining room. She knew it was remiss of her to leave them at all, but truly, there was no other way of allowing them the time they needed to speak openly and honestly. It would be that, she was certain, which would be the basis for a happy marriage. She knew it was that way with herself and her Brian. More than just matching people, Rebecca was determined to ensure the matches she made were ones where the participants would be happy for their lifetime together.

She made certain to make a bit of noise as she came down the stairs and then opened the door to the dining room—just in case the couple was doing something they shouldn't be. She was a little surprised to find them sitting by the fire, each with a glass in their hand, talking.

Lord Willington stood. "Ah, Lady Preston, we were hoping you would rejoin us soon. I've just ordered dinner."

"Excellent. I have to admit I am quite hungry," Rebecca said, coming farther into the room.

Lord Willington refilled the glass she'd drunk from earlier and handed it to her. As he did so, he leaned a little toward her and whispered, "You were right, my lady, I am no longer a boy."

She smiled. So, he had tested his ability to control his passions. As she had expected, he'd come through the experiment admirably.

It was all Emilie could do to keep the smile on her face and behave in a polite manner after she'd recovered from Lord Willington's kiss. He was absolutely and thoroughly a dangerous man, she decided. She didn't know what it was about him, but when he moved close to her, her mind just seemed to go numb. She didn't think. She couldn't. Not with him so near. Not with the heat radiating off his body, making her so warm. Not with his enticing scent of sandalwood, leather, and man enveloping her.

She had gone into the dining room still undecided about whether to follow Lady Preston's advice and tell his lordship the honest truth about her feelings toward him—confused though they were. But then he had captured the conversation and been the one to be completely open and honest with her.

As she told him, she still couldn't believe Lady Preston's descriptions of both of their personalities had been so uncannily accurate. He was, in fact, as passionate as the lady had said. But as he pointed out, he was no longer a nineteen-year-old boy unable or unwilling to control himself. Oh, no, he'd proved that very well.

His kiss still made her knees weak and her insides melt as she remembered it even as she lay here in the bed she was sharing with Lady Preston. Emilie had never been so disappointed as when he'd pulled back and proved himself able to withstand his urgings. She had wished... well, but she should *not*. She should be happy—no, grateful—that he'd resisted. She might not have been able to do so herself.

And it was that—both the fact he had, and she hadn't, wanted to end their kiss—which made her so annoyed. Where was her conviction that she didn't want to marry? Where was her determination that men were horrible, self-absorbed, untrustworthy creatures? He was continuing to challenge her long-held beliefs, and she did not like it.

She thought of her brother-in-law visiting the opera singer. Of the men she'd danced with at balls who'd only spoken of themselves without a thought of her. It was still true, she decided, men were awful. But Lord Willington?

Was it possible he had somehow risen above others of his sex? How could he be so damnably sweet and considerate? It truly was the most vexatious thing!

She hated the man. He'd hurt her.

But she could feel herself liking him more and more and it just made her all the more annoyed. What was it that Lady Preston had said in the carriage? Emilie was stubborn. Once she believed something it was extremely difficult for her to change her mind. And yet somehow Lord Willington was doing just that. He was changing her mind about him. He was making her think maybe, just maybe, she'd been wrong.

Gabriel had never been so relieved to settle himself into a chair at Powell's.

"You look like you've had quite a day. What a sigh!" Lord Uxbridge said, his extremely broad shoulders bouncing with silent laughter.

Gabriel hadn't even noticed him sitting there. His back had been to the door, and Gabriel had taken the first empty seat he'd seen.

"You wouldn't believe," Gabriel agreed. "And not just today, but the past forty-eight hours."

"Really? Well, let's get you a glass of rum and you can tell me about it. I've been itching for some good entertainment." He lifted a hand and motioned to a footman.

"Entertainment? Well, yes, I suppose you will find it so. I can assure you there was very little of that in it for me," Gabriel told him. He did sit up however and lean forward toward his friend. "I do first need to make a confession."

"I'm no priest, but go ahead," the man said, with a wide smile.

Gabriel gave a little chuckle. His friend was in fine form tonight. "I'm certain you're aware I didn't exactly believe you when you told me about Lady Preston being so wonderful in her matchmaking skills and accurate with her predictions."

Ox nodded but didn't say anything.

"Well, yesterday she proved herself to me quite thoroughly. I am here to admit I was wrong, and you were right."

Ox began to chuckle once again. Luckily, the footman came with their drinks before his friend could utter his "I told you so" that Gabriel could see was ready to pop from his mouth.

"Well, then, here's to enlightenment," Ox said, raising his glass toward Gabriel before taking a sip.

Gabriel did the same, enjoying the sweet burn of the alcohol as it slid over his tongue and down his throat.

"Now, tell me all that's happened," Ox prompted after Gabriel had drained a good amount from his glass.

"Well, it started with Lady Preston deciding Lady Emilie and I needed some... assistance, I suppose, with our courtship." He paused to take another sip of rum. "Somehow, she decided I was unhappy or perhaps annoyed with Lady Emilie."

"And were you?" Ox asked.

Gabriel waved a hand. "It's irrelevant." He honestly didn't want to admit he was actually annoyed with himself for allowing his emotions to become engaged when it came to Miss Preston. "The point is Lady Preston invited me and Lady Emilie out to Greenwich for a picnic."

"Ah, that sounds lovely."

"It was, actually. We talked and got everything aired out, so it was quite productive as well." At least that's what he wanted the ladies to think, so it wouldn't hurt for Ox to think so as well.

"On our return to London, unfortunately, we were driven off the road by an idiot driving much too fast in a phaeton—engaged in a race, of course."

"Oh, dear! I hope no one was injured," Ox asked, showing concern.

Gabriel shook his head sadly. "The driver broke his arm and got a concussion from having been thrown from the coach, but luckily neither I nor the ladies were injured in any way, aside from some bumps and bruises."

"I am sorry to hear about the coachman but relieved no one else was injured."

"Yes, but the coach ended up nearly on its side in a ditch!" Gabriel told him.

"Ugh! I do hope the idiot who ran you off the road had the grace to stop and help."

"Thankfully, he did," Gabriel conceded. "But still, I spent the rest of the day seeing to the driver, the horses, and gathering men to right the coach.

We ended up having to spend the night at a tiny little tavern in a nearby village."

"Oh, really?" Ox said, lifting his eyebrows nearly up to his hairline.

"It was after we arrived there that Lady Preston told me things about myself I would never have shared with anyone—but she just... *knew*."

Ox burst out laughing, turning the heads of some nearby gentlemen. "Of course she knew," he said. "You gave her your time and day of birth when you met her, didn't you?"

"I did, but..."

"She uses her astrological charts and can uncover absolutely uncanny knowledge from the placement of the stars. I have to admit I don't entirely understand it, but she was spot on with me as well."

Gabriel just shook his head in wonder. "Well, it was a very interesting experience, let's put it that way."

"And what of Lady Emilie?" Ox asked.

"Apparently, while I was gone taking care of matters, Lady Preston did the same with her—telling her how much she knew of the young lady's personality."

Ox chuckled and nodded. "Actually, I meant to ask how she handled the whole affair with the accident and then staying the night at the tavern."

"Oh! That girl is the most level-headed creature I've ever had the pleasure to know. She was not unduly upset by the accident, although she was uncomfortable spending the night away from her family, but that's understandable."

"Indeed, with only you and Lady Preston with her, it could be disconcerting for a young lady with little experience."

"Actually," Gabriel lowered his voice and sat forward so only Ox could hear him, "for a good part of the evening, it was only the two of us in our private dining room. Lady Preston decided to give us some time, er, alone."

"Really?" Ox too kept his voice low.

Gabriel nodded. "She went up to her room and didn't come back down for over an hour."

"And you were with Lady Emilie for that amount of time?"

Gabriel shrugged. "Of course. It did give us a chance to talk, which I believe we both appreciated."

"Which is probably why the lady did that," Ox said, with a knowing smile, as he sat back again.

"Indeed."

"And now? Are things better between you and Lady Emilie?"

This time it was Gabriel's turn to smile. "Oh yes, much."

A few nights later, Emilie had recovered enough from the excitement of her trip to Greenwich to accompany her mother to Lady Ovingham's party. She was happy to see her friends again.

"Oh, Lady Emilie, how wonderful it is that you are here!" Miss Merrill said upon seeing her.

"Where have you been?" Miss Smyth asked.

"Oh, please do say it was somewhere exciting," Miss Merrill added.

Emilie just laughed. "It *was* exciting, but perhaps a little too exciting." She told them a brief version of the picnic, accident, and then having to spend the night at a tiny tavern in an unknown village.

"You spent the night alone with Lord Willington?" Miss Merrill whispered in awe.

"No! My goodness! Don't even begin to think that, Miss Merrill," Emilie said quickly. "I spent the night with Lady Preston. We shared a room, in fact. Lord Willington was there as well, but I can assure you we were properly chaperoned the entire time," she fibbed.

"Oh, of course," Miss Merrill said, looking a little crestfallen. "What a shame Lady Preston was there. Otherwise, you could now happily be engaged to his lordship." Emilie's friends giggled at the thought, but Emilie didn't find it amusing at all.

She gave them a stern look. "I would never do such a thing, I assure you."

Her friends immediately sobered. "Oh, no, of course not," Miss Merrill said quickly.

"You may not, but I'm sure there are many who would," Miss Smyth replied.

Sadly, Emilie had to agree, but as she was thinking of what to say to such a comment, her friends' eyes widened, both of them looking over Emilie's shoulder. She turned and found Lord Willington approaching.

He bowed to the three of them and then held out his hand to Emilie, a warm smile playing on his lips. "May I have the pleasure of this dance, Lady Emilie?"

Emilie's gaze snapped to the center of the room where couples were beginning to line up for the first dance of the evening. She turned back to his lordship. "Why, thank you, my lord. I would enjoy that greatly." She placed her hand in his and allowed him to lead her onto the floor.

As they danced and made light, meaningless conversation, Emilie realized Lord Willington was in an excellent mood. He was light on his feet and smiling at her every time her eyes met his. Perhaps that kiss had done something to him as well.

Over the past few days since their adventure, she had hardly been able to stop thinking of his kiss whenever her mind was unoccupied, but then, it was only the second time in her life she'd been kissed. And to be honest, she almost wondered if or when the man would simply disappear just like he had the first time. She forced herself to believe the best of him, however. And, in truth, he did not seem as if he was about to disappear. But, of course, she hadn't expected him to do so the last time either.

She would stay optimistic, she decided—for now.

# Chapter Twenty-One

"Lady Emilie," Lord Willington said as he came up to her later that evening. She had been about to seek out some refreshment with her friends, but he was frowning at her rather sternly. She was very confused. He'd been all smiles and sweetness when they'd danced earlier. What could have happened in the meantime?

"My lord?" she asked. She indicated to her friends to go on without her.

"I am extremely annoyed with you," he said, still glaring at her, although he'd had the good manners to nod a greeting to her friends before they'd gone off without her.

"I, er, I can see that, but I don't understand why."

"Because you are ruining my reputation!"

Her mouth dropped open. "Your... your reputation, my lord?"

"Yes, my reputation as a man colder than a block of ice in winter. I can tell you I worked very hard to develop that reputation and now... People are coming up to me and asking why I'm smiling!" He sounded peeved, but Emilie noticed one corner of his lips was twitching with mirth.

"Oh no!" she said, as if horrified. She put her hand to her mouth and looked up at him with distraught eyes. "I am so very sorry, my lord. I... I don't know what to say. Please, sir, tell me what I can do to make things right again."

His lips twitched again as she joined him in his little farce. "You will have to dance with me once more and this time... this time no smiling!"

She thought about that for a moment. "You do not think people will comment on our dancing twice in one evening?"

He lifted one shoulder in a nonchalant way. "No, just so long as it is clear that I am *not* enjoying your company."

A little bubble of laughter burst from her mouth, but she quickly clamped it down. "I see. And, er, am I, too, not to enjoy myself while we dance?"

"Oh, no. You can have as much fun as you like. But I assure you, I will not." And with that, he held out his arm for her to take as he led her out onto the dance floor once again.

Emilie was impressed. While she was charming and smiling, Lord Willington truly did manage to maintain a look of boredom or, if he smiled at all, it was nothing more than a cold, polite smile— throughout the entire dance.

As they executed a turnabout, she looked around at the assembled guests to see if anyone was actually noticing Lord Willington's dour expression. Disturbingly, she found Lord Brice staring straight at her.

That would have been bad enough, but to make matters worse, he was speaking with Lady Findlater, the most notorious gossip of the *ton*, as he did so. What in the world could Lord Brice have to speak with Lady Findlater about? And why was he looking at her in that way as he did so? Emilie didn't like this at all.

Thank goodness, Lord Willington was completely oblivious to what was occurring at the other end of the drawing room. Emilie shuddered to think of how he might react if he was aware of what his "friend" was up to. To ensure he didn't, she continued in her silly attempts to break his lordship of his dour expression.

She hated the fact that she had seen Lord Brice. Now she was imagining many others were staring at her as well. It *was* her imagination, wasn't it? She looked around and found Lady Findlater speaking with another older matron and then watched as that woman hurried to the side of another lady. The third woman turned to look at Lord Willington. Goodness, maybe he'd been right, and people were discussing his reputation as a cold fish. Well, if so, he was doing an excellent job of *not* smiling now.

As he was returning her to the side of the room where her friends were—with their refreshments, which Emilie was now quite desperate to partake of—she spotted her sister speaking with another matronly looking woman, although she probably couldn't have been much older than Eliza. Strangely, Emilie's sister turned at the same moment and looked right back at her.

The hair on Emilie's arms prickled. Her sister did not look happy, not happy at all. Emilie began to wonder if she was the one people were gossiping about or Lord Willington. She couldn't think why anyone would be talking about her. Well, there was nothing Emilie could do about it now, and she was certain she would be hearing from her sister before too long.

It was the very next morning, in fact, when Eliza came over to pay Emilie a call. Wisely, she brought Georgie with her. There was no better way to make sure Lady Tremelling was kept much too busy to pay attention to the sisters' conversation.

"You are still carrying through with your revenge plan," Eliza quietly said as she sat down next to Emilie.

No good morning. No pleasantries whatsoever. She got straight to the point. Emilie was a little taken aback, especially because she'd all but decided *not* to carry through with that plan. She'd been thinking about it ever since Lady Preston and she discussed it while sitting in the sideways coach waiting for Lord Willington to return. She'd thought about it even more that night as she lay wide awake replaying *That Kiss* in her mind over and over again—and still wishing he hadn't had quite so much control over his passions.

"I don't—" Emilie started, frowning at her sister.

"You *must*. You absolutely must carry on with it, Emilie." Eliza had hardly ever spoken so forcefully.

"All right, but why? What's happened? I noticed people talking last night. I'm certain I was simply being paranoid, but I could have sworn they were speaking about me. Or was it Lord Willington?" Emilie asked.

"Yes, people were talking. Thank goodness Livia Penderton is such a good friend! She told me what they were saying." Eliza stopped speaking and looked down at her hands folded in her lap.

Emilie put her hand on top of her sister's. "What were they saying?" She wasn't entirely certain she actually wanted to know, but she *had* to know.

Eliza let out a breath. "They were saying it was clear that you are completely smitten with Lord Willington. You're making a fool of yourself before him and all the *ton*, pushing yourself at him as you're doing. And it's abundantly clear that he, being the cold man he is, is not interested." She looked Emilie in the eye. "It's known he's looking for a marriage of convenience, not love. He has told quite a number of people, apparently, that he disdains love matches and simply wants to marry a young woman from a good family who will not burden him unduly."

Emilie could feel herself going cold as her sister spoke. She was throwing herself at Lord Willington? Well, she supposed she was. She was attempting to make him fall in love with her and, from what she could tell, it was working. The fact that her own emotions were beginning to become engaged as well was beside the point. She was certain her anger at the man would override any softer feelings she may have developed for him when she came to that point.

"Well," Emilie said after thinking about this for a minute, "it is true that I'm trying to engage his interest."

"But you are doing so to make him fall in love with you, not the other way around," her sister hissed.

Emilie glared at her for a moment. "I am *not* falling in love with him while he, most certainly, is falling in love with me."

"How do you know?" Eliza asked, speaking normally again.

"Because he kissed me. When we were at that tavern a few days ago, he kissed me—quite passionately, I might add."

Emilie's sister's mouth dropped open. "He did?"

"Yes."

"Then why was he looking so bored when he danced with you a second time last night?"

Emilie nearly laughed. "It was a joke! He said I was ruining his reputation as a cold fish and the only way I could make up for it was to dance with him while he looked bored. I was shocked he was able to maintain a straight face the entire dance—although I did catch his lips twitching a number of times."

"A… a joke? He was doing it deliberately?"

"Yes!"

Eliza sighed. "All right, then. And you are certain he's the one who is smitten and not you."

"Absolutely," Emilie lied. She might pay for that later, but she was becoming more determined by the minute that she had to rein in her own emotions and return to simply hating the man.

"And you are still carrying through with your plan?"

"Yes!" she reassured her sister.

Eliza just shook her head. "I have to say I'm impressed with your acting skills. It's almost a shame you can't take to the stage." Finally, Emilie's sister allowed a small smile to grace her face.

"Why, thank you. I'm certain it's all the Christmas plays we put on every year."

Eliza gave a little laugh. "That's true. You were always excellent in them as well."

"In truth, I've been trying to be more like Amelia," Emilie admitted.

Eliza gave a little laugh and nodded her head, understanding immediately. But then she tapped her chin as she thought about it. "That's excellent, but don't forget to be yourself as well. It was you who he fell for all those years ago when Amelia was right there."

"Oh, I am. I'm trying to do both," Emilie said.

She then tilted her head a little and looked at her sister. Something had been nagging at her ever since Eliza had suggested this plan of revenge. Now was as good a time as any to ask.

"Eliza..." Emilie began slowly.

Her sister raised her eyebrows suspiciously.

"Why are you so determined that I go through with this plan?" Eliza opened her mouth to speak, but Emilie held up her hand to stay her. "Yes, I know now I've got to save my reputation but before this. You've been very... set on it. Is there a reason?"

Eliza let out a little huff. "I love you, you silly thing, and I want you to be happy. You deserve happiness. You deserve love. It's why Mother went to this Lady Preston. We all just want you..."

"To not have a marriage like yours?" Emilie asked quietly.

"Yes. Please don't think Alford and I don't like each other. We do! But... we don't love each other. You deserve to marry someone you love and who loves you with all their heart." She reached out and took Emilie's hand. "You deserve to be treated better than Willington has treated you. All women do. We deserve respect. Willington has shown you no respect whatsoever. He kissed you and fled. No man should be allowed to get away with that.”

Gabriel was working in his study that morning going over the estate books when there was a knock on the door. He was more than happy to be disturbed, so he called out for whoever it was to enter.

Mrs. Gibson, his grandmother’s lady’s maid, hesitantly inched into the room.

“Mrs. Gibson, come in. What is it that I may do for you?” he said, encouraging the woman. He’d had very little interaction with her woman, but she’d been with his grandmother for probably his whole life.

“I do beg your pardon, my lord,” she said, her voice so soft he could barely hear her.

“Not at all. I am just doing the most boring of tasks and happy to be given an excuse to put it aside.” He gave her a warm smile, hoping to put the woman at ease.

“Oh, thank you, my lord. It’s just... well, your grandmother—”

Gabriel jumped to his feet startling the woman. “Is she all right? Did she fall and hurt herself? Is there something else ailing her?”

The poor woman looked terrified. “She told me not to bother you, but it’s just so unlike her,” the woman started again. She began to wring her hands.

Gabriel let out a frustrated sigh. "Of course, she did. What is wrong, ma'am? Or should I just go up and—yes, why don't I do that." He started toward the door.

"Oh, my please, my lord, please don't let on I told you. She'll be ever so cross with me."

He paused as he was about to pass her and gave her an awkward pat on her shoulder. "Have no fear Mrs. Gibson, after all these years it is unlikely my grandmother would turn you off for telling me she was ill."

"Oh, no, I don't expect she would. It's just... well... when she gets cross, she doesn't speak to me," the woman admitted. "It's very difficult and upsets me so."

"Ah, of course. I understand. Well, have no fear, I won't give you away." He turned and continued out toward the door. "I assume she is in her room?"

"Yes, my lord. She is still abed."

Gabriel gave a nod and strode out the door. He took the stairs two at a time, thinking of the excuse he would give to be invading her bedchamber.

He stopped just in front of the door to her private sitting room and knocked, knowing she wouldn't be in there but would probably be able to hear him. When there was no answer, he moved one door down and knocked on her bedroom door.

A weak voice called out. He couldn't make out what she said, but he assumed it was permission to enter.

He opened the door and strode into the room with a smile on his face. "Good morning, Gran." He stopped when he saw her still in bed. "What's this? Didn't feel like getting up today?"

"Oh, Gabriel." Her voice was nearly as quiet as Mrs. Gibson's had been and sounded hoarse.

He quickly gained her bedside. "What is it, Gran? Are you unwell?" he asked, showing his true concern.

She shook her head slightly. "I'm afraid I am just a bit... feeling a touch languid today."

"I am sorry to hear that." He sat at the edge of her large tester bed. "You have been going pretty hard ever since we arrived in London. Perhaps it's just all catching up to you?"

She smiled. "Yes, that must be it. Do not have a care for me. I'm sure I'll be well enough before too long."

"Well, I should hope so. I had come up to ask if you wanted to go for a drive in the park this afternoon. Do you think you'll be up for it?" He asked as he took her small, limp hand as it lay on her coverlet.

"Oh, no dear. I don't think... not today."

"Tomorrow then," he said.

"I... I don't know. I'll see how I feel then." She attempted to give him a brave smile, but he could see even that seemed to be almost too much for her. Her eyes drifted closed.

"Of course. Well, then, I'll leave you to your rest." He leaned forward and placed a gentle kiss on her forehead.

"I don't feel warm, do I?" she asked, sounding half-asleep already.

"Feverish? No, not at all."

"Oh, good. I'm just tired then." She slid herself down a little farther under her covers.

Gabriel reached out and adjusted her pillows for her and then got up to quietly leave the room.

Mrs. Gibson was standing out in the hall. "Well?"

"You were absolutely right to come and fetch me, Mrs. Gibson. If she's not feeling better by this afternoon, I'll have the doctor in," he told her, keeping his voice quiet so as not to disturb his grandmother.

The woman nodded. "Oh, thank you, my lord."

He returned to his study but just couldn't focus on his work. The way his grandmother had looked so... so old and shrunken in the huge bed. Usually, her vibrance made her look years younger, but now it was so easy to see just how very old she was. He had to think about it for a few minutes, but he believed she was close to seventy if not past that exalted age. He shook his head. Well, it was no wonder she was tired.

But when Gabriel went up to check on her again a little after three that afternoon, he found her sound asleep. Mrs. Gibson was sitting with her doing some mending.

"She hasn't been asleep all day, has she?" he asked the woman quietly.

She just nodded, her forehead furrowed with worry.

Gabriel frowned and nodded. "I'll go fetch the doctor."

"Oh, thank you, my lord," the woman said, sounding relieved.

He called for his phaeton, but when it arrived, he realized he didn't know of any doctors in London. He'd never been sick, nor had any of his friends. He stood there for a good minute trying to think of what to do when suddenly it occurred to him that Lady Tremelling would probably know of someone. And then not only could he get the information he needed, but he would have an opportunity to see Lady Emilie as well.

That thought put a bounce in his step as he hopped up onto the bench and took the reins.

# CHAPTER TWENTY-TWO

Rebecca was both horrified and furious when she heard the gossip going around. She was paying a morning call on Lady Wraxley, known to be a good friend of Lady Findlater. For someone in Rebecca's line of work, it was very important she keep up-to-date on all the latest gossip, so she'd made sure to maintain an acquaintanceship with the lady.

"You were the one who paired them, weren't you, Lady Preston? Or am I mistaking the matter?" Lady Wraxley asked, peering at Rebecca over the rim of her teacup, just before she took a sip.

"Yes, and I stand by my decision," Rebecca said, giving the woman as pleasant a smile as she could. It wasn't easy, but it was necessary.

"I'm certain that is the only reason why Lord Willington is paying the girl any attention at all. But it is obvious he doesn't enjoy her company. Is it possible you—" the woman started.

"Of course he does," Rebecca argued, unable to keep herself from cutting off the woman's words. "Lord Willington is not the sort of man..." She paused for a breath and the opportunity to choose her words carefully.

"To be led by a woman?" Lady Wraxley supplied. "I beg to differ. He is exactly that sort of man. Why look at how he dotes on his grandmother."

"Just because he is solicitous toward Lady Willington—" Rebecca tried again.

"I hear the betting books at White's and Boodle's are filled with speculation over exactly when he's going to throw the girl over and just how badly she's going to react." The woman gave an unpleasant little chuckle. "Some say he'll wait until the end of the Season. Others say he wouldn't be so cruel—for certainly once he is finished with her, she'll have to immediately turn around and try for another husband. On the other hand, if her heart is truly broken, perhaps she'll just leave Town. And then there are wagers whether she'll return next Season or not."

Rebecca was speechless at the cruelty of the *ton*. But then she chastised herself. She should know better by now.

Lady Wraxley, however, was clearly enjoying it all. The rotund woman let out a titter behind her gloved hand. "Why, Lady Preston, the possibilities are endless!"

"The one outcome no one seems to be considering is they are truly falling in love and will marry," Rebecca pointed out.

At that, Lady Wraxley truly burst into peals of laughter. "Lady Preston, you are too amusing! Goodness, I must tell others how humorous you are."

Still laughing, she turned and walked away to spread her tales to her other guests. Rebecca could hear her tittering, "fall in love and marry."

Rebecca stood there seething for a few minutes before she could get herself under control once more. With a swift shake of her head, she allowed her anger to dissipate and her logical mind to take command of her thoughts. What was she going to do about this?

Well, first of all, she needed to inform Lady Emilie and Lord Willington. Lady Tremelling and Lady Willington would probably have to be told at the same time. Yes. That was what she must do and then perhaps one of them would come up with a plan of how to combat the gossip—and if they should at all. Perhaps it would simply blow over as so many of these things did.

Wishful thinking wasn't a bad thing, was it?

Before Eliza and Georgie left, Emilie had been reminded most urgently by her niece that she'd promised to make a frock for Georgie's stuffed bear.

"Yes, my sweet, I know, but you're going to have to be a little patient. I can't sew as quickly as your mama can," Emilie had told Georgie.

"It's because you don't practice as much as I do," Eliza had said *sotto voce* in the direction of their mother.

Lady Tremelling had laughed and agreed.

"Well, be that as it may," Emilie continued, redirecting her attention back to her niece, "I shall work on it this very day and see if I can't get a fair way into finishing it. All right?"

Georgie only nodded because her mouth was full of her thumb.

"And what do you say to Auntie Emilie?" Eliza reminded her daughter.

"Thank you, Auntie," Georgie said, reluctantly removing her thumb.

"You are most welcome," Emilie said, standing back up.

Eliza gently stopped her daughter from putting her thumb back into her mouth. She gave her mother a little kiss on the cheek and headed toward the door. Before they could get there, however, there was a knock on it from outside.

The footman jumped to answer it. A gentleman's voice was clearly heard saying, "The Marquess of Willington to see Lady Emilie, if you please."

The footman turned to see if it would be all right to let the man in. Emilie's mother gave a short nod ,and the man backed up, opening the door fully.

"Oh, Lady Emilie, Lady Tremelling, were you about to go out?" Lord Willington said, looking about the entrance hall where they'd all congregated.

"No, no, not at all, my lord," Lady Tremelling said, reaching a hand out toward the man, so he could place a kiss on the back of it.

"They were just saying goodbye to me." Eliza scooped Georgie up into her arms and headed out the door with a cheery wave.

A little "Goodbye!" could be heard from Georgie as they left.

"Do come in, my lord," Emilie's mother said, heading toward the stairs. She led the way up to the drawing room with Emilie and Lord Willington following.

"What a lovely surprise this is," she said as she took a seat in a chair closer to the unlit fireplace.

"I do hope I'm not intruding or—"

"Not at all! Not at all," her mother said quickly, indicating he take a seat on the sofa.

He did so. Emilie took the matching chair to her mother's.

Lord Willington sat forward. "I was wondering, my lady, if you might know of a physician you would recommend."

"Oh dear! I do hope you are feeling all right?" Lady Tremelling exclaimed.

"It is for my grandmother. Sadly, she is not feeling very well," he answered.

"I am so sorry to hear that," Emilie said.

He turned toward her, his face softening. "Thank you, Lady Emilie."

Her mother was clearly thinking. "I have always used mister... no, that's not right. He's a surgeon. You need a physician." She tapped her chin as she thought. With a little jump, she sat forward. "I know! Samuelson. Yes, that's his name. Mr. Samuelson."

"Ah, excellent," Lord Willington said. "Thank you so much."

"I believe I have his address..." She got up and wandered out the door, still deep in thought.

Emilie and Lord Willington both watched her go. His lordship had a little smile on his face.

Emilie gave a little laugh. "Well, if that was all it took to get her to leave us alone for a few minutes, I might have requested you to ask her something before this."

He turned his smile on her. "I think this is just an extra special opportunity."

"Yes, it is and I am going to take advantage of it," Emilie informed him.

He tilted his head and lifted his eyebrows. "Oh?"

"I have been thinking, my lord..."

"Hmmm, is this a good thing or a bad thing?" he asked, when she paused for dramatic effect.

She gave him a look. "It is a good thing for me, but I'm not so sure about you."

"Oh dear." He sat back. "Yes?"

"You mentioned the other night that I was ruining your carefully crafted reputation," she began.

He only nodded.

"And then to regain it, you managed—and I will have to say I was most impressed—to maintain a straight face throughout our dance."

He gave her a broad smile. "Thank you."

"I am not certain that is something to be proud of, however. In fact, I am determined to make you laugh. In public."

He burst out laughing. When he had regained control of himself, he said. "In public? Well, good luck to you! I won't do it. I tell you that I have very carefully created this—"

"Fiction," Emilie finished for him.

"It is not fiction," he protested.

"It most certainly is. You are *not* a cold fish. In fact, just the opposite, if you ask me."

"Which is why I never asked you," he pointed out, his lips still quirked up in a little half smile.

Emilie just crossed her arms over her chest.

"As I was saying, I have carefully crafted this reputation, and I do not intend on allowing you to destroy it just like that." He too crossed his arms.

"But what if you can't help it?" she asked, releasing her arms to rest her hands in her lap.

"I do not lose control in public," he informed her.

"Well, I am determined to prove you wrong and get you to laugh."

"Shall we make a wager on it?" he asked with a lift of an eyebrow.

"A wager? That I can make you laugh?"

"In public," he added pointedly.

Emilie nodded, accepting the correction. "And what will I win when you do so?"

He burst out laughing again. "Oh my, you are certainly sure of yourself, aren't you?"

She smiled. "Yes, I am. Now, what will I win?"

He sat back crossing his arms over his chest again as he thought about it. His eyes strayed toward the window. "If you win—you will not, by the way—you... Let's see, you do not seem to be the sort of girl who values clothes above all else so buying you a new gown wouldn't do. Do you paint? Ply a needle? Enjoy riding?"

"I sketch, am worse than anything at needlework, and greatly enjoy riding and driving a phaeton," she answered.

"Driving a phaeton?"

She gave a little shrug. "My brother taught me how to drive his, and it was incredibly fun. I understand why so many men drive one."

"All right, then, if you win you may drive my phaeton in the park one afternoon."

"With you next to me, smiling and laughing at everything I say," she added.

He gave a little chuckle and then a nod of his head in agreement. "And if I win—"

"Which you won't," she slipped in.

"Then you must dance only with me and allow me to escort you to the park, and whatever parties you were planning on attending—for a week."

Oh, she liked that! So either way it went, she would get what she wanted—either an enjoyable drive in the park, or many more opportunities to carry out her plan to make him fall in love with her. This was perfect!

"You have a deal, Lord Willington." She held out her hand to him. He took it and gave her a firm handshake.

They had just let go of each other when her mother walked back into the room waving a small piece of paper. "I am sorry that took me so long. I had thought I'd written Mr. Samuelson's address in my book, but I couldn't find it. Eventually, I had to ask the housekeeper. Luckily, the butler knew."

Emilie frowned. "You asked the housekeeper, but it was the butler who knew?"

"Yes, that's what I said," her mother gave Emilie a confused look as if she couldn't understand why her daughter was having trouble understanding her. "In any case, here it is, my lord." She handed him the piece of paper.

He glanced at it and then stood up. "Thank you, my lady. I shall drive there directly and hopefully be able to bring the man to my grandmother right away."

"Oh, I wouldn't count on him being able to come immediately. He is quite busy. But I'm sure he'll be able to visit her before the evening is through."

He bowed to her and then to Emilie. "Thank you again." And then he strode purposefully out of the room.

After he'd left, Lady Tremelling turned toward Emilie. "Well, what did you say to have him laughing so uproariously? I was about to rejoin you when I heard him all the way down the hall."

"Oh, it was nothing, Mama. Just a joke I told him which he found amusing," Emilie said, standing up.

"Well, I am very glad you are getting along. Perhaps before too long we'll be heading to the modiste to order your wedding trousseau." Her mother looked so happy at the prospect that Emilie didn't have the heart to tell her it wasn't going to happen, whether Lord Willington proposed or not. Emilie was not going to marry.

# CHAPTER TWENTY-THREE

Rebecca handed her visiting card to the footman who answered the door at Lord Willington's home later that afternoon. "I am here to see Lady Willington, if she is at home?"

The man shook his head sadly. "I'm very sorry, my lady, her ladyship is unwell. In fact, Lord Willington is out right now fetching the doctor."

"Oh dear! I am so very sorry to hear that. Well, please convey to her my most sincere hopes that she recovers quickly."

The footman nodded and closed the door as Rebecca turned and descended the steps.

Well, that made things a great deal more difficult, she thought as she got back into her coach. Hopefully, Lady Tremelling would be accepting visitors.

She was bowed into the Tremelling's home not a quarter of an hour later, much to her relief.

"Why, Lady Preston, what a lovely surprise," Lady Tremelling said, as she stood to greet Rebecca.

"I'm afraid you may not think so when I inform you of the reason for my visit," Rebecca said. She nodded to Lady Emilie, who had also stood and given her a little curtsy.

"Oh? Is there something wrong?" Lady Tremelling asked as she indicated Rebecca take a seat. "No, wait. Do not tell me. Not until we are well fortified with a cup of tea." She went to give the bell pull a little tug.

"You might want something a little stronger," Rebecca said under her breath as she watched Lady Tremelling.

"I beg your pardon?" Lady Emilie asked.

"Nothing!" Rebecca said quickly. She gave the girl her best smile but feared it might not be as positive as she would have liked.

She was sure of it when the girl just gave her head a little tilt as she looked at Rebecca curiously.

They passed the time while they waited for the tea in meaningless pleasantries, but as soon as it was brought and poured out, Rebecca was about to say what she'd come to say when Lady Emilie put down her teacup without taking a sip.

"I fear I know the reason for your visit, my lady," the girl said, folding her hands in her lap. "But truly, there is nothing for you to worry about."

Her mother lowered her own teacup. "What are you talking about Emilie? Lady Preston, what is it you came to tell us?"

"It is about the gossip being spread, isn't it?" Lady Emilie asked.

Rebecca let out a little sigh. "Yes, I'm afraid it is." It was a relief that she was already aware of it. It did make things so much easier.

"What gossip?" Lady Tremelling asked, looking from Rebecca to her daughter and back again.

"Oh! Do you not know, my lady?" Rebecca asked.

"No!" the lady said, beginning to frown.

"It's nothing, Mother. I saw Lord Brice whispering something to Lady Findlater last night as Lord Willington and I were dancing. They both turned and looked straight at me."

"Oh no!" her mother exclaimed, furrowing her brow.

"Is that who started it?" Rebecca asked. "You clearly know even more than I."

The girl gave a little shrug. "It was just luck which made me turn toward them when I did. I didn't learn what was said until this morning."

"What was said? Who told you?" Lady Tremelling asked.

"Eliza did when she visited," her daughter told her.

"Eliza? While I was playing with Georgie?" Lady Tremelling asked.

Lady Emilie nodded and then turned toward Rebecca. "My sister, Lady Alford, visited with her daughter, Georgiana," she explained.

"Emilie, I insist you tell me what this gossip is immediately!" an increasingly anxious Lady Tremelling said.

Her daughter sighed, but Rebecca allowed her to impart the unpleasant things that were being said—they were about her, after all.

"It is being spread about that I am throwing myself at Lord Willington, and he is not at all happy about this since he is trying to find a girl who will enter into a marriage of convenience with him."

Rebecca nodded, although she also added, "I heard you are making a fool of yourself by trying to get him to come up to scratch. Some people are saying he's putting up with it because he is being forced to court you—although no one quite knows why. Lady Wraxley thought it was because I was engaged to find him a match and I suggested Lady Emilie."

"Oh dear," Lady Tremelling whispered.

"Apparently, the betting books at the gentlemen's clubs are filled with speculation," Rebecca added.

"Oh, dear." This time Lady Tremelling shook her head as well and continued to do so for nearly a full minute. "What are we to do? We cannot allow Emilie's reputation—"

"As I said, I have it well in hand, Mother," Lady Emilie interrupted.

Her mother turned toward her, confusion writ over her face. "What? How?"

The girl turned toward Rebecca. "Lord Willington was here a short time ago—sadly, his grandmother isn't doing well, and he wanted the name of a doctor to see to her. He came to ask my mother for a recommendation."

Rebecca nodded when Lady Emilie paused.

"While my mother was getting the direction of the physician she's used on occasion, I told Lord Willington I thought I could make him laugh—in public. He thought the idea ludicrous and extremely amusing. We entered into a little bet of our own whether I could do this." Lady Emilie gave Rebecca and then her mother a broad smile. "I am fully confident I can, actually, make him laugh, and then the gossips will be proven wrong."

"But what if you can't?" her mother asked, still looking worried.

Lady Emilie just looked at her mother. "Even if I don't say anything so amusing that he would laugh, I think he would anyway just to allow me to win. In either case, he's going to be paying me a great deal of attention over the next week in order to give me the opportunity and prove to me that I can't do it." The girl gave a chuckle. "You see? Even if he doesn't laugh, it will be clear that he is interested in me, and it is not just me throwing myself at him."

"That was very clever, Lady Emilie," Rebecca admitted. "I do hope your plan works."

The girl gave a little shrug. "How can it not?"

Gabriel was severely disappointed when, upon reaching the address given to him by Lady Tremelling, he found the doctor away from home. The woman who answered the door just scowled at him. He was forced to remain on the doorstep while she told him the doctor was out and it was unknown as to when he would be returning. Gabriel left his card and requested the man attend to his grandmother as soon as possible. The woman gave him a curt nod and then slammed the door in his face.

"Well, I think I might be having a word with the doctor if and when he ever comes, on the manners of his housekeeper," he muttered to himself as he climbed back up onto his phaeton.

As soon as he got back home, he went straight up to his grandmother's room. She was still sleeping, and Mrs. Gibson was still sitting by the window with her sewing.

"Mrs. Gibson, have you had tea? A break of any sort?" he asked the woman softly.

She just shook her head.

"Well, then, please go straight away downstairs and get yourself something. Perhaps a walk in the garden as well. You need it and deserve it for sitting here all this time."

The woman gave him a grateful look. "Thank you, my lord. You'll stay with her while I do so?"

"I will," he assured her.

As she left, he pulled the chair she'd been sitting in closer to his grandmother's bed and settled himself. He'd been clever enough to briefly stop by his study on his way up and grab a book to read.

He wasn't sure how much time had passed, but he'd gotten a good way through his book when he heard his name being whispered. He looked up to find his grandmother reaching out a tremulous hand.

He jumped up, taking it as he sat on the edge of the bed. "How are you feeling, Gran?" he asked gently.

"Just tired, that's all," she said with a hoarse throat.

He poured her a glass of water from the pitcher on her bedside table and then assisted her to sit up in order to drink it.

She nodded gratefully after swallowing some. "What are you doing here, you naughty boy?"

He smiled. "Nothing. Just reading."

"Why aren't you out visiting your Lady Emilie?"

"I already did, this afternoon," he informed her.

"Oh?"

"Yes, you would not believe that girl. She told me she is determined to make me laugh out loud in public! Me!" he chuckled.

His grandmother smiled. "That would be a feat. You hardly even smile when you're in public."

"Well, I do have a reputation to maintain, you know."

"Yes, I do. You have carefully crafted a reputation precisely the opposite of your mother's," Gran said.

This gave Gabriel pause. He'd never even thought of that. She was right, though. His mother had been bright and vivacious. The men had not-so-secretly called her Willing Willington for how easily she'd slip between the sheets of any man's bed. And yet despite that, people liked her—even the ladies.

"Yes, I suppose you're right."

"Isn't that the reason why you have such a reputation?" she asked.

"No. I just don't like sharing my feelings."

"Or even acknowledge you have any?"

He gave a little shrug.

"You were such a lively boy," she said, running a hand down his arm. "Just like your mother, so full of life and joy and passion. What happened, Gabriel?"

He gave her a little smile as he too remembered how he'd been as a child. "I grew up, I suppose."

"And your mother's behavior embarrassed you?"

"How could it not?" he answered a little harshly.

She patted his arm again and nodded.

"I don't know how Papa put up with it," Gabriel said.

Gran sighed. "He loved her, and he accepted who she was—the good and the bad." She looked at him and smiled. "I'm sure you understand. Do you not feel that way about Lady Emilie?"

"What? No! I am not in love with her," he protested immediately. What a thought! He could barely believe his grandmother believed it.

She gave a little chuckle. "Hmmm," she said, clearly unconvinced. "Well, when you do fall in love, I am certain you will feel the same way."

"Gran, I've told you..."

"Yes, yes, you want a loveless marriage. A marriage of convenience," she said, sliding down her pillows once more. "Well, you go and see if you can find yourself such a match for I will not do so. And if you succeed, remember, I will not be there to hear your wails of regret. Now, go on and let an old lady sleep." She allowed her eyes to close slowly.

"I'll sit right here with you," he said, switching back to the chair.

Opening one eye, she squinted at him. "Afraid I'll kick the bucket before you return?"

Gabriel laughed. "Should I be?"

"No! Now go away like a good boy."

"I promised Mrs. Gibson I'd stay until she returned from her tea. It's all right. You go back to sleep."

She gave a little *harrumph* but did so anyway.

# CHAPTER TWENTY-FOUR

It took Lady Willington a few days to recover, but once she did, she and Gabriel were once again seen attending the best parties the *ton* had to offer.

He hadn't realized how eager he was to see Lady Emilie until he got his grandmother settled in a little gilt chair surrounded by her admirers and friends. She shooed him off, and he was more than happy to go in search of the young lady.

And then he stopped midway across the ballroom.

He'd suddenly remembered their wager. He couldn't go see her! He couldn't speak with her! If he did, she was going to do her best to make him laugh, and he would surely have a hard time not doing so. He always wanted to laugh when he was around Lady Emilie. She simply made him happy and lighthearted—how could he not?

Even though he could now see her standing by the potted plants with two of her friends, he heaved a sigh. She was looking especially beautiful this evening. He didn't know what it was, but her cheeks were pink, her gown was of the palest green making her beautiful green eyes stand out so he could even see them from this distance, and she was laughing, which always brought him joy.

But no, if he wanted to win this bet—and he most certainly did—he would have to avoid Lady Emilie for a week at least. Surely, she would forget about the silly wager by then. But just seeing her standing there and knowing he couldn't approach, made him feel like a boy confined to his room on a sunny summer day.

This was probably going to be the hardest week of his life.

Wondering what he might do instead of speaking to Lady Emilie, he looked around for Ox and Miss Ellison. They were present at nearly every party he attended and, being so tall, they were easy to spot. Oddly enough, they didn't seem to be here this evening.

With a sigh, Gabriel turned and headed into the card room. There seemed to be only one spot open at a table near the windows. He headed for it before anyone else could claim the seat.

"Evening gentlemen," he said, placing a hand on the empty chair. "Mind if I join in?"

The three men already there glanced up at him, then the one holding the deck of cards said, "No, not at all. Actually, we'd be happy for a fourth. Then we can play whist. Any objections?" He looked about the table. A chorus of "don't mind" and "excellent idea" had Gabriel taking a seat.

He and his partner across the table had just won their second hand when Gabriel felt a hand clap down onto his shoulder. He looked up. "Ah, Tremelling, good to see you."

"I'm sorry I cannot reciprocate the feeling," Lady Emilie's older brother said.

"Oh?"

"Why are you not dancing with my sister? Have you tired of her already?" Tremelling asked, his eyes narrowing.

"No! Not at all. I just—"

"Good then let me escort you to her," Tremelling said. It wasn't a question, it was a command, and Gabriel knew if he truly wanted to court Lady Emilie, he would have to do as her brother said.

He excused himself from the game and followed Tremelling out into the ballroom. About halfway across the room, Gabriel began to wonder if he might be able to avoid speaking with Lady Emilie— maybe not entirely as he was heading over to her just now, but that didn't mean he had to have an extended conversation with her. If he didn't ask her to dance, then they would have to talk and then he might very well be in trouble of losing his reputation and their wager. Yes, dancing would be better—much more difficult to hold a conversation while dancing.

Tremelling clearly noticed Gabriel's slowing walk as he was thinking this through. He, once again, put a guiding hand on Gabriel's shoulder, and this time he kept it there until they reached Lady Emilie's side.

"Look who I found lurking in the card room, Em," Tremelling said as they approached her.

She cocked her head a little to the side. "Avoiding me, my lord?"

"Er... not exactly..." he hedged.

"Why would you avoid her?" Tremelling asked, frowning at Gabriel.

"I wasn't!" Gabriel defended himself despite the fact that it was a flat-out lie.

"You are not good at telling falsehoods, my lord," Lady Emilie said with a laugh.

Gabriel's lips quirked up, but he immediately straightened them, so it could not be seen that he might have found her comment amusing.

She turned to her brother. "We have a wager going. If I can make him laugh in public, he's going to allow me to drive his phaeton in the park. If I can't, then he gets to escort me to parties for a week."

Tremelling gave a little chuckle. "Doesn't seem like a fair wager to me. Good job, Em, in either case you win."

She quickly put a finger to her lips. "*Sh*! Don't tell him that!"

Gabriel nearly had to slap a hand to his mouth to stop himself from laughing. He took in a deep breath and then schooled his features into an expression of ennui. Goodness, this was a lot more difficult than he thought it would be! He cleared his throat. He had to get them off this topic, and there was only one way to do so.

Holding out his hand, he asked, "Lady Emilie, would you honor me with this dance?"

She gave a little snort of laughter. "Oh, you think I won't be able to make you laugh if we are dancing?"

He gave a short nod of his head. "It's much more difficult, if not sometimes impossible, to converse while dancing. And I do believe it is a country dance that is forming just now, so we will be separated almost more than we will be together."

Lady Emilie giggled. "Very clever, my lord." She put her hand into his and allowed him to lead her onto the dance floor. He nodded to Tremelling as he did so. The infernal man was outright laughing at him.

Emilie found her brother already sitting at the breakfast table the following morning. "Good morning, Evan."

He didn't even look up from his paper. "Good morning."

Emilie helped herself to some toast and a boiled egg before seating herself at the table. She ate in silence for a few minutes but then couldn't help but blurt out what was on her mind. "Why did you bring Lord Willington over to me last night?"

Evan slowly lowered his paper. His eyebrows were slightly raised as he turned to look at her. "Should I not have?"

"I would have thought if he'd wanted to dance with me he could have very well come over to me himself. He didn't need your prodding."

"Well, considering your silly little wager, I imagine he *was* avoiding you."

"Quite possibly, but what's that to you? If I remember correctly, you were absolutely set against him at first," she pointed out.

"Yes, but then he and I spoke, and I changed my mind."

Emilie nodded. The thing was, it would be so very much easier for her to carry out her plan if her brother didn't get involved. "This is a good thing, but I would still rather if you left things up to me and didn't push him at me—or me at him."

"I would be more than happy to leave things up to you, but I'm not certain you would be able to manage—" He didn't finish the thought as their mother entered the breakfast room just then. Evan rose to greet her.

"Good morning, Mama," Emilie said.

"Good morning to you both. Do I sense a whiff of tension in the air?" She looked from Emilie to Evan and back again.

"I was just requesting my brother leave—" Emilie started.

"She thinks she is able to manage—" Evan started at the same time.

Lady Tremelling held up a hand and stopped them both. "Does this have to do with Lord Willington?"

"Yes," Emilie answered.

"It does," her brother said.

"In that case, Tremelling, you will please allow your sister to handle the situation," their mother said.

Emilie had to catch her mouth from dropping open in surprise.

"But—" Evan started.

"She has been doing a very good job of it so far, and I don't want you disturbing all that she's done so far by sticking your nose into something which doesn't concern you. Do you understand?" she said, taking a firm tone just as she did when they were children.

Evan opened his mouth but shut it again without saying anything. With a bit of a huff, he sat back down and lifted his paper once more.

"Thank you, Mama," Emilie said, also retaking her seat.

"Do not make me regret this," Lady Tremelling said.

Emilie nodded, but she was grateful for the vote of confidence her mother had just given her. She'd also, unwittingly, just helped Emilie with her plan. She wondered, as she continued to nibble on her toast, if she should ask Eliza to have a word with Evan as well just to make sure he didn't try to "help" her again. She might just do that.

Gabriel wasn't certain, but he had a feeling Lady Emilie had gone easy on him a few evenings ago when her brother had intervened and forced the two of them together. Tonight, he wasn't sure how he was going to avoid seeing Lady Emilie, but he'd had no choice but to escort his grandmother to Lady Ayres's soiree this evening.

"Where have you been, old boy?" He was greeted by Ox soon after seeing his grandmother settled.

"Here and there, but mostly there, looking after my grandmother," Gabriel responded, happy to see his friend after more than a week.

"You're a good man," Ox said, nodding his head. Then he gave Gabriel a little half smile. "I am supposed to be fetching refreshments. In fact, why don't you come with me, and you can pay your respects to my lovely fiancée?"

"I would be happy to!" Gabriel said, falling into step with Ox as he headed toward the refreshments room.

"I have to admit when I didn't see you around I figured it was because of the gossip going around. Thought it rather clever of you, to be honest, even though it is more detrimental to Lady Emilie than yourself," Ox said as he waited to pick up a couple of glasses of lemonade.

Gabriel frowned. "Gossip? About Lady Emilie?"

Ox turned to him. "Have you not heard? But then, if you've just been at home caring for your Gran..."

"I haven't heard anything, and I did attend Lady Meriton's ball the other night."

Ox turned to pick up the glasses. "Don't know how you haven't heard, then." He turned around with the lemonade to face Gabriel and sighed. "I really hate to be the one to tell you this, but you should know."

"Out with it, Ox." Gabriel hated it when people told you they had something important to impart and then hemmed and hawed their way to telling you.

His friend moved away from the refreshments table, allowing others to get their own drinks and to give them the illusion of privacy in the crowded dining room. "It's being said Lady Emilie is throwing herself at you in an attempt to bring you up to scratch. Everyone knows you're looking for a marriage of convenience—one to match your reputation as someone who abhors the softer emotions. People are wondering why you are giving her any attention at all and are beginning to wonder if you might be in financial straits or have some other problem, making it imperative that you court the girl." He paused and then frowned as Gabriel took in all he'd said. "There's something going about the clubs…" He screwed up his face as he tried to remember. "Something involving Lady Emilie, Tremelling, and you when you and Tremelling were at school together?"

Gabriel ground his teeth together, deliberately holding his mouth shut so his scream of rage would burst from his throat.

"Er… take deep breaths, my friend. Deep breaths," Ox advised.

Gabriel managed a nod and did as his friend recommended. He focused on simply breathing in and out. It would not do to make a scene. It would help nobody, especially not Lady Emilie. In and out. In and out.

"There's a good lad. Calming down a bit?"

"Thank you, Ox, for sharing this with me," Gabriel managed to say after unclenching his jaw. His voice sounded a great deal calmer than he would have thought.

"I, er, am sorry."

"No. It is none of your doing."

"Do rather have to wonder whose doing it is, though," Ox said, shifting his eyes toward the drawing room as if the person responsible would be standing there ready to admit to spreading the rumors.

# CHAPTER TWENTY-FIVE

"I have to admit," Gabriel told Ox, "I'm not yet at the point where I care. At the moment, all I can think of is Lady Emilie's reputation. I must see to that first and foremost. She does not deserve to have such horrid things said about her."

"Couldn't agree more, old man."

Gabriel's mind began running through possible ways he might negate the rumors. What could he do to show society that he was enjoying Lady Emilie's company? That he *wanted* to be courting her? That she was not, in any sense, throwing herself at him?

"Well, er, maybe now is not the best time for you to speak with Miss Ellison."

Gabriel refocused on Ox. "What? Oh! Er, no, perhaps not, Ox. I am terribly sorry. Another time."

The two men nodded to each other, and Ox went off to deliver the lemonade while Gabriel continued to let his friend's words circulate around his head.

Immediately, he was once again fighting the urge to bellow at all the imbeciles in the drawing room and in society. He wanted to shout and rage and scream and defend Lady Emilie with every breath he took, but he knew he could do none of that. Instead, he focused on his breathing again.

As he exhaled for the fifth time, the answer came to him. How obvious! Of course. He was an idiot for not thinking of it immediately.

Their wager. He would allow Lady Emilie to win their wager. He would laugh at something she said. He would show the *ton* that he was not just courting the girl because he had to.

He wanted to dance with her, every dance. He wanted to laugh at everything even mildly amusing that came from her beautiful mouth. He wanted to escort her out into the garden and kiss her soundly, no matter who saw them go or who was nearby when he did so.

Well, he couldn't do any of that, but he could allow her to win their wager, and that's what he would do.

He was halfway across the room when it suddenly occurred to him he would have to do this stealthily. She probably had no idea of the horrid things being said about her. If he just suddenly burst out laughing at something she said no matter how funny it was or not, she would certainly become suspicious. No, he had to do this in such a way...

But then, wouldn't he be doing exactly what Lady Preston had said he should not—keeping secrets from her. Not being open and honest. Well, he had to admit to himself that he'd never been completely honest with her. He'd never told her about her brother's actions all those years ago. But then, he did like being alive, and Tremelling had suggested he might not be for very long after he told Emilie the truth. He truly did believe in honesty—to a point.

He came to a complete halt. But if he was honest with her, she would surely be hurt.

"Lord Willington? Is everything all right?" a woman's voice interrupted his musings.

He refocused his eyes and found Lady Findlater watching him very closely. He nearly laughed out loud. She was in all likelihood the one who started the gossip. Well, then it should be she who stopped it.

"Yes, my lady, I do beg your pardon, I was just looking for Lady Emilie. You wouldn't happen to know where she is?" He gave her a polite, if cold smile.

The woman turned to look toward the wall near where Lady Emilie and her friends had been hovering for most of the evening. Indeed, she was there, watching the dancers and giggling with her friends.

"Ah, yes, of course. I see her now. My thanks." He gave her a slight bow and continued on his way, now certain they would be watched by precisely the person he wanted watching. Good.

"Lady Emilie, Miss Merrill, Miss Smyth." He bowed to them.

"Good evening, my lord," the girls said in near unison, each of them dropping a little curtsy.

He smiled. "If you will excuse me, ladies." He turned toward Lady Emilie. "Lady Emilie, might I have a word?"

She cocked her head slightly, but before she could say a word Miss Smyth said, "Miss Merrill, I am absolutely parched. Shall we go and see if we can find some lemonade?"

"I would love to," Miss Merrill replied with a little giggle. "You will excuse us, I hope?" she asked Gabriel.

He gave the girls a grateful nod of his head. "Of course."

As soon as they were gone, he turned to Lady Emilie. But once he had her complete attention, he found himself unsure of how to begin. And he was still absolutely certain Lady Findlater was still watching.

"My lord? Was there something you wanted to discuss with me?" Lady Emilie asked.

"Er, yes." He cleared his throat and made sure his back was turned toward Lady Findlater. He then spoke so quietly Lady Emilie had to lean toward him slightly to hear. "I have some rather disturbing news, I'm afraid."

Lady Emilie's smile slipped off her face, and she raised her eyebrows.

"I have just learned there has been some, er... well, gossip—"

"You just learned of it?" she asked, standing straight and away from him again.

He blinked. "You know of it?"

"Yes! My sister told me the day after it began. It was the day you came to ask my mother for the name of a doctor." Her lovely face softened again, her lips forming a slight smile.

"The day we made our wager?"

She nodded.

His mouth nearly dropped open as he put everything together, and then he burst out laughing. "Oh, my goodness, Lady Emilie, you *are* the cleverest thing!" he said, no longer keeping his voice so quiet that no one could hear him speak.

Lady Emilie put her hand to her mouth to hide her own laughter, but Gabriel could see it in her eyes. "I thought you knew, and that's why you went along with our silly wager," she said after a moment while she got a hold of herself.

"No. I didn't. I just... I was simply charmed by the idea," he told her.

"Well, now, my lord, you not only know the truth of it, but have lost the bet," she said, allowing a big grin to emerge.

"Yes. Oh dear, yes I have." He shook his head ruefully, keeping his laughter in check. As he did so, he managed to catch Lady Findlater standing much closer than he had anticipated. "Well, there is nothing for it then. You will have the honor—one I have never granted to another soul, mind you—of driving my phaeton in the park. Just name the day and time."

Emilie was so shocked when Lord Willington threw his head back and burst out laughing—in public! She nearly did the very same but managed to hold hers back behind her hand. The poor man had felt so bad about the gossip, but when he had put everything together—well, really his reaction could have gone either way. Either he would be annoyed she had tricked him or, as he had done, he'd have found it amusing. Thank goodness, it had been the latter.

"Would tomorrow be too soon, my lord?" Emilie asked in answer to his offer to allow her to drive his phaeton.

"Not at all. I will be delighted." He paused and then turned toward the center of the room where couples were lining up for a country dance. "May I have the pleasure of this dance?" he asked, bowing and holding out a hand.

"I would enjoy that immensely, thank you," she said, as she placed her hand in his. She could feel the heat of him even through his gloves and hers, and it sent tingles of warmth and awareness up her arm.

How was it that they had gone from discussing the unpleasant gossip flying about to Emilie being so extremely aware of this man? His eyes were dancing with mirth, his cheeks slightly flushed from laughing, his alluring smile gracing his lips—lips Emilie had kissed and... she realized with a start, wished she could do so again.

As they took their places for the dance, Emilie nearly felt as if she were walking across a soft feather mattress of happiness. It was the oddest sensation; almost as if the rest of the world no longer existed. All she saw was Lord... no, not Lord Willington. Gabriel. The same young man she had fallen in love with when she'd been fifteen. Yes, that's what it was. He was looking as alive and vibrant now as he had so long ago.

Gone was the dour-faced serious man he had become in the intervening years. Gone was the practiced ennui, the cool gaze, and colder polite smile. The man she was dancing with right now was Gabriel. The Gabriel she knew. The Gabriel she loved.

Oh goodness. She wasn't supposed to have done that. She'd promised Eliza she would not fall in love with him again. But she couldn't deny it, not when he was looking at her like that. Not when he was smiling and looking at her as if she were his world.

*Now* what was she going to do?

Rebecca stood back, watching the dancers go through the complicated steps of a country dance. In truth, she wasn't so much watching the dance as two dancers in particular—Lord Willington and Lady Emilie. They both looked as if they were in a dream, each watching the other without a glance to either their left or right to even notice the other dancers around them. She was quite amazed they didn't bump into anyone.

For a short time earlier, she'd been nervous that everything she'd worked so hard for was going to come unraveled. Lady Findlater had seemed to be on the hunt this evening, determined to prove the truth of the gossip being circulated.

Rebecca had nearly cried out loud when the woman had accosted Lord Willington as he was making his way—albeit very slowly, as if deep in thought—across the room toward Lady Emilie. She'd watched anxiously while he'd spoken a few words to her and then continued with more determination toward his target.

Lady Findlater herself, had even followed him, placing herself close enough to overhear their conversation but not quite close enough to be noticed. Rebecca had watched the lady's expression as it grew ever more unhappy—something which made Rebecca quite hopeful. And then when Lord Willington burst out laughing at something Lady Emilie said, the lady looked absolutely furious for a moment and then rather chagrined.

Rebecca celebrated—silently.

Lady Emilie's plan had worked! There could be absolutely no doubt now that the girl was not throwing herself at the gentleman nor was he merely putting up with her because he was being forced to. It was more than obvious to whoever happened to glance their way now they were, indeed and most assuredly, in love.

Oh, yes, it most definitely was time to celebrate. Rebecca wondered if there was any champagne to be had.

Gabriel was about to take a sip from his glass of rum when someone slapped him on his shoulder. He nearly spilled his drink down his front and looked up to protest when he saw Ox's broad, smiling face come around in front of him.

"So? Have you asked her? Spoken with her brother? Decided on a date yet?" The large man settled into the chair next to Gabriel as he set down his glass on the table next to him.

Gabriel laughed and held up his hand. "You are getting far beyond me!"

"What? How could this be? I—and all the *ton*—heard you laughing at something Lady Emilie said. And we all watched as the two of you floated through a dance afterward. Goodness, but you had eyes for no one else."

Gabriel feared he was blushing. "Oh dear, were we so very obvious?"

"Obvious? I suppose you could call it that, my boy. If you call a horse galloping hell for leather through the streets of London a touch upsetting."

Gabriel laughed. "Well, I have not asked her to marry me just yet, but I most certainly shall do so—soon."

"Is there something you're waiting for?" his friend asked, lifting one inquisitive eyebrow.

"My grandmother. I want to speak with her about it and make certain she has no objections. I'm sure she won't, but she has excellent discernment when it comes to people. I want her opinion on the matter before I make the final plunge."

Ox just grunted. "Well, if you must."

"I must," Gabriel said, with a smile. He paused and then added, "I can hardly believe I am having such feelings."

"What? But surely you knew it would happen. I told you it would, didn't I?"

Gabriel gave a chuckle. "You did, and I didn't believe it. I do now, and truly, it is amazing."

What was even more incredible was the fact that Gabriel could feel such strong emotions and not get overly carried away by them. He had not whisked Emilie out to the garden, even though the doors had been so close and tantalizing, nearly calling for him to pass through them, Emilie on his arm. He had not kissed her soundly as he'd wanted to rather desperately. He had controlled himself, behaved like a gentleman, and simply enjoyed the lady's company.

Oh yes, he was astounded at his own self-control and overjoyed he'd managed his passion so well. He supposed the real test would come when he did propose, but surely, if he was able to behave so well at the party earlier that evening, he would be able to do so after she had agreed to marry him. And hopefully her family would be agreeable to a quick wedding because he wasn't certain just how long he would be able to maintain such control over himself.

# CHAPTER TWENTY-SIX

The very next evening at Lady Rossburke's soiree Emilie was accosted by Lord Willington almost the very minute she walked into the room.

"Good evening, Lady Emilie," he said, before bowing over her hand and placing a kiss onto her gloved knuckles.

"Good evening, my lord," Emilie said, trying and failing to keep the enormous smile from her lips.

"I do hope you have been keeping well?"

She raised her eyebrows and gave a little laugh. "Since you saw me at last evening's party? Yes, my lord, I am happy to say I am hale and hearty."

"Excellent, I am so very glad to hear it because I plan on dancing with you twice this evening, if not three times," he said, his voice deepening ever so slightly. It sent a shiver of excitement down Emilie's spine.

"My lord!" she said reprovingly. "To dance with me three times would be beyond the pale, as you very well know."

A small smile tugged on his lips. "I do not care one whit. I simply wish to spend time with you—as much time as I may."

"Well, you may dance with me twice, and after that, perhaps we shall perambulate about the ballroom. Would that satisfy you?" In truth, she wanted to spend time with him as well. She so enjoyed his company and oddly even if they ran out of things to say to one another—which didn't happen often—just being silent in his company brought her nearly as much joy as when they did speak.

He bowed once again. "I will accept that. Now, I do believe the orchestra is about to begin the first dance of the evening. Shall we?" He held out a hand and Emilie gently placed her own into it.

Was it possible for a heart to burst with happiness, she wondered as she watched Lord Willington circle with the other lady in their quartet. She was certain she was smiling broad enough to be seen down the length of the drawing room.

At the end of the dance, instead of taking her back to her mother or her friends, he kept a hold of her hand.

"My lord?" she asked, tugging gently to get him to move.

"You promised me two dances," he reminded her.

"Not two in a row!"

"Whyever not?" he asked with a lift of an eyebrow.

"It's not seemly!" she said more quietly as people began drifting toward them in preparation for the next dance.

"Puff!" He expelled a breath of air through his lips. "As if I care about what is seemly or not."

"I know you care about what others think," she countered.

He lifted a negligent broad shoulder encased in his handsome black coat. "At this moment, all I care about is being with you. Now, pay attention, we need to align ourselves with the others."

Emilie looked around and found two lines had formed, one of men, the other of women. The music started, forcing Emilie to quickly jump into line for the country dance.

Somehow, Lord Willington kept her giggling through most of the dance with his clever observations. She ventured a few of her own as well, and they were having a grand time when her eye was caught by her sister, standing on the edge of the dance floor. Eliza was staring straight at her, a concerned expression on her face. Emilie gave her a nod. When she turned about once again, Eliza nodded back and then moved toward the corner of the room where they might speak without being overheard.

As soon as the dance was over, Lord Willington took her hand to forestall her from leaving the dance floor. She looked up at him questioningly.

"You promised to perambulate after our dances," he reminded her.

"Now?"

He simply gave a lift of his dark eyebrows, obviously questioning her. "Will you go back on your word?"

"No, but after two dances in a row people would begin to talk, if they aren't already, my lord. We just overcame one round of gossip. I do *not* want to become the subject of yet more."

"Hmm... very well. On one condition will I let you go to your friends." His face took on a very serious expression.

"Oh? And what might that be?"

"That you stop *my lording* me and call me by my given name." His lips remained neutral, but Emilie could see the smile dancing in his eyes.

She nodded. "Very well, but only when we are in a more private setting. To do so here would not be appropriate."

"Very well. I suppose you are correct. So, for example, when I call upon you tomorrow, you will call me Gabriel?"

Emilie's eyes widened. "You are going to call on me tomorrow?"

"I do have such intentions if you do not mind?" He answered with a nod of his head.

Emilie's heart began to flutter in her chest, and she began to feel so light as if her feet might just lift off the floor any moment. "Er, no, I do not mind. Not at all."

"Excellent," he said, giving her a little smile. "Then I shall allow you to retire to your wall and your friends. But I shall be claiming our walk before too long, so don't get too comfortable."

She gave him a little nod and then went off to find her sister. She smiled at a few acquaintances as she passed them but did not stop to talk. She even passed Lady Willington who, thankfully, looked quite comfortable sitting and watching the dancers, with another lady by her side.

Eliza grabbed Emilie's arm just as she'd passed the older lady. "What do you think you're doing?" she said in a loud whisper.

Emilie drew down her eyebrows. "What do you mean? I'm—"

"Dancing twice in a row with Lord Willington?" Eliza asked, her eyes boring into Emilie's, and she still hadn't let go of her arm either.

"He is going to pay a call upon me tomorrow," Emilie told her sister. She tried her best to keep her smile from her face but was certain she was failing.

Eliza frowned even harder. "He's going to..."

Emilie nodded and giggled.

Her sister's grip on Emilie's arm loosened. "And your plan? Are you still committed to it? Or have you so lost yourself—"

"No!" Emilie softened her voice. "No, I am still committed to it." She heard herself say the words but her heart... her heart ached at the thought, and she began to feel chilled.

Eliza nodded and let go of her arm altogether. "So, you'll turn his proposal down," Eliza confirmed. "And say what? Have you thought it through?"

"No, I haven't," Emilie admitted. "I didn't realize he would declare himself quite so soon. I'm sure to come up with something."

"Don't rely on that. Think it through beforehand. He has to know and understand why or else this will all have been for naught."

"Yes, you're right..." Emilie said, trying to remember precisely why she was going to turn down a marriage proposal from a man she—

She stopped that thought right where it was. She didn't love Gabriel. She *couldn't*. He was a horrible, selfish, thoughtless man.

Only he wasn't.

She knew that now, which was why she suddenly felt as if someone had just dropped a freezing cold, soaking wet blanket over her shoulders.

Yes, he'd broken her heart all those years ago, but he'd explained himself to her. He had been afraid of getting carried away by his passions.

It still didn't excuse the fact that he'd never contacted her again after their first kiss. That was what she was punishing him for. Yes, she had to keep that thought at the forefront of her mind. He may be an exceptional gentleman thinking about others, being so sweet and kind and thoughtful—goodness knew she'd never met another man who behaved so. Not even her brothers-in-law were so thoughtful, at least not according to Eliza. And she knew for a fact that Amelia's husband was not only *not* caring, but he was unfaithful as well.

Emilie hardened her heart. For all the horrible, thoughtless, selfish men she would turn down Gabriel's proposal. She would simply have to set aside her own feelings and make an example of Gabriel. She would get over him... eventually. And she would be the best spinster aunt ever.

Emilie blinked to clear her eyes. She turned her face toward the wall and cleared her throat. "I... I think something must have flown into my eye," she explained to her sister. Yes, that was all, just a piece of dust or something. She blinked a few more times for good measure and tried very hard not to think about anything but the happy, independent, lonely future which awaited her.

Gabriel was speaking with another gentleman with whom he'd had some interesting debates on the current issues of the day. The man was beginning to get into another, but Gabriel was all too aware this was neither the time nor the place for such a discussion.

"Oh!" The man glanced around the drawing room filled as it was with beautiful ladies and gentlemen paying court to them. "Er... yes, of course, you are right. I do beg your pardon."

"Not at all," Gabriel started to say. He was interrupted by Lady Fareham, one of his grandmother's friends.

"I do beg your pardon," she said.

"Yes, my lady?" Gabriel immediately turned toward her, rather relieved to be freed of his friend just at this moment.

"Your grandmother has sent me over, my lord. She is feeling very tired and wishes to go home," the lady said, rather apologetically.

"Oh! Of course! I, er, yes, of course. Please tell her I will be with her momentarily." As the woman walked away, he scanned the walls searching for Lady Emilie. He found her standing just across the room under a painting of their host's very imposing father.

He quickly made his way over to her. "Lady Emilie, I do hope you will excuse me?"

She smiled up at him with a slight tilt to her head. "What for, my lord?"

"I'm afraid I will not be able to perambulate with you, after all. My grandmother is not feeling well and needs to go home. Will you forgive me?"

"Of course! By all means, you should care for your grandmother," she said quickly, much to his relief.

"Excellent. I do thank you for your understanding, and I... er, I will see you tomorrow?" He smiled at her, certain she understood his meaning. He'd been wondering if he should speak to her brother first but decided that, considering how independent-minded Lady Emilie was, she would probably prefer if he spoke with her and then Lord Tremelling.

"I shall look forward to it... Gabriel."

He couldn't help the enormous grin that must have been covering his face. "Good evening, then, Emilie." He bowed over her hand before running off to see to his grandmother.

In the darkness of their coach, Gabriel could hear the rustling of his grandmother's silk gown against the leather of the seat even above the clopping of the horses and the rattle of the wheels against the stones of the street.

"Are you all right, Gran?" he asked, trying to peer through the dark toward her.

"Er, yes."

That didn't sound very definitive. He reached across the coach for her hand and found it resting on her knee. "What is it? Are you feeling unwell?"

"No!" She paused and then said again, modifying her tone, "No, I am quite well. Tired and..."

"And?"

"I have something to tell you, Gabriel," she said softly.

He waited for a moment for her to continue and then prompted her when she said nothing. "You know you can tell me anything, Gran. What is it?"

"We'll speak when we get home." She gave his hand a gentle squeeze and then withdrew her own from his grasp.

Gabriel sat back. What in the world could she have to tell him that made her so nervous she was fidgeting. Never in his life had he seen his grandmother fidget. She was a model of poise and grace.

They reached their home soon enough, and Gabriel assisted his grandmother to alight before following her into the house. She went straight to the drawing room and from there to the window where she looked out onto the street. Her hands were clasped tightly together at her waist.

Gabriel came over to her and pried them apart to hold in his own hands. "Gran, whatever it is—"

"I overheard Lady Emilie speaking with Lady Alford, her sister," his grandmother blurted out. She kept her gaze firmly on some distant point over his left shoulder. "Lady Alford asked Lady Emilie if her plan was still in play. Lady Emilie said it was. She confirmed to her sister that she was expecting you to propose tomorrow and said she would turn you down. Lady Alford reminded Lady Emilie that she had to tell you why, to... to make you understand." She shifted her gaze to his eyes. "I don't know what it is you are to understand, but... but she has been playing you. She has never been interested in marrying you. It's all been some sort of... plot to get you to propose. I simply do not understand why. Why she would do this." His grandmother's voice broke, and she looked uneasy. Never had Gabriel seen his grandmother so upset.

And then her words sank in.

It was all a plot, a ploy to get him to propose. What was all a plot? Her allowing him to court her? Could she have actually made him fall in love with her? Was she so good of an actress that she feigned falling in love with him as well—for he was certain he had seen such emotion in her eyes, read it on her face, in her smile, even in the tilt of her head. Was it all a ruse?

He let go of his grandmother's hands and turned away. "I... I don't understand."

"Neither do I, but Gabriel..."

He held up a hand to stop her words. "No, Gran, you were right to tell me. I... I *was* planning on proposing to Lady Emilie tomorrow. I told her I would call on her."

"And she is planning on refusing you."

Gabriel nodded. He understood, but... but his heart... he didn't feel anything. Nothing. It was as if it had stopped beating. He was aware of his breathing, so he knew he was still alive, but his heart? No. It was slowly disintegrating like a lump of sugar in a cup of coffee. Black, black coffee. Bitter, acidic, and foul on the tongue.

"I beg your pardon, my lord." The voice seemed to come from far away.

There was a slight pressure on his arm. He turned to see Gran looking at him with such sorrow. "Willington..."

"My sincere apologies for disturbing you, my lord, but this was delivered this evening by hand. The man who brought it looked like he'd ridden a long way, he was so coated with dirt from the road. He said it was quite urgent." The butler held out a silver tray with a note on it. "I nearly sent a footman to you, but... well, I hope I did the right thing by waiting until you got home."

Gabriel shook his head as if that could toss out the thoughts that were running rampant through his mind. He reached for the missive, broke open the plain wax seal, and forced himself to focus on the words in front of him.

His eyes first dropped to the bottom to see who it was from. Thetford. One of his closest friends from school. The only one who had stuck with him after the fiasco with Tremelling and Lady Emilie. He returned to the top of the page and began to read. There wasn't much there. It was clear that it was hastily scribbled.

*Willington,*

*She's dying. The babe was stillborn, and she's dying.*

*I can't bear it. I don't know what I will do if she—*

*The midwife and doctor are trying to stop the bleeding but*

*please come. Make haste.*

*Thetford*

It was so disjointed. Thetford was a brilliant correspondent and had always been the best at writing essays of any of the boys—but this...

He looked up at his grandmother who was standing there clearly waiting anxiously for an explanation.

Gabriel swallowed, his mouth suddenly dry. "It's Thetford, my friend from school. His wife is dying, and he's requested I come immediately."

He turned to look out the window. It was a clear night, but moonless—so dark he could barely see the houses across the street. He couldn't go now. He would need to wait until first light. That would give him some time to pack and... Well, he wasn't certain he would be able sleep after what he'd learned tonight. But he would lay down. Yes, he needed to try. He would have a very long ride tomorrow. He wondered if he could ride straight through. He would try. For Thetford, he would certainly try.

# CHAPTER TWENTY-SEVEN

Emilie got dressed with a great deal of care the following morning. Her maid was still shaking her head over the dark circles under her eyes, but it had been nearly impossible to sleep the night before. Her mind had whirled with possible explanations she could give Gabriel today after he proposed and she turned him down.

Should she tell him exactly what she thought of men? But she knew him to be an exception. Should she tell him that she was still furious over the fact that he'd never contacted her? But she wasn't—not really. And he had apologized. Perhaps she should tell him that she was using him as an example to all men. But that wasn't really fair, was it? And what other men would know or even care? She supposed she could tell him he'd broken her heart all those years ago, and therefore she was breaking his now.

That was as close to the truth as she could get. The only problem was her heart was now recovered.

In fact, he had been the one to heal it with his thoughtfulness, his kindness—not to mention *That Kiss*. Oh dear, her heart was not only mended, but it was full. It was full of him. Of her love for him.

Yes, he'd broken her heart, but he'd mended it as well.

"Tilt your head back, Lady Emilie!" Mary's voice broke through Emilie's musings. She tilted her head back.

"Thank you." Her maid was sounding a bit frustrated. Emilie must not have heard her request the first time. "And look up, please."

Emilie looked toward the ceiling as Mary gently dabbed at the loose skin now sagging under Emilie's eyes due to her lack of sleep. The cooling cream she put there felt good. She then topped the cream with half slices of cucumber resting just under Emilie's lower eyelashes.

"There now, stay like that for about five minutes and then I'll wipe it off. It should get rid of all evidence of a sleepless night."

"Thank you, Mary. I was just so nervous and excited. I could not stay asleep for more than half an hour at a time."

Her maid smiled down at her. "Is it Lord Willington?"

"Yes. He asked to call on me today."

Mary gasped and then clapped her hands. "Oh, Miss, how wonderful! I'm so happy for you. And I completely understand. I don't think I would have been able to get a wink of sleep either."

Emilie nodded as best she could without allowing the cucumber to fall.

After thinking about it all night, the only solution Emilie could find to the problem of what to say to Gabriel was... yes.

She would say yes to his proposal. She would say yes because she loved him with all her heart.

Eliza would forgive her. She was sure of it.

Despite his worries, Gabriel had actually been able to sleep a little before he roused himself the following morning. It was a good thing too, considering he had nearly a hundred miles to cover today.

Thetford had been Gabriel's closest friend. He'd literally fought for him in school. Afterward, they had gone to Oxford together, graduated and had come to London to see what life had to offer them. William had met Miss Stelles not long after they'd arrived. He'd been introduced to her once before by her brother, who'd also been at university with them. William and the young lady made a connection the first time they'd met, and it only deepened throughout the Season. They were married by the summer.

Gabriel could hardly believe it had only been three years ago. It seemed like an age. So much had happened. Will's mother had died—his father had passed years ago—and both of Gabriel's parents. Will and his bride hadn't even returned once to London in that time; they were happily ensconced in his home, Red Castle, and much preferred country living. Gabriel could still remember the letter he'd received from Will telling him of his joy when he learned they were expecting a child. His friend had written his hopes for it to be a girl even though he knew he should wish for an heir. He figured they had plenty of time to have all the children they desired.

And now...

Gabriel couldn't even imagine the distress his friend must be in. It only made him feel a little bit guilty that he was using his friend's suffering so as not to think of his own. The hard ride was helping as well.

Emilie was in the dining room slowly nibbling on a piece of toast when her mother joined her. Jumping to her feet, she said, "Oh, Mama, I am so glad you are here. I can't decide whether I should ask Cook to make biscuits for Lord Willington's visit or cake. Or perhaps tarts, her apple tarts are delicious."

Lady Tremelling just stopped, stared at her daughter and then turned away to help herself to some of the food on the sideboard. Emilie was certain she had done so more to hide her smile than out of hunger. Emilie noticed her shoulders were shaking ever so slightly.

"Are you laughing at me?" she demanded.

Her mother cleared her throat before turning back to her. "No, dear, not at all. It's just, well, you have been fighting against this match ever since Lady Preston suggested it and now…"

Emilie sighed. "Now I have given in to the inevitable?" she finished for her mother.

"Well, yes." Lady Tremelling sat down opposite Emilie and began to pour herself a cup of tea.

"I suppose I've finally given up fighting it. Is that so bad of me?" Emilie asked.

"No! Not at all. It's excellent, in fact, and couldn't make me happier." She reached her hand across the table toward her daughter.

Emilie took it for a brief moment to allow her mother to give her hand a squeeze and then both retreated to continue eating. "I fear I don't know Lord Willington's particular tastes very well. I don't know how he takes his tea or what he likes to eat with it," Emilie continued.

"How about we ask Cook to make her biscuits—they are so buttery and wonderful there isn't anyone who doesn't like them—and a small batch of tarts?"

"Yes, that does sound good." Emilie thought about it for a moment and then said, "He might not even want anything to eat. He might simply get straight to the point."

Her mother nodded, her mouth full so she couldn't reply right away. "Or he might want to sit and relax with you for a moment before declaring himself."

"Yes, he could." Emilie just couldn't stay still. She got up and began pacing back and forth, wringing her hands. "I don't know what to expect. Will he get down on one knee? Might he give me a ring? Or..." She spun toward her mother who was merely watching her with an amused look on her face as she consumed her eggs. "Perhaps he'll take me shopping and want me to choose my own ring. There's also the possibility that there is a particular ring in the Willington family jewels for the wife of the marquess." She stopped her pacing for just a moment as an idea struck her. "But if that's the case, it must now belong to his grandmother. I couldn't take a ring right off her finger. And speaking of his grandmother, do you think she likes me? I've hardly spoken a word to her since they came for that horrid meeting when we first learned it was he who Lady Preston had chosen for me."

Her mother opened her mouth to answer, but Emilie continued on. "I do need her to like me considering how close she and Gabriel are. I'm certain she will continue to live with him—us."

She was interrupted by the entrance of Evan. He stopped at the threshold, surveying his sister and mother. "Good morning," he said hesitantly as he joined them.

"Good morning," they said in unison.

"I don't suppose you have heard the good news?" Lady Tremelling asked.

Evan cocked one eyebrow. "Good news?"

"Lord Willington is coming today to propose," Emilie told him.

"Oh!" A smile spread across his face. "Congratulations, sister." He came over and gave her a quick hug.

"Thank you, but it may be a touch too soon to say as much. I mean, he didn't specifically say he was coming to do that, but it was the feeling I got when he asked if he could call on me."

Evan nodded as he headed over to help himself to some breakfast. "I'm sure you are right, even though he hasn't spoken with me yet. I imagine he will once he's spoken with you."

"I'm sure. Well, he has to, doesn't he?" Emilie asked.

Evan nodded as he filled his plate. "He does, at least, if he wants to marry you. We'll need to draw up a marriage contract."

"Yes, although I believe he's well off—not in dire need of my dowry, in any case," she said, taking her seat once again.

"Oh, yes, he is." Evan sat down at the head of the table. "I checked."

"Of course you did," Emilie said dryly.

"It is his duty to do so for any gentleman interested in pursuing a closer relationship with you," her mother reminded her.

Emilie just nodded. "Well, in any case, I'm certain he will be in to see you once he has spoken to me."

"And you *do* intend on accepting his proposal?" Evan asked.

Emilie took in a deep breath. "I do."

Gabriel walked his horse into the yard of the Running Hound Posting Inn. They were both exhausted from traveling all day. A groom came running from the stables.

"Take good care of him, we've been traveling since dawn," Gabriel told the boy, handing over a coin. It was more than he usually gave, but it would ensure his gelding was well taken care of.

Inside, the innkeeper took one look at him and said, "Ale and a hearty meal for ye."

"Yes, please," Gabriel said, dropping into a chair at a close by table.

The man brought the ale over right away. "Food will be out of the kitchen in but a few minutes, sir."

"My thanks. Would you possibly have a horse I could use to get me to Thetford and Red Castle?" It wasn't common for posting inns to keep horses for rent, but Gabriel asked anyway, just in case.

The man narrowed his eyes at him. "A horse was left here just yesterday. It's for Lord Willing... Willingburg? Willing..."

"Willington?"

The fellow snapped his fingers. "Yes! That's it, Lord Willington."

"I am he," Gabriel said, perking up.

"Ah yes, well, the groom who brought it said you'd be here in the next few days heading to Thetford and would have need of the horse. He asked that you leave yours for him when he returns. Paid for the lodging and care of both horses."

Gabriel could feel his anxieties slip away. "Excellent. My Shadow could use a few days' rest, and I'll be able to journey the rest of the way without worry."

The man nodded. "Right you are, my lord. Right you are."

The sixth time Emilie passed her mother, Lady Tremelling finally said something. "Emilie, can you not sit like a proper young lady?"

Emilie stopped and turned back toward her mother. "No, I cannot. I don't know if even the most proper of young ladies would be able to do so when waiting for a gentleman who is now..." She peered at the clock on the marble-topped table against the far wall. "Three hours late. I just—"

Evan came into the room cutting off her words. "Has he not come?"

"No, he has not," Emilie told him, crossing her arms.

Her brother's eyebrows dipped dangerously low over his eyes.

"Could you, perhaps—"

She didn't even get to finish her sentence before Evan said, "Yes. I'll see if he's at Powell's, and if not, I will not hesitate to confront the man in his own home!" With that, he spun on his heel and stormed out of the room.

Emilie turned back to her mother. "Well, I must say, Evan certainly is the best brother a girl could hope for."

Her mother chuckled. "Indeed. I am quite proud of him."

About an hour later Evan returned. The moment he slammed into the house, pounded up the stairs, and then into the drawing room, Emilie knew it would not be good news he brought.

"You didn't find him," she said, as her brother entered the room.

He frowned. "No. He's left Town."

"He's left London?" she repeated back, unable to believe it.

Evan nodded. "He wasn't at Powell's, so I went to his home. The butler told me he left very early this morning."

Emilie just stared at her brother for a moment before crossing her arms over a chest that was practically exploding with fury. "Well, fine. I'm glad the selfish, horrible man has left. I hope he stays away—this time for longer than six years. Forever!" And with that, she walked out of the room.

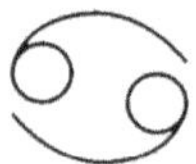

# CHAPTER TWENTY-EIGHT

Gabriel arrived at Red Castle close to nine that evening. He was exhausted, as was the horse he was riding. Gabriel's legs were a little wobbly as he got off the animal. He'd been on horseback for over twelve hours with only one brief stop along the way.

The door was opened before he even had a chance to ring the bell. "Lord Willington?" the gaunt butler asked.

"Yes." He gave the man a smile as he handed over his saddle bag to a waiting footman. "I assume Lord Thetford informed you I was coming."

"Indeed, my lord. He has said very little in the past forty-eight hours—since her passing," he added softly and with a distressed look. He cleared his throat and then continued. "But he did say you were on your way."

"I got here as quickly as I could."

The butler nodded. "Much more quickly than we expected. We are grateful for your haste. If you will follow me, I will show you to his lordship. I'm certain he would like to see you right away."

"Of course." Gabriel looked down at his clothing, covered in grime from riding all day. He was certain he smelled rank, but if William wanted to see him right away, Gabriel was certain he would forgive him his filth.

The butler led him to the left after ascending the grand stairway. Gabriel had only ever been to the right where the public rooms were, and the floor above where there were guest rooms. The west wing must be the family's private quarters. They entered a comfortable-looking drawing room despite its grand proportions. It led to a small study with a beautiful, delicate lady's escritoire. A door in the corner of that room led to another sitting room where the butler stopped. He gestured to the far side of the room. In the corner was an ornate ceramic heating stove, next to which was a closed door, next to which was...

William sat on the floor, his back to the wall staring off into nothing.

"He has been there for the past three days," the butler said quietly.

"Three days?" Gabriel asked.

The butler nodded. "The moment she went into labor he stationed himself just outside of her room." He nodded toward the door. "At first he would pace as her ladyship's moans and screams emanated from the room. She had a midwife with her, and later a surgeon was called in. When that happened he sat there, only getting up once to speak with them... afterward. Since then, he hasn't moved. We've tried to get him to eat, but he takes the merest nibble and then pushes it aside. And he has let no one enter her room."

Gabriel frowned. "Do you mean..."

The butler nodded, looking even more pained than before. "She and the babe are still inside. No one has been allowed to go in to clean or... or anything."

Gabriel closed his eyes for a moment, sighed, and then nodded.

He strode up to his friend and crouched down next to him. "Will."

William looked up briefly and then buried his face in his hands and began to sob. Gabriel could just make out the words, "Sh-sh-she's gone!" He began to rock back and forth repeating the words. "She's gone. She's gone."

Gabriel shifted to his knees and grabbed a hold of his friend, pulling him into a hug. "I know," he whispered. "I know. And I am so sorry." He let Will cry on his shoulder for a good five minutes, then he gently pulled away.

Will tried to stem his tears, hiccoughing as he did so. He wiped a hand across his stubbled cheek to brush aside the tears. Looking up at Gabriel, he said, "It was a girl." He began to weep again, but more softly this time, crying for his child.

Gabriel just waited patiently for tears to abate again. "Why don't we get you to bed? Nothing more can be done here."

"No! No, I can't leave her!"

"Will, you said so yourself. She's gone. You need to let her go. How can she rest peacefully if you are here holding her back?"

His friend looked up at that. "Do you... do you believe I am stopping her from going... going..."

"To her just rewards? To join all those we've lost?" He paused. "I don't know. But I do know it does neither of you any good if you stay here. You can't bring her back, no matter how hard you may wish for it."

His friend began to cry again, but he also allowed Gabriel to help him up.

With the butler's assistance, they guided him through the door at the other end of the wall.

Will's bed chamber was large with a huge tester bed dominating the room, complete with a canopy that peaked like a crown in the center. There was also a seating area close to another ceramic stove, and it was there that Gabriel led his friend.

They sat together on a settee. Gabriel turned toward Will. "Do you want to tell me about it?"

Will shook his head, before slumping against the cushioned back. "How am I going to go on without her, Gabriel? She was... she was everything. My light. My love. My joy."

Gabriel put a consoling hand on Will's arm. "I know. But you will find a way. I know you. You're a strong person, and you *will* get through this."

Will just shook his head. "I don't know how."

"I think a little bit at a time. One day will follow another and the pain will lessen."

"It will never leave me."

"No, it will not, but it *will* get better," Gabriel told him. He'd spoken with his grandmother about how one dealt with the passing of someone close when his parents had died. She'd recalled how she'd managed after her husband had passed, and that was what she'd told him. One day after another and the pain will slowly fade.

William looked at him. "Thank you for coming."

Gabriel gave him a slight smile. "Always."

Looking around his room as if he'd never seen it before, William said, "I suppose I should let you bathe and get some rest. You must be exhausted."

"And the same goes for you," Gabriel said.

William nodded.

Gabriel gave his leg a pat and stood. Just outside the door, the butler stood waiting patiently.

"I have ordered a bath for him and for you, my lord. If you would follow me, I shall show you to your room."

Gabriel nodded and followed the man wearily as he was led into the other wing of the house.

Two days later Emilie was curled up in the window seat in her bedroom when there was a knock on the door. "Enter," she called out.

Her mother came in but stopped just inside the room. "What is this that I hear from Mary? She said you told her you didn't need her to help you dress this evening because you're not going out? But you know we have Lady Carlyle's soiree tonight."

"I'm not going," Emilie told her mother. "I see no reason why I should—well, except maybe to see my friends, but they'll get along just fine without me."

"Emilie!" her mother protested.

"Mother, what do you expect me to do, simply go back on the hunt for a husband?"

"Yes!"

"Well, I am not going to. I am not going to marry. This whole experience has simply confirmed what I've known since I was fifteen. Men are horrible creatures, and I refuse to tether myself to one."

"Emilie..." Lady Tremelling started, coming forward.

"No, Mother. I know you think I should marry, but I won't. I am not going to marry some man only to be ignored by him. He will continue living his life, having his mistresses, going to clubs, and whatever else it is men do while I am stuck at home caring for the houschold and raising his children, unable to do what I want. I have no interest in doing this. I am *not* going to marry."

"All men are not so bad," her mother hedged. "Your father was a very sweet man. He remained faithful to me for over twenty years and gave me four wonderful children."

"Are you sure he was faithful? Are you certain he was the man you thought he was?" Emilie challenged her.

"Yes, I am sure," her mother countered immediately.

"Amelia thinks her husband is faithful. She has no idea he sees his opera singer when he comes to London. I assume he simply tells her he has business in Town."

Lady Tremelling just sighed. "I know. I will have to tell her this, but I just... I couldn't do so in a letter. I'll tell her when I see her next."

"Or maybe I'll return to Tremelling before the end of the Season and tell her so myself," Emilie offered.

"No, Emilie, you will not. I still want you to go to parties and look for a husband. I know you are disillusioned now, but once you meet the right man."

"I'd thought I had met the right man!" Emilie said, jumping to her feet. "Lady Preston assured us so. She said we were soulmates, Gabriel and I. Well, she was wrong, wasn't she?"

Her mother's gaze dropped, and a frown creased her forehead. "I am extremely disheartened by the mistake, but I'm sure she never could have foreseen he would have disappeared the way he did."

"Abandoned me," Emilie corrected. "Left without a word!"

"Yes," her mother admitted. "He has been a horrible disappointment."

"Ha! That is the kindest way to put it. I would rather say—"

"That's enough, Emilie. We agree he has behaved abominably, but I still want you—"

"I'm sorry, Mother, but no."

Her mother sighed but finally accepted Emilie's *no*. "Perhaps in another few days or so you will change your mind. You simply need some time to get past this disappointment. I understand, my love."

Before Emilie could argue with her once again, her mother gave her a nod and left the room.

The following week Rebecca happened to see Lady Willington at Lady Emmerton's garden party. It was an annual affair that almost no one missed for it was one of the events of the Season, and only a select number of people were invited each year. This was the first time Rebecca had ever been sent an invitation, and she was making the most of it, speaking with as many people as possible.

"Lady Willington, good afternoon," Rebecca said, coming up to the elder lady as she stood under the shade of a large awning.

"Oh, good afternoon, Lady Preston," the lady responded, giving her a polite nod.

"I don't believe I've seen either you or your grandson for some time. Is everything well?" Rebecca asked, giving her a solicitous look while trying to keep her avid curiosity from her face.

"Oh, yes, I find I just need a little more time before entertainments than I used to."

"I understand. And his lordship?"

"He is out of Town, visiting with a friend who has recently lost his wife," the lady answered.

"Oh, dear, I am so sorry to hear it. But how very kind and considerate of Lord Willington to come to the aid of his friend in such a difficult time." So that's where he'd been.

"Indeed. Willington is very good that way."

Rebecca gave the lady a sly little smile. "I'd actually been wondering if he and Lady Emilie had eloped and I hadn't heard of it," she said with a little laugh. "I haven't seen her either."

"Oh, goodness no! In fact, that reminds me, I've been meaning to ask you to call upon me," Lady Willington said.

Rebecca noticed she wasn't smiling when she said this and worried something might be amiss regarding the relationship between Lady Emilie and his lordship. "Yes, of course."

"I was thinking I should wait until Gabriel returns, but so far there is no word as to when that might be."

"I see. Well, just let me know when you would like me to come—"

"I think we will give him another day or so to get in touch and then I will inform you. Good day." And with that, the woman walked off, leaving Rebecca very worried indeed.

# CHAPTER TWENTY-NINE

Gabriel joined William in the breakfast parlor. It had been just over a week since he'd arrived, and his friend was beginning to look better already. The funeral had taken place four days ago and now William simply needed time to heal.

"How are you feeling today?" Gabriel asked his friend, sitting at the head of the table.

William just nodded and continued to pick at the food on his plate, not really eating anything.

Gabriel filled up a plate for himself from the offerings on the sideboard and seated himself next to his friend. He placed a hand on William's arm. "You need to eat."

William looked up, giving Gabriel a sad little smile. "I know." Dutifully, he dug his fork into the sausage on his plate.

Gabriel turned back to his own breakfast.

After a moment, William said, "Do you know, I don't think I've asked you even once since you got here how *you* are doing."

Gabriel gave him a little smile. "I think you've been a little preoccupied—and rightfully so."

"Yes, I suppose so. But still... how are things going for you?"

Gabriel took a sip of his coffee. As he put down his cup, he gave a little shrug. "It's rather a long story."

"What is?"

"How things have been going for me recently," Gabriel explained. "You see, not a quarter of an hour before I received your note, I was prepared to propose to a young lady."

"Truly?" Will's eyes widened and the first glimpse of a smile could be seen on his lips—the first smile Gabriel had since he'd arrived.

"And then my grandmother told me something she'd overheard which made me change my mind. Before we even had the opportunity to discuss it further, my butler came in with the letter from you. I left at first light the following morning, and have been trying not to think of it ever since."

"All right, now you must tell me this long story because I want to hear every bit of it," William said, before turning his attention back to his plate.

Gabriel was gratified to see his friend begin to eat with more enthusiasm. Could distracting Will with his own problems be just what his friend needed?

Lady Renwick's soiree was a lovely affair. There was dancing in the drawing room, which had been opened to include what was normally the music room, judging by the pianoforte in the corner. They also had a card room for the gentlemen, and there were so many people in attendance they had opened the library to guests as well. It was there Rebecca found Lord Tremelling speaking with his elder sister, Lady Alford, in a quiet corner well away from anyone else.

"Good evening, Lord Tremelling, Lady Alford," Rebecca said, approaching them.

"Good evening, Lady Preston. I hope you are well this evening?" Lord Tremelling said, giving her a slight bow.

"I am thank—"

She was abruptly cut off by Lady Alford who'd turned to her brother and whispered furiously, and rather loudly, "You must tell her, Evan!"

He glared at his sister. "I will if you will."

She huffed and crossed her arms.

"Tell me what?" Rebecca asked, looking from one to the other.

Lord Tremelling looked to his sister.

"Fine!" she said before turning back to Rebecca. "Emilie had been planning to get her revenge on

Lord Willington for not contacting her six years ago."

Rebecca blinked and then nodded. "She made me aware of this."

Lady Alford's mouth dropped open slightly. "She told you?"

Rebecca nodded. "Yes, when we were trapped in my coach after it had overturned."

"Oh. And you were all right with it?" the lady asked, astounded.

"No! Not at all. I urged her to tell Lord Willington," Rebecca answered quickly.

"But she didn't," Lord Tremelling guessed.

"Not as far as I know," Rebecca admitted.

"Yes, well, I asked her about it at Lady Rossburke's party," Lady Alford said, sounding slightly reluctant.

"Oh?"

"She said she was still planning on carrying out the plan, and after she refused his suit, she would explain to him precisely why." Lady Alford took in a deep breath. "But while she was explaining this to me, I noticed Lady Willington standing not too far away, behind Emilie."

Rebecca widened her eyes in shock.

"But she's an old lady," Lady Alford said quickly. "Surely, her hearing can't be what it once was. She probably didn't hear a thing.

Rebecca narrowed her eyes at this. "She has never had any problems with her hearing—not as far as I know."

Lady Alford winced, as well she should. "But that's not all," she said, turning to look at her brother.

He sighed and nodded, ready to disclose his part. "Six years ago when I discovered Willington kissing my sister..." he started.

"Yes?" Rebecca prompted him, even though her mind was already reeling from Lady Alford's confession.

"You know I left with him early the following morning."

Rebecca nodded. "Your sister told me as much."

"Yes, well..." He took in a deep breath. "What she doesn't know is he never got in touch with her ever again because I told him if he did I would kill him."

"He told Lord Willington this after hitting him and telling all their mutual friends to shun him," Lady Alford added.

"Er... yes," his lordship admitted.

Rebecca could not believe what she was hearing. "So, he *didn't* want to avoid her? He only did so because you threatened him and ruined him socially."

Lord Tremelling nodded and then dropped his gaze to the floor—as well he should, thought

Rebecca. "I have to admit, I'm now rather ashamed of my behavior," he admitted.

"I should expect so! Lady Emilie knows nothing of this?" she asked him.

"No. Nothing." He barely lifted his gaze.

Rebecca could do nothing more than close her eyes for a moment. "So, all this time she thought him a despicable, thoughtless man," she said, looking directly at Lord Tremelling. "And so, she plotted to get her revenge against him for something he didn't even do willingly, and his grandmother has learned of this plan." She finished by looking at his sister who just nodded ever so slightly. "And in all likelihood, Lady Willington informed his lordship of Lady Emilie's duplicity."

"It's worse," Eliza whispered.

"Worse? How could it possibly..." Rebecca asked, trying as hard as she could to keep her voice down when really she wanted so much to scream.

"Emilie had changed her mind and decided to accept his proposal," Tremelling told her.

"She fell in love with him," Eliza added.

"But the bounder never showed up after he asked to call on her!" Tremelling said with a slight growl to his voice.

Rebecca narrowed her eyes at them. "When did he do this?"

"A week ago," Lord Tremelling snapped.

"He asked to call on her the same evening Emilie and I spoke," Lady Alford told her.

"Before or after?" Rebecca asked.

"Before. It was how we got onto the subject of whether she was going to turn him down or not." Lady Alford's mouth pursed in anger. "But then he never even showed."

"That was when we learned he'd left Town," Lord Tremelling put in.

Rebecca opened her mouth to say something, but then closed it as she began putting everything together in her mind. The night of Lady Rossburke's party Lord Willington asked to call on Lady Emilie the following day. She was then overheard by his grandmother as she spoke with Lady Alford about her plans to spurn him, but, in fact, she'd decided to accept his proposal. It was entirely likely Lady Willington told her grandson what she'd overheard for he did not show at Lady Emilie's home and, sometime later, left London. "So now where does your sister stand with regard to this relationship?" she asked the siblings.

"She's furious with him, as you can imagine," Lady Alford answered.

"She refused to come to this party. My mother said she is refusing to even consider getting married now," Lord Tremelling added.

"Well, she never really wanted to in the first place," his sister said.

"But she'd changed her mind," Rebecca reminded them.

Lady Alford frowned. "She fell in love."

"But now she's just angry," Lord Tremelling added.

"But she's angry because she *thinks* Lord Willington abandoned her a second time, but he never would have done so to begin with," Rebecca pointed out. And it was entirely possible he'd been called away to help his friend before he had a chance to call upon Lady Emilie.

"Er, no," Lord Tremelling admitted.

"You need to tell her this," Rebecca insisted.

"But he did abandon her this time," he pointed out.

"He may or may not have," Rebecca said.

"What does that mean? He didn't come," Lady Alford insisted.

Rebecca shook her head. "I spoke with Lady Willington yesterday at Lady Emmerton's garden party. She told me her grandson had left to console a friend whose wife was dying."

The siblings just stared at her dumbfounded for a minute.

"So... he may not have abandoned her deliberately?" Lord Tremelling asked.

"Surely, he would have sent her a note telling her this," Lady Alford said.

"He would?" Lord Tremelling asked, turning to his sister.

"It's quite likely, in his haste to get to his friend, he forgot to do so," Rebecca told them.

"Humph!" Lady Alford crossed her arms.

"And now Lady Willington has asked to speak with me," Rebecca said.

"Probably to tell you what she overheard," Lord Tremelling said, nodding.

"Yes," Rebecca agreed. "I shall have to tell her everything."

"Everything?" his lordship asked, sounding a little panicked.

She glared at him. "Yes. Everything."

"We did all this because we wanted to protect our sister," Lord Tremelling argued.

"Yes!" Lady Alford agreed immediately. "All we wanted was for Emilie to be happy."

"I understand, but I doubt Lady Willington will be sympathetic." She sighed. "Thank you for your honesty—both of you. It would, of course, have been best if you'd told all this to Lady Emilie... in fact, I strongly suggest you do so—with haste!"

"Why?" Lord Tremelling asked. When she looked at him incredulously, he defended himself. "He did not show when he said he would and didn't send a note."

Rebecca nodded. "That was very bad of him, but honestly, can you blame him? He had just learned he was going to be spurned."

"You do think his grandmother told him?" Lady Alford asked.

"I do. So, I repeat, you need to tell your sister everything. Both of you." She looked from one to the other.

Neither one met her eyes.

# CHAPTER THIRTY

It was late in the evening by the time Gabriel finished telling William his tale. He'd managed to put it off until dinner simply because he hadn't wanted to relive the entire thing himself. He knew, however, it might very well help William, so he finally steeled himself and told his friend the whole story. After he finished, he drained the last of the whiskey from his glass.

"What are you going to do?" William asked, getting up to refill Gabriel's glass as well as his own.

Gabriel just looked at his friend curiously. "What do you mean? I'm... I'm going to forget her. She was going to refuse my suit. I will—"

"No."

The word was simple and spoken quietly and shocked Gabriel to no end.

"What do you mean?"

"I mean, no. Do *not* do that." William said, settling himself back down into his chair.

"She was going to—"

"I understand," William said, holding up a hand to stop Gabriel's words. "I understand you believe what your grandmother told you."

"What she overheard!" Gabriel argued.

"Yes, what she overheard. But what if she was wrong? What if Lady Emilie changed her mind? What if she misheard?"

Gabriel frowned. He hadn't considered any of that.

"Or even if she did truly mean what your grandmother thinks she said, if you love her, is she not worth fighting for?" William persisted. He sat forward in his chair. "You said you love her, did you not?"

Gabriel could only nod. His mind was throwing *what-ifs* and *perhaps* this way and that.

"If you love her, Gabriel, you must fight for her. Fight *with* her, if need be, but do not simply give in." William was beginning to get passionate through his words. "If you love her, do not accept she is going to turn you down. Why is she planning on doing that?"

"Because she thinks I deliberately stayed away..."

"Yes, but you didn't. Tell her so!"

"And face the wrath of Tremelling?" Gabriel asked, astounded. "He'll challenge me to a duel!"

"Then fight him. But make sure Lady Emilie knows the truth. Make sure she knows you love her and have done so since you were nineteen bloody years old!" He had risen to his feet and was practically shouting. "You *cannot* let her go!"

Gabriel, too, stood. He took two steps forward and grasped onto his friend. This was no longer about him and Emilie. This was William who hadn't had a choice but to let the woman he loved go. Gabriel put his arms around his friend who then collapsed into tears. He'd been so good all day. He hadn't cried once. Gabriel had been hopeful he'd begun the process of mending. Clearly, he'd been wrong.

He just stood there and let his friend sob on his shoulder.

"*Shhh*... it's going to be..."

"No! It's not going to be all right!" William said, suddenly standing away from him. The tears were still running down his face. "It's not! She's gone. My Louisa is gone. But your Lady Emilie... she's still here. Gabriel," he grabbed onto Gabriel's shoulders and shook him gently. "You cannot just give up. You have another chance. Tell her the truth or get her damned brother to do so. But do not—"

"I don't know she'll believe me, William," Gabriel said quietly. "I... was going to propose. I told her I would call on her."

"Yes, this is good."

"But then I left to come here, to you," Gabriel explained, hoping his friend would understand the implications.

He didn't. William just shook his head in confusion.

"I didn't tell her," Gabriel said.

William frowned and sniffled. "You didn't tell her you were coming here?" He pulled out his handkerchief and wiped his face.

"No."

"You didn't send her a note explaining..."

"No," Gabriel said again a little louder. He was such a fool. He hadn't even thought of doing so. He was so angry and hurt by what his grandmother had heard, so concerned for William, he hadn't even stopped to think.

"But you have to tell her. You have to go back and explain."

Gabriel took a deep breath. "Do you really think she'll believe me? After everything?"

William understood. Gabriel could see it in his eyes. "I will go with you. I will explain it all to her. She will believe *me*."

"What? No! I couldn't ask—"

"You are not asking. I am telling you."

"But William..."

"No, Gabriel. This is good. This is very good." William dropped his arms from Gabriel's shoulders and looked around the parlor. It was the one just outside of his bedchamber—and hers. It was where Gabriel had found his friend when he'd arrived just over a week ago. "I... I keep thinking..." William's voice trembled through his words. He cleared his throat. "I keep thinking I'm going to see her. That she's... that she's going to come from her room any second." He turned back to Gabriel. "I need to leave here. It's too painful. I'll come back to London with you. I'll explain everything to your Lady Emilie and then... then... I'll go someplace. I don't know where, maybe the Continent, maybe America or India. It doesn't matter. I need... I need to get away. To leave this place."

Gabriel didn't know what to say to his friend. He understood his desire to leave, but...

"We will pack tonight and be on the road first thing in the morning." William strode away, calling for a footman. Gabriel could only stand there feeling rather dumbfounded.

His friend, deep in mourning, was going to return to London with him so he could fight to get Emilie to love him as much as he loved her. He couldn't imagine.

William came back into the room a few minutes later. "My groom will take my second pair of horses to the Running Hound tonight. We'll leave first thing tomorrow morning and arrive in London that night. We'll take my curricle."

It didn't seem as if Gabriel had a choice in the matter.

# Chapter Thirty-One

The following morning the dreaded summons came from Lady Willington. Rebecca didn't even need to see the note to know what it said. She groaned when Connor, her butler, presented it to her with her midmorning cup of tea.

"I don't even want to see it," she told her faithful servant. "If it's from Lady Willington, she is demanding I call upon her this afternoon."

"May I?" Connor asked, picking up the missive.

"Be my..." she started to say and then changed her mind. "Yes, please open it and see what time she wants me."

He did so, scanned the contents, and then placed it back onto his tray. "Two o'clock."

Rebecca let out a sigh and nodded.

At precisely that hour, she was knocking on Willington's door.

"Good afternoon, my lady," Rebecca said, after she'd been shown into the drawing room where the elderly lady sat by the fire despite the fact that it was unseasonably warm out.

"Lady Preston." Lady Willington nodded. "Please, do have a seat." She indicated the chair across from her.

Rebecca sat at the edge of the chair, her stomach clenched with anxiety. "Have you heard from your grandson?" she asked.

"No. I have not. I have decided to take matters into my own hands. He is not going to marry that odious Lady Emilie. I can't understand why you continued to promote the match despite the fact that they were clearly unsuited for each other."

Rebecca opened her mouth to dispute the fact, but the lady held up a hand stopping her.

"You will do as my grandson requested weeks ago and find him a suitable girl from a good family. A marriage of convenience."

Rebecca sighed. "So, you *did* overhear Lady Emilie speaking with her sister at Lady Rossburke's."

"I most certainly did. Am I to understand you knew of this?" The woman glared.

"I learned of it... recently," Rebecca hedged.

"And you did not think to inform me or my grandson?"

"I urged Lady Emilie to reconsider. And I told her to be honest with him, to discuss her concerns."

"Well, clearly she did not heed your advice, for she told her sister she was going ahead with this deplorable plan."

"No, clearly she did not. However—" Rebecca started.

"I expect you to have a list of suitable girls for me no later than Friday, is that understood?" the lady interrupted.

That was only three days away! Rebecca opened her mouth once again but was cut off before she could even start.

"There should be at least five girls, if not ten, on the list. They must be from good families, not in dire financial straits—I do not want my grandson to be expected to save some profligate family members—and pleasant to look at."

"Of course, but—"

"By Friday," the woman reiterated.

"Yes, my lady, however you—"

"That is all. You may leave. You have a great deal of work to do in very few days." The woman lifted an eyebrow.

There was nothing Rebecca could do. She had been dismissed. She stood, curtsied to her ladyship, and left. She hadn't even been given a chance to tell her that Lady Emilie had changed her mind. That she had fallen in love with Lord Willington and was going to accept his proposal. And now... now she had to cobble together a list of eligible girls for a man who had the most perfect young lady within his grasp. Goodness, she hoped Lord Willington returned soon.

By the time she climbed out of her carriage in front of her own home, Rebecca had made a decision. While she would certainly put together such a list for Lady Willington, she was also going to continue in her efforts to get Lady Emilie and Lord Willington together. She was not ready to give up on this match. She knew deep down it was right, that they were destined for each other. Soulmates.

Gabriel and William arrived late that evening to Gabriel's home in London. The journey back had been a great deal easier than his ride to Red Castle. He and William had taken turns driving and had chatted nearly the whole way. William was doing so much better and even he acknowledged as much.

"Willington, you have returned!" his grandmother said from the top of the stairs as he and William were divesting themselves of their hats and gloves.

"Yes, Gran. I'm sorry I didn't have a chance to send word," Gabriel said, coming to the foot of the steps and looking up at her.

She just nodded. "Come to the drawing room as soon as you have washed."

"I've brought Lord Thetford with me," he told her.

"Very well." She turned and walked away slowly.

William looked at Gabriel. "Why do I feel like a school boy coming to stay for a holiday?"

Gabriel just laughed. "Come, I'll see you to your room."

A quarter of an hour later, Gabriel joined his grandmother in the drawing room as she'd requested. He was surprised to find William already there sitting and chatting with Lady Willington. His friend had somehow changed and washed even faster than he had, and he'd been proud of how quick he'd been.

"How very difficult," Gabriel's grandmother was saying. "You poor boy. I am so very sorry." She reached out and patted Thetford's hand.

William just nodded and murmured, "Thank you."

"Ah, Willington," she said, turning to look at him as he took a seat across from her and William. "I must tell you, I met with Lady Preston this afternoon."

"Oh?" Gabriel frowned. What in the world would have driven her... a terrible feeling stole over him.

"I told her I wanted a list of eligible young ladies for you by Friday," his grandmother told him.

"Eligible...? Gran—" Gabriel began to protest, but she cut him off.

"You will not have to even think of that dreadful girl ever again—although, I suppose you will meet her in society. That can't be helped," she said, looking thoughtful.

"But I want to think of Lady Emilie," he told her.

"Lady Willington, Gabriel is in love with her. He cannot simply throw that away," William said, adding his voice to the conversation.

She frowned at him. "I do not know how you got such an idea in your head, but he is not in love with Lady Emilie. She is a scheming, spiteful girl who Willington will—"

"No, I will not!" Gabriel cut in.

His grandmother's head whipped around to look at him in shock. "You..."

"Will not cut her, forget her, or anything else you might have been about to say. Thetford is right. I love her, and I *am* going to ask her to marry me."

"But Gabriel!" Lady Willington protested.

"I know you overheard her tell Lady Alford that she was going to turn me down should I do so. Well, let her. Let her try. I will not accept it. Instead, I will do everything in my power to convince her that I am the right man for her—even if I have to risk the wrath of her brother and tell her the truth of what happened six years ago."

Lady Willington's eyes went wide. "What happened six years ago?"

Gabriel cocked his head. "Did I never tell you this?"

"You haven't told me anything."

Thetford shook his head in disbelief and gave a little chuckle. "Wait till you hear this story."

"It will explain everything," Gabriel said before he began his tale.

Sometime later, Lady Willington was shaking her head in disgust. "So, it was all Lord Tremelling's doing? And you still want to marry the girl?"

"It was, but he has since regretted his actions. He told me so himself before he gave me permission to court his sister," Gabriel told his grandmother.

She released a breath. "And that is why she planned on turning down your proposal, to get revenge on you."

"Indeed," he said.

"She wanted to hurt him as much as he hurt her," Thetford said quietly.

"But he hadn't done so willingly," Lady Willington argued.

"She didn't know that," Gabriel said.

"But you must tell her!" she insisted.

Gabriel just smiled. "And so I shall. Tomorrow."

# Chapter Thirty-Two

Emilie was finishing the dress she'd promised to Georgie for her stuffed bear when the door to the drawing room opened and her sister came in followed by Lady Preston.

"Oh, is that for Georgie?" Eliza said, coming forward to examine the little dress.

Emilie ignored her sister for a moment to make her curtsy to Lady Preston. "Good afternoon, my lady."

The lady didn't smile beyond a brief polite lifting of the corners of her mouth as she acknowledged Emilie's greeting. "Good afternoon. Your brother will be joining us shortly."

"He will?" Emilie looked to Eliza who seemed to be examining the dress with even greater attention.

"He and your sister have something they need to tell you," the lady informed her.

"I shall order some tea while we wait for Tremelling," Eliza said, moving toward the door.

"Are there not bellpulls?" Lady Preston said, stopping her from leaving the room.

Eliza paused. "Oh, yes, but I'd like to..." Her voice petered out as the woman glared at her.

Emilie had no idea what was going on. She looked from one woman to the other. "What—"

"Have you ordered tea?" Evan asked as he came into the room.

"I was just about to," Eliza said. With a slightly guilty expression she moved to the bellpull and gave it a yank.

"Although we might end up wanting something a little stronger," he said, turning to look at Lady Preston. He bowed. "Good afternoon, my lady."

"Good afternoon, my lord. I believe you know why I am here and have requested your presence?" Lady Preston asked.

"I do not," Emilie piped in.

Evan's gaze dropped to the floor for a moment as he nodded.

"What is going on here?" Emilie asked. Clearly, they knew something she did not, and she didn't like it.

Unfortunately, the maid entered just then bearing a tea tray. "I beg your pardon, my lady. I just assumed this was why you rang."

"Er, yes, it was. Thank you," Eliza told the girl.

"Is there cake?" Evan asked, seeming to be much more interested in the tea tray than normal.

But Emilie was becoming frustrated. It seemed as if they were all deliberately keeping something from her and she wanted to know what it was—now. "Evan!"

Her brother jumped and spun around to face her. "Em? Can a man not want to have a piece of cake before he is—" he stopped.

"Before he is what?" Emilie asked.

"Yes, of course you can," Eliza said, filling in the awkward silence that was threatening. She sat down on the sofa and began pouring out.

Emilie just wanted to grind her teeth together. Lady Preston didn't look any happier. But just before Eliza was about to hand the lady her tea there was a scratching at the door. The footman came in.

"Lord Willington and Lord Thetford to see you, Lady Emilie." He stepped aside to let the two men into the room.

Emilie's heart tightened in her chest, and she found herself staring at Lord Willington. She looked at him closely, searching for some sort of injury or remains of an illness—something that would have kept him from meeting her when he said he would. She knew he'd left Town, but maybe it was for a good reason. It couldn't have been to attend a relative on their deathbed. His parents were already gone, and his grandmother was with him here. She immediately chastised herself. There *was* no reason. It was purely cowardice, that was all.

But then, why was he here now? And who was this man he'd brought with him?

"Oh, thank goodness, Lord Willington, you have returned," Lady Preston said as she sketched him a curtsy.

He bowed. "I have." He turned to the company at large. "Lady Emilie, Lady Alford, Lord Tremelling." His bow encompassed them all. "May I introduce to you my good friend Lord Thetford?"

The gentleman with him bowed. He was fair with dark-blond hair and blue eyes, which looked rather striking next to Lord Willington's dark hair and eyes, but he was not nearly as handsome. He was thin whereas Lord Willington was broad, shorter, and more spare-looking next to Lord Willington's athletic build.

"Goodness, Thetford. I haven't seen you in ages," Evan said, coming forward to shake his hand.

"Been in the country," the man explained without any sort of elaboration.

Evan accepted this and said no more. Emilie got the impression they weren't good friends, but perhaps they'd known each other at school.

It was strange, Emilie thought, watching the gentleman. He had an odd air about him. He seemed quiet and small despite his size.

"Please come in and sit down. We were just serving tea. Would you care for some?" Emilie said, gathering her wits and remembering her manners.

The gentlemen did so and soon they were all seated sipping tea.

Lord Willington started first. "I, er, actually came to apologize, Lady Emilie."

She looked at him, raising her eyebrows. "Oh?" She was not going to make this easy for him.

"Yes. I said I would call, and I did not. I'm afraid I was so distracted I completely forgot to send you a note explaining my absence to you. I should have done so." He looked so contrite Emilie was almost taken in. She quickly steeled herself, however.

She merely nodded. "Indeed, you should have. And are you here to explain yourself? You need not. Your prior behavior made your absence quite understandable—expected even."

He had the grace to wince.

"It was because of me." "It was my fault." Somehow the words seemed to come from both Lord Thetford and... Evan?

Emilie looked from one to the other. "What was your fault, Evan? What did you have to do with him not visiting when he said he would, Lord Thetford? I am exceedingly confused," she admitted. When neither man spoke right away, she narrowed her eyes at her brother. "Evan? Did you do something? Say something to Lord Willington?" She stopped. She would have liked to have an open and honest conversation, but in Lord Thetford's presence, she could not.

It was Lord Thetford who started first. "Willington was coming to see me when he should have been with you, Lady Emilie. You see, I... I needed him desperately."

Emilie could only tilt her head silently asking why. The man understood, naturally, but dropped his gaze to the teacup in his hands.

He took in a deep shuddering breath. As he did so, Lord Willington put a steadying hand on his shoulder. "It's all right, William, you don't have to—"

"Yes, I do!" Lord Thetford answered with more force than expected. He turned to Emilie. "My wife... she..." He took another deep breath. "She died. In childbirth. The babe as well."

Emilie's heart constricted. "Oh, I am so very sorry. Please accept my most sincere condolences."

He nodded as everyone else chimed in theirs as well.

"Thank you, all. It rather... destroyed me. Gabriel was the only one I could think of who could help me get through the first few days. We grew up together, went to school together, and have been like brothers our whole lives."

"I received Thetford's note urging me to come as soon as I returned home from the Rossburke's. I got on the road to him first thing the following morning," Lord Willington explained.

"So, you honestly *did* mean to come?" Emilie asked. She didn't know why her eyes were stinging.

"I did. Truly, I did," he said softly, looking her straight in the eye.

A lump formed in her throat.

"I thought—" she began.

"You thought he was not going to show just like he didn't six years ago after his visit during the Easter holiday," Evan said. "You thought he wouldn't visit and wouldn't write."

She turned toward her brother, now feeling very confused. Why was he reminding them all of this?

He sat up taller. "It wasn't that he didn't want to see you anymore," Evan said, looking straight at her. "He did it because after I forced Gabriel out of our house at daybreak, I... I threatened to kill him if he did."

Emilie frowned. "What?" The word whispered from her throat, which was becoming tighter by the moment. She turned toward Lord Willington.

He nodded. "It's true. I wanted... I wanted very much to visit you. To write to you. To continue our... acquaintance," he said lifting one side of his mouth in an adorable little smile.

"You did?" Emilie had to swallow hard to get the words out.

"Truly, I did," he said.

She turned back to her brother. "But you stopped him."

"Yes. I was protecting you," Evan said, trying to defend himself.

Emilie could only close her eyes. She didn't know what to feel. There were so many emotions roaring through her—anger, frustration, hurt, and... and love. Love for Gabriel who had wanted to be with her and couldn't for fear her brother would harm him.

"When Lady Preston introduced us again," Gabriel began. Emilie opened her eyes again. "I was terrified of what Tremelling might do, to be honest. But it wasn't my fault that she thought we would suit."

"You are soulmates," Lady Preston put in.

"I saw how hurt you were when Willington didn't contact you again," Evan said, taking up the story. "And I saw the interest—along with the anger—in your eyes when he came to meet you. I realized what I'd done was wrong, so I gave him my permission to court you."

"I didn't know any of this," Eliza said, joining in the story. "So, I encouraged you to get your revenge on him for breaking your heart so many years ago." She paused and looked at Emilie. "I'm so sorry."

Emilie shook her head. "It wasn't entirely your fault. I agreed, ultimately." She suddenly realized Gabriel knew nothing of her plan. Her eyes flew to his. Strangely, though, he looked as if none of this was a surprise to him. "Did you know?"

He gave her a sad little smile. "My grandmother overheard you talking with Lady Alford at the Rossburke's. She told me after we got home."

"But she had no idea of your history or why you wanted to get your revenge on Lord Willington," Lady Preston put in. "When I explained it to her, she understood. She wasn't happy, but she understood."

Emilie found her hands were shaking. She put down her teacup with a clatter.

"The reason I came today," Gabriel said, standing. He took the few steps over to her and lowered himself onto one knee. "Was to ask if you could look beyond all this and consider—truly consider—marrying me. I love you, Emilie," the last words came out as a whisper, as if he were becoming overwhelmed by his own emotions.

She couldn't hold back. Emilie threw her arms around Gabriel's neck, finally releasing the tears that had been threatening.

His hand gently rubbed up and down her back until she could catch her breath and force the tears away. She pulled back and looked Gabriel in the eye. "I love you too. I was so upset when you didn't call last week because I was going to throw my plan out the window and truly accept your proposal, no matter what. I was going to forgive you for what happened six years ago because you'd proved yourself to be true—and then..."

He shook his head, that smile teasing his lips again. "And then I didn't show. Oh, Emilie, I am so sorry."

She sniffed and nodded. He pulled out his handkerchief and handed it to her. After she'd wiped her nose and eyes, he put a finger under her chin, forcing her to look up at him. "Did you say you love me?"

She laughed. "Yes, I did."

"Does that mean...?"

"Yes, I will marry you, Gabriel Willington. Happily."

A sniff came from somewhere behind him. Gabriel turned to smile at whichever lady would soon be needing another handkerchief. He was surprised when he saw William surreptitiously wiping a tear from his cheek.

Tremelling must have noticed as well because he stood up suddenly. "Thetford, I think you and I need a drink. What do you say we repair to my study to partake? Of course, any ladies who would like to join us are more than welcome," he added.

"Goodness, I know I need one," Eliza said, standing as well.

William did so as well and the three of them made their bows and curtsies before leaving the room. That left only him, Emilie and Lady Preston.

Strangely, the lady didn't seem overly eager to leave just at the moment.

Gabriel got to his feet but kept a hold of Emilie's hand. "My lady, I don't know how you did it or how you knew to persist in the face of... well, everything, but may I just say how happy I am that you did?"

She gave a little snort of laughter. "I believe I told you the very first time you came to my home that I rely on horoscopes, my lord. They have never steered me wrong."

"Oh, yes, you told me the same," Emilie said. "What did you say we were?"

"You are a Taurus, Lady Emilie. It is known to be the most stubborn of all the signs, which is how I knew that only when you came to a conclusion on your own would you accept it. I assume you no longer believe all men are horrid, selfish creatures?" she asked with a smile twitching on her lips.

"Oh no! I still believe that most sincerely," Emilie said. "Lord Willington, however, is an exception to the rule. I believe my brother is as well, although I'm not sure I'll ever be able to forgive him for threatening Willington the way he did."

Lady Preston just shook her head. "And you, my lord, were born under Cancer. They feel everything most acutely, just as you do your passions. And they are known to empathize with others so strongly that they may do harm to themselves while trying to make things better for others."

Gabriel could feel his face heat with the veracity of her words. "I suppose that does describe me," he admitted.

"Did you not follow Lord Tremelling's dictates to the letter despite the fact that it hurt you and Lady Emilie?"

"But he threatened Gabriel with bodily harm!" Lady Emilie argued.

"He did, but he didn't need to. If your brother had known of Lord Willington's sun sign, he would have known all he needed to do was tell him he would be deeply hurt if Lord Willington persisted in courting you. And we also saw evidence of this when his lordship ran off to assist Lord Thetford despite the fact that you were waiting for him to propose. It was not at all to his advantage to do that, but he did so anyway because he knew his friend was in distress, and he put him above any feelings of his own."

"I was also upset because I'd learned of Lady Emilie's plan for revenge," Gabriel put in. "But on the whole, you are right. Even if I hadn't known, I would have run to Thetford's aid."

"It's quite incredible this zodiac," Emilie said.

"It is," Lady Preston agreed as she stood. "And now I think I will say my adieus. I am so very happy everything worked out—not that I thought for a moment they would not. I am always right about these things."

"Thank you for everything, my lady," Emilie said, getting to her feet as well.

"Yes, thank you, and I'm certain my grandmother will be extolling your brilliance to everyone and anyone in society who will stop to listen—and that will not be a small number of people, I can assure you."

The lady curtsied. "Thank you, my lord. And please send my thanks to Lady Willington as well."

Emilie watched the door close behind her. "I should have offered to walk her out," she said quietly.

"Perhaps," Gabriel agreed.

She turned and looked up at him, smiling. "But then I would not have had the opportunity to spend some precious time alone with you."

"Oh, my love, have no fear, we will have a great deal of time alone."

"You promise?"

He chuckled. "I promise."

He then did what he'd been wanting desperately to do for over a quarter of an hour. He leaned down and kissed his bride-to-be with all his love.

# ABOUT THE AUTHOR

Meredith Bond's books straddle that beautiful line between historical romance and fantasy. An award-winning author, she writes fun traditional Regency romances, medieval Arthurian romances, and Regency romances with a touch of magic. Known for her characters "who slip readily into one's heart," Meredith's heart belongs to her husband and two children.

Meredith loves connecting with readers. Sign up for her monthly newsletter at http://meredithbond.com/blog/newsletter-sign-up/ to receive free short stories and get all her news before anyone else. And don't forget to find her on-line:

**Website**: http://www.meredithbond.com

**Facebook**: https://www.facebook.com/meredithbondauthor

**Amazon**: http://www.amazon.com/Meredith-Bond/e/Boo1KI1SNE

**Instagram**: https://www.instagram.com/meredith_bond/

**Bookbub**: https://www.bookbub.com/authors/meredith-bond

**Newsletter**: http://meredithbond.com/subscribe/

**Please don't forget to leave a review wherever you buy books.**

# Other Books By Meredith Bond

**Zodiac Regency**
*The Determined Debutante*
*The Willful Wallflower*
*The Count and the Chameleon*
(coming soon)

**The Ladies' Wagering Whist Society**
*A Hand for the Duke*
*Jack of Diamonds*
*The Games She Played*
*A Trick of Mirrors*
*A Bid for Romance*
*An Affair of Hearts*
*Love in Spades*
*Token of Love*
*King of Clubs*
*Christmas in the Cards*
*Deck the Halls*

**The Merry Men Series**
*An Exotic Heir*
*A Merry Marquis*

*A Rake's Reward*
*A Dandy in Disguise*
*My Lord Ghost*
*My Gentleman Thief*
*Under the Mango Tree*
*A Spanish Dilemma*
*When Hearts Rebel*

**The Storm Series**
***Storm on the Horizon***
***Bridging the Storm***
***Magic in the Storm***
***Through the Storm***

**The Children of Avalon Trilogy**
*Air: Merlin's Chalice*
*Water: The Return of Excalibur*
*Fire: Nimuë's Destiny*

*Falling*
*Falling for a Pirate*
*Falling Through the Air*

*Chapter One: A Fast, Fun Way to Write Fiction*
*"In A Beginning," a short story featuring Lilith*

www.ingramcontent.com/pod-product-compliance
Lightning Source LLC
Chambersburg PA
CBHW040515170726
48295CB00012B/204